Standby

a novel

Kenneth S. Spiegelman

**Outskirts Press, Inc.
Denver, Colorado**

This is a work of fiction. The events and characters described herein are imaginary and are not intended to refer to specific places or living persons. The opinions expressed in this manuscript are solely the opinions of the author and do not represent the opinions or thoughts of the publisher. The author has represented and warranted full ownership and/or legal right to publish all the materials in this book.

Standby
All Rights Reserved.
Copyright © 2009 Kenneth S. Spiegelman
V2.0

Cover Photo © 2009 JupiterImages Corporation. All rights reserved - used with permission.

This book may not be reproduced, transmitted, or stored in whole or in part by any means, including graphic, electronic, or mechanical without the express written consent of the publisher except in the case of brief quotations embodied in critical articles and reviews.

Outskirts Press, Inc.
http://www.outskirtspress.com

ISBN: 978-1-4327-3446-6

Library of Congress Control Number: 2009924039

Outskirts Press and the "OP" logo are trademarks belonging to Outskirts Press, Inc.

PRINTED IN THE UNITED STATES OF AMERICA

Acknowledgements

One of the things I learned while writing this book is that a novel never happens without the support and guidance of some wonderful, giving people. I will try and acknowledge all of them. I will, of course, fail miserably in this regard. So, for those of you that I neglect to mention know that your efforts and assistance were not in vain and I will always thank you for your help.

To my sisters, Michelle and Jennifer, you are my original gentle readers. Thank you for always having my back. I love you both.

To their husbands, my brothers, Steve and Barry, thanks for being funny; well, most of the time.

To my boys, Michael, Bryan, Benjamin and David, I love you all. You are my greatest creations.

To Emily Joffrion, the original editor of this book, thanks for your patience, guidance, and your giggle. You are still the finest English teacher I know. Those kids in Japan were blessed the day you decided to leave South Florida and travel abroad to teach.

To David Rosenwasser, the best literature professor at Muhlenberg College, it is an honor to call you my friend. Thanks for your advice while this book was in its embryonic phase.

To Patti, the finest lawyer I know.

To Dr. G, who gets me and helps me get me.

Lastly, to my close circle of friends, in no particular order, Mark Samson, Gary Siegel, Mark Tate, Martin Berger, Suzie Silverman and Joey Waldman, thank you for honoring me with your friendship. You have each, in your own way, and at different times, helped me restart and refocus my life. I am a very lucky guy.

Dedication

    This first one is, of course, for my Mom and Dad. Thanks for being the inspiration for so many of my stories, the audience of my jokes, and the anchor in my chaotic world. I love you both.

    "If you look deeply into the palm of your hand, you will see your parents and all generations of your ancestors. All of them are alive in this moment. Each is present in your body. You are the continuation of each of these people."
    -Thich Nhat Hahn-

Prologue

He floated in an anesthetic haze, really a state of delirium that was, by necessity, a very good thing for him. He was in a great deal of pain, actually an excruciating amount of pain. During the times when he was awake he noticed that he could only see out of one eye and on those occasions when he tried to talk, nothing came out but guttural sounds.

So, instead of trying to talk, he tried to gather a sense of his surroundings and, more importantly, precisely how he got here.

He remembered the plane, and the rush to the seat. Then he drifted off to sleep again.

He awoke with no concept of time, no concept of how long he had been asleep, although things were brighter now, and after a time he came to realize that what must have been bandages on his face had been removed. Still, his vision seemed strange, almost as if it lacked depth.

He slept again.

He awoke when the horror began. There were two women, were they nurses? There were two of them and they were scrubbing his face and his arms and his legs. The pain was tremendous and he screamed throughout the process. His screams sounded alien to him. Then he realized that his tongue was missing. He realized this because he knew that when he was nervous he had the habit of chewing on his tongue, but now there was just a rough feeling stump. Were those stitches?

The nurses always talked to him during the scrubbings. Telling him to bear down, hang on, breathe, and focus on something pleasurable, anything in an effort to distract him from the horrifying pain of his daily existence.

They kept referring to him by name, but he could never respond. Only scream.

He was back on the plane, right there in seat 1J. He was drinking champagne and eating snacks. Then there was a crappy movie and he felt tired so he drifted off to sleep. There was a bump and he woke up. He tried to get back to sleep but he couldn't. He wanted to go to the lavatory, but he couldn't get up. He dreamt that he was stuck in his seat.

There was another bump and then the captain announced something about migrating pelicans. Did pelicans really migrate? He dreamt the pilot said something about a rough landing and that everyone should assume brace positions. He dreamt that he yelled to the flight attendants that he couldn't brace because he was stuck in his seat and they yelled back to do the best he could.

He dreamt he felt the plane rise and drop, drop and rise, rapidly, over and over again. He dreamt he heard the engines screaming and the passengers screaming, and the pilot's voice on the intercom, also screaming. In his dream he thought that pilots shouldn't scream, should they?

He dreamt that everyone was screaming, but he was calm. He was peaceful, objective, almost a witness to everything. He dreamt of feeling peaceful and calm.

Then, in his dream, the plane began coming apart but his seat rose up above everything, and he could look down and see it all, like a child imagining floating above everything in a hot air balloon. Then, in his dream, he was not floating anymore, instead, his seat stopped rapidly and he felt ripping pain in his wrists and then his arms flailed up but he was still stuck in the seat.

He landed in something very soft and extremely foul smelling and he was on fire. He knew this because he could smell it, but not really feel it and he knew that, in that moment, that the burns must be terrible for him to smell them but not feel them. And the smell was overpowering and it was the smell of gasoline and oil, and burning flesh, and shit, and those things were burning, and there was screaming. Then he realized that only one person was screaming, and it was he, and his screams made no sense, even to him, they were garbled, nonsensical, and he felt like he was drowning. And only he screamed. No one else. There was no other noise save the moaning sounds of a plane burning after its crash. No sounds except for his scream.

And when he awoke from this dream, he was soaked in sweat.

And he was screaming.

Chapter 1

"Mommy, why is that man's face leaking?"

"Alison Reese, come back here right now!"

Larry Jones opened his eyes from his short nap and realized that the little girl was talking about him. He sat up, wiped the drool from his face, brushed the cookie crumbs off of his belly and tried to straighten his now wrinkled suit and overcoat. He grimaced. Wasn't this suit supposed to be travel friendly? Wrinkle free?

He smiled at the little girl and held out his hand.

"Would you like the last cookie?"

He watched as her face turned red and her eyes welled up with tears, her lower lip quivered uncontrollably and she turned and screamed to her mother, "Mommy, the stranger just talked to me! You told me not to talk to strangers! But he talked to me! Stranger Danger!!!"

Larry glanced up at the little girl's mother and opened his mouth to apologize but she was already glaring at him and scooping up her little girl.

"Paging passenger Singh to the Service desk"

Larry Jones sat listening to the calling of the Deacon Air Flight 721 standby list passengers, knowing that he was so far down the list that he would never make this flight from Los Angeles to Miami. He glanced down at his old Timex and prepared himself to wait for the morning flight.

"Paging Standby Passenger Rogers".

"Paging Standby Passenger Diaz".

Here he sat at an obscure gate in Los Angeles International

Airport, hoping against hope that his name would be called so he could catch this flight home. Home? Now that was an interesting word choice. A wife at home who couldn't care if he lived or died. No kids and now even his dog expressed a great deal contempt toward Larry. No longer content to rollover and get a pleasant belly rub when Larry walked in the door from another business trip, the dog now simply grunted, lifted his leg, and passed vicious gas upon Larry's arrival. Much the same reaction that Larry's wife offered, he thought, allowing himself a chuckle. That was the first time the young couple seated across from him offered even the slightest acknowledgment that he was even there. Before the chuckle, Larry was just another anonymous face in the crowd. But now, with the mild chuckle generated from his own imagination, he received the glance people usually reserved for the screaming child in the corner. "Oh, isn't that sad?" "Gee, I hope he isn't sitting near us on the plane." "Is there a movie on this flight?"

"Paging Standby passenger Hurwitz."

Larry was sure that he wasn't going to get on this flight. Getting a break like getting a standby seat on an earlier flight wasn't the way Larry's life worked. He stood up, scratched his gradually balding head, and took off his wrinkled jacket.

Larry was always picked last on sports teams, cars always drenched him with puddles, his milk always curdled, and he was a virgin until his wedding night. He was married to a somewhat plump and homely youngest daughter of the local banker who assured Larry a vice presidency in the new branch of his S & L right after Larry married that daughter. Larry married her and was taught all about sex by a woman homelier and portlier than he, but a woman who apparently had a great deal of sexual experience, so much in fact that when they finally culminated their marital bliss she muttered, in between puffs on her cigarette, "Well Larry, you've made an honest woman of me, but you are one terrible lay".

Unfortunately, his skills never improved as each session ended with some similar insult. "I've had better." "I might as well have married the produce department at the local stop and shop for all the good you do me" "Dammit Larry, move your hips!" "Not tonight honey, I have a headache" "Not tonight honey, you suck."

"Paging Standby Passenger Rietzek."

Standby

"Paging Standby Passenger Rubens."

"Ladies and Gentlemen, the plane is now full and we can accommodate no more standby passengers."

Larry set about trying to figure out how he would spend another night at a cheap airport hotel. With a sigh, he threw his overnight bag over his shoulder, a bag that never exceeded the measurement box that the airlines always had at the ticket counter. That was Larry, always making sure that his needs fit within the size box of the airlines. He looked around and saw a planeload of passengers who crammed all their worldly belongings into their oversized carry on bags, oversized briefcases, purses, diaper bags and all manner of carry on paraphernalia.

Larry turned from the gate and began strolling toward the hotel reservations desk where the line had already begun to form.

Around that time, Edsel Dodger, the self-proclaimed "West Coast's King of Adult Paraphernalia", jumped into his limousine and shouted to the driver to hurry up with the bags, that he was late, very late and need to get to the airport pronto. He sat down and smoothed out the almost imperceptible wrinkles in his white linen suit.

The driver slammed the trunk shut, jumped in the drivers seat and turned to the back to say, "On my way, boss!"

He glanced at Edsel but the only response he received was Edsel holding up his grossly oversized Panerai wristwatch, tapping it anxiously with his well-manicured forefinger, as the panel between driver and passenger closed.

Looking at the bar in the limo, Edsel realized that this driver knew his business. His favorite tequila, Don Julio Blanco, 100% Blue Agave, was sitting in a very cold ice bucket with a very clean glass at its side. He poured himself a glass and swallowed it quickly, savoring the crisp liquid and the warmth in his chest before pouring another and settling back to read the paper during the ride to the airport.

Edsel's attention was drawn to an article on page three. The article was on the crime page and told the story of another drug deal gone bad with two men left dead at the scene. That, in and of itself, made it like so many other stories in the paper that day. But it was the last line of the article that made Edsel's skin crawl.

"Unidentified sources inside the police department say that this appears to be the work of a new Croatian drug gang. Sources say this because the murders were particularly violent, with the victims having both been brutally beaten prior to death, their noses having been shot off, and each was left with one neat bullet hole in the forehead."

Edsel began to sweat and quickly downed two more shots of tequila.

"Boss, are you awake?"

Edsel didn't respond.

"Hey, boss, we're here!"

Edsel looked up, realized they had reached airport and jumped out the limo. He handed the driver a hundred dollar tip and grabbed his bag.

He walked over to the skycap and handed him his genuine purple alligator suitcase while swinging his man-purse in his other hand. Well, he liked to think of the bag as his executive travel bag, but he knew that those around him called it a "man-purse" whenever they thought he was out of earshot.

"Sir, I'm sorry, but Flight 721 is closed, and I don't think you will make it and I sure don't think your, um, luggage will make it."

"Listen, mate…" Edsel had a habit of calling everyone "mate" when they weren't doing things just so. He even affected an annoying British accent while doing it.

"Listen, that bag needs to make Flight 721 cause I've got an important, a very important conference in Miami and that bag needs to be there. It just needs to be there."

Edsel also had an annoying habit of repeating himself when he wanted something.

"But sir, I don't make the airline rules, I just move the bags."

"What's it going to cost me? How about if I just take it carry on?"

"No sir", said the progressively more nervous skycap, a pimply faced young man who was probably handling his first real job, and facing his first real crisis, " I, I just can't, um bend the rules and check this bag."

"Listen mate, I told you once, I told you a gig-gillion times, that bag and I need to be on that flight to Miami, or I will have your skinny little ass, get the picture!"

Standby

"What seems to be the problem here?" In walked the skycap's supervisor. Now Rufus Schwartz was a man who knew how to solve a problem. Rufus immediately had this problem sorted out. See, he knew that the slightly bizarre piece of purple leather luggage was never going to make that flight. He also knew that the chances of "mister fancy man purse" making the flight were around 50-50 although the odds favoring fancy boy were slipping by the moment. However, in the face of this conundrum Rufus saw an opportunity.

"How can I be of assistance?"

"How can you be of assistance? Well, mate, I will tell you how you can be of assistance, you can tell Howdy Do-Nothing over there to get my very important suitcase on Flight 721, right about now, or I will have his skinny ass in a sling. Understand chum?"

Rufus simply sighed. "Sir, I am sure some sort of accommodation can be reached."

Edsel Dodger didn't get to be where he was in life without recognizing a shakedown. However, he was also practical enough to know that this Rufus fella held the key to his making Flight 721 in his not yet outstretched hand.

"What's it gonna be mate?"

"Well, sir, as I see it we have a conundrum. You see, I want you to make your flight, and you want to make your flight, and I would like to help you make your flight, but I am just not sure that we can fulfill each other's needs the longer we stand here and talk about your very nice piece of unique luggage."

The "man purse" opened and Edsel slipped Rufus three one hundred dollar bills. He knew it was a somewhat high price to pay, but his luggage, unique in color and make up for a reason, had to get to Miami with him.

Rufus, for his part, wasn't done the negotiations. As quickly as Edsel had slid him the money, was as quickly as it disappeared.

"Wow, sir, this is one heavy bag. I believe I am going to have to take it over to the scale, make sure it meets the weight limitations of the airline. Very full flight you know." And with that, Rufus began dragging the purple monstrosity across the parking curb to the scale.

That was more than Edsel could bear.

"Hey, mate, that suitcase costs more than you make in a year, and what's in it… Well, let's just say that what's in it doesn't take too well being dragged across the concrete."

That was certainly all Rufus needed to hear. Amazing the things people will tell you about their luggage and the contents of it.

"Well, sir, I certainly understand your concern and I recognize the value of such a fine piece of traveling accessory. Indeed, sir, I have been a humble porter for over thirty years now and I don't think I have ever seen such a fine and unique piece of equipment. But I am sure that a man of your intelligence and obvious good taste knows that rules are rules, and the rules say that I gotta weigh this here bag."

"You are gonna make me miss this flight…"

"No, sir, with respect, you being so late is why you are gonna miss this flight."

"I am of a mind to ask for your supervisor. But I am in a hurry, what is this gonna cost."

"Cost? What cost? I check bags in for no charge. But I have to do my job you see, rules being rules and all. I mean do you know how expensive airline tickets would be if all of us here porters threw out our backs out moving very heavy luggage. Certainly not luggage as noticeably fine as this luggage. But heavy bags. I mean I got corns, calluses, and bunions you wouldn't believe…."

"Enough, mate, just shut up, where is your supervisor?"

"Johnny", he said to the pimply faced young man who started with Edsel, "where is the supervisor?"

"Ain't you the supervisor?" asked Johnny, just starting to come to terms with what he was observing, but not quite sure about the shakedown itself.

"Well, sir, that's right, I am the supervisor. So it seems we are back to our conundrum."

Edsel grunted and then handed Rufus another couple of hundred dollar bills.

"Tsk."

Another hundred-dollar bill slipped into Rufus' hand. Rufus smiled.

"Well, sir, your bag is all checked to Miami on Deacon Air 721. Do enjoy your flight."

"Right, thanks…" Edsel dashed off to the security gate.

Rufus called after Edsel, with very little enthusiasm, "Oh sir, want your boarding pass? First class and all." Edsel ran back and snatched the boarding pass and murmured, "asshole."

Rufus smirked in return and when Edsel turned away, he dropped the purple luggage into the bin of luggage that would definitely not make it on to Deacon Air 721.

Chapter 2

Larry trudged back out towards security carrying his simple carry on over his shoulder, thinking to himself, what sort of hotel should I get? What is that company per diem again? Did he have enough money for a decent meal or will it be fast food again? Should he call Felicity and let her know he missed the red eye and wouldn't be home until tomorrow? Perhaps later he would call, right now she would be in the middle of one of those late night talk shows she loved so much, with her nightly quart of ice cream and can of diet soda. She hated to be disturbed during that time and he knew if he called he would get a ration of it. No, he would wait until later, when he was in the hotel and would call to let her know he wouldn't be home until tomorrow afternoon. Not that she would care. But when all else is gone it seems appropriate to keep up appearances.

He sighed and walked on, so mired in his own thoughts that he nearly missed the page.

"Paging standby passenger Jones. Larry Jones, report to Gate 16 for immediate departure."

Larry kept walking toward the exit.

"Paging Standby Passenger Jones. Last call for Flight 721."

Then it connected in his brain. He had actually caught a break. He got a standby seat on the redeye. He would be able to get home by morning and might even get a chance to make it to his beloved Hurricane game the next afternoon.

He quickened his pace and arrived at Gate 16 breathless.

"I'm Larry Jones."

The bespectacled and rather gruff young woman looked at him

Standby

with some measure of dismay, "Well, Mr. Jones, it's your lucky day, last standby seat is yours, and it's in first class."

First class? Did he hear correctly? He assumed it would be another non-reclining middle seat.

"It's Seat 1J, but sir, you are going to have to check your bag, because the overheads are all full."

"But my carry on is size matched for the overhead compartments and it has all my business materials, and, and, and…"

"Sir, it's your choice, take the seat and check the bag, or give the seat to someone else. The pilot is waiting and he is closing the door to the plane in about eight minutes."

"Okay, well, you seem trustworthy enough, you can check my bag."

He was handed his boarding pass and practically bounded down the Jetway, pleased with his good fortune. Larry, who had never tasted champagne in his life, was handed a glass (well, a plastic cup shaped like a fancy glass) as he entered into the first class section of Flight 721, and he sat down in the oversized chair. He drank his champagne, and enjoyed the way the bubbles tickled his nose. He closed his eyes, leaned back, and enjoyed the peace of first class travel.

Chapter 3

"Hold the damn plane!" Edsel Dodger was alternately running down the concourse toward Gate 16, and stopping to pick up one of the very fancy Italian loafers that kept slipping of his feet. He just had to make the flight. His meeting in Miami was too important to miss.

"Hold the plane!!!" He skidded to a halt in front of Gate 16, sweating and holding his left shoe.

"I'm sorry sir, but the plane is boarded full and the pilot is closing the doors," replied the same gruff young woman who had just helped Larry.

"Well, open them, don't you know who I am?!?"

"No, sir, I don't, perhaps you could show me your boarding pass."

"Here."

She took it and typed a few strokes into her computer.

"I'm sorry, sir, but seat 1J was already filled."

"How could you fill it when I have a boarding pass for it?"

The gate agent looked at Edsel and his steadily increasing state of agitation and said the only thing that came to mind "Seems as though we have a conundrum…."

Dodger shook his head in disbelief. Another "conundrum". Maybe they should change the name of this airline to "Shakedown Air". He knew this gate agent was looking for money. Alright, so be it.

Standby

"How much do you need?"

"Sir?"

"What's it gonna cost me?" asked Edsel as he placed his man purse on the counter.

"Sir, this isn't about money."

"Listen, love, everything is about money. This airline ticket costs money, this bag costs money, that lousy hairdo of yours costs money, well, maybe not that hairdo cause I'm guessing you got that thing with a bowl of soup, but this bag certainly costs money, and I have money for you if I can get on this damned airplane!!!"

The gate agent reddened.

"Sir, I don't take bribes."

"Bribes, honey, this isn't a bribe. This is commerce. This is America. This is supply and demand. You have the supply of seats and I have the demand for a seat. I also have a goddamned boarding pass for my goddamned seat and I am here at your goddamned gate, before the plane has left and you won't let me get on the goddamned plane! Now I have to get to Miami, on this flight, for a meeting critical to my business! Don't you know who I am?"

"Well, yes sir, you are Mr. Dodger, originally assigned to seat 1J, but you were late beyond boarding time and your seat was assigned to a standby passenger."

That is when Edsel's luck changed for the other agent at the gate was a frequent visitor to one of his establishments and had a bit of fetish for the monkey's paw, one of Edsel's personal favorites, which required a particularly limber back.

"Sir, perhaps I can be of assistance, I am the supervisor here, perhaps you would like to step over to the side here and I will see if I can help you with this problem."

"Well, mate, if you can help me I would certainly appreciate it" said Edsel as he walked to the far side of the counter to discuss his issues with the supervisor.

"Mr. Dodger, I first wanted to tell you what an admirer I am of you and your noble work. Your 'monkey's paw' has changed my life. When I think about it I just can't wait to get home. I mean, where did you get the idea for such a wonderful invention?"

Edsel ignored the pleasantries.

"Alright, listen, mate. I am in a bit of a bind, a real bind; I need to be on that plane, do you understand. I have, or should I say, had a ticket and a seat on that plane which is going to Miami and that is where I need to go and where I need to be in the morning.

The supervisor listened attentively. Dodger continued, "Can I tell you something confidentially??"

"Yes, absolutely Mr. Dodger", he said, speaking sotto voce.

"I have a deal, a lead, on a new product which will make the monkey's paw look like something out of the middle ages. And, I tell you what, get me on that plane and I will get you a sample before they come to market...."

The supervisor immediately blushed. "Well, sir, that sounds wonderful. I am not really supposed to do this but I tell you what. Write your contact information down on this piece of paper while I go on the plane to check for you and find you a seat and I will come back out and help you out." And then, sotto voce again, "Why don't you give me a personal contact number."

If there was one thing Edsel Dodger knew in this world, it was that sex made people tick. From the demure housewife who enjoys her romantic soap operas, to the traveling businessmen with a penchant for hotel porn, to the Mormon father of 9, who needs his 'monkey paws' delivered in plain brown wrapper to a drop box in Colorado, instead of Utah. Yes, he definitely knew what made people tick. Sex, in all its normalcy and deviancy. That's what it was and that was why he existed. "Thanks mate."

The supervisor immediately went down to the plane to check things out while Dodger put his man purse on the counter and opened it up to get a pen out and then wrote his contact information on the paper.

Just then, the supervisor came running out of the plane and grabbed Dodger by the arm and dragged him down the Jetway to the plane.

Dodger yelled "Slow down, I gotta get my shoe on still........"

"No time, no time!!!!"

Edsel chased him with his shoe in hand.

Chapter 4

Larry was just dozing off when he heard a commotion. He was in the place just between sleep and awake. That strange place where voices and other noises can become part of your dreams. The commotion became part of a dream where his wife was shouting at him to "Wake up, wake up, wake up!"

He woke up.

To a rather annoyed airline employee telling him he was in Mr. Dodger's seat.

Larry had no idea who Edsel was but this flight attendant was waiving a boarding pass in Larry's face. Larry took the boarding pass and sure enough it said that Edsel Dodger was assigned to Seat 1J on Deacon Air flight 721.

"But, wait" said Larry, "see I was given this seat from the standby list and I was all ready to go and…"

"Sir, honestly, do you think we give first class seats to standby passengers?" said Royce in his most snooty tone.

"I don't know but I was given this boarding pass and told to sit here"

"Give me your boarding pass"

Larry obliged him.

Royce took both boarding passes and whispered in the ear of the senior flight attendant who, after a moment, walked over to Larry and said "Sir, I'm sorry there seems to have been a mistake. Um, you see, Mr. Dodger here has seat 1 J"

Larry responded, "Okay, no problem, do you want me to move to another seat?"

"I'm afraid that isn't possible. The plane is full."

"Oh, so what am I supposed to do?"

"Well, you will have to get off the plane and the ticket agents will assist you." This was one of those moments that define a man. Most men would've stood their ground and held the seat they had been given. Not Larry. Larry wasn't most men. He didn't engage in confrontation. He did what the Larry's of the world do; he got off of the plane. As he walked off the plane he heard the senior flight attendant say to the man who took his seat, "and I want to thank you for you promising to send me the paw" even though it was all said sotto voce, of course.

Larry took the boarding pass offered to him by the flight attendant and walked off the plane. As he left he heard

"Arrivadderci mate!"

That was most definitely not said sotto voce.

Chapter 5

Larry heard the plane doors close behind him and the engines fire up even as he was walking up the Jetway, preceded at a quick pace by the flaky ticket agent who first came on the plane to tell him he had to get off. He arrived at the top of the jetway only to see a line of twenty standby passengers waiting to talk to a harried young woman at the gate counter who was busy screaming at her supervisor for help as he skipped away for the exits kissing a piece of paper.

Larry waited in the line and the hours passed as he waited for his turn with the young woman who was supposed to provide him with assistance for a hotel and money for a meal. Just as it was his turn to get the counter the young woman said she was going on break and that Larry should wait for the next agent who would be coming out shortly.

Another hour passed while Larry dozed at the counter waiting for assistance. He was long past the time of calling home to let his wife know that he wouldn't be home on the redeye. Truth be told, he was long past caring about calling her. He was tired. He was hungry. But he was terrified to leave the line.

Then, a young man arrived who said he worked with the airline and he was there to help and if Larry would just give him the boarding pass. Larry took it out of his now wrinkled coat pocket and as he passed it to the helpful young man he glanced and saw the name printed on the boarding pass.

Edsel Dodger.

Larry couldn't understand. There must have been some mix-up

on the plane and the flight attendant must have given him the wrong boarding pass. Then it hit him; his briefcase was on the plane, along with his luggage.

"Well, sir, under the difficult circumstances and as you were the purchaser of a first class ticket, we have arranged for a room at the airport luxury hotel along with a car service to take you to the hotel, a first class ticket for tomorrow's morning flight at 11:00 AM, and $200 for meal money, of course, a successful guy like you probably knows how better to put $200 to use, wink wink…."

"Huh, no wait, there must be a mistake."

"No mistake sir, except on our part. We value your business and want to make it right, so if you will just come with me out to curbside, we will get you to your limo and get you to the hotel. Please accept my apologies sir, but you sure look like you could use some rest. And let me say, I've spoken with Royce, and like him, I am so very excited for your new product."

"New product? There must be some kind of mistake"

"Sir, if you please, follow me…"

Larry followed. He followed this helpful young man out of the airport and to the curb where a very large stretch limousine was waiting for him. Larry again turned to the helpful young man and said

"I'm sorry; there really must be some mistake"

"Again, sir, the mistake was ours and we apologize. Now you go along with this car and there will be a car waiting for you at 10 am tomorrow outside the lobby to bring you back here for the next flight." With that, the helpful young man was about to close the door, and just before he did, he leaned in and said "And don't worry about your luggage, it's already in the trunk."

Larry relaxed finally and assumed everything was fine. He knew his luggage was now in the trunk, so he felt more relieved about his business materials, although he was still concerned about his briefcase, but that mainly held some notepads, cheap hotel pens, and an old picture of his wife. Of greater concern was his asthma inhaler. That was also in that briefcase.

Upon arrival at the hotel he was immediately escorted to his room by a very helpful young bellman who kept asking for his card or contact information and kept saying how he was just so excited for

Standby

the new product line. Larry nodded politely and assured the young bellboy that he would get him some information although he was certainly curious what this young man would do with hanger covers.

Then he entered his room.

In his life Larry had never seen anything so opulent. It was almost dizzying the amount of glitter in the room. The room was enormous. Larry thanked the bellboy and asked when his suitcase would be delivered. The bellboy assured him it would be soon and told Larry that he could go relax in the bedroom and the suitcase would be delivered to the suite.

When he walked into the bedroom, a bed that was larger than his entire bedroom at home amazed Larry. He kicked off his old worn shoes, loosened his belt and took off his tie and then lay down on the bed just to relax for a second.

Before he knew it, Larry was asleep. Just moments after falling asleep, Larry heard a knocking at the door. Not quite sure what was going on he looked through the peephole and saw a small woman standing outside. Figuring he must have ordered room service before dozing off, and feeling hungry, he opened the door. He was greeted by the the most beautiful, petite woman he had ever seen in his life. "Hello", she said, "Percy sent me."

Larry wasn't sure who this Percy was, and he was hesitant to let this woman into his room, never having done anything like this. "Ma'am, I, um, didn't order or ask for an escort."

"I'm not an escort. Just a special massage for you."

Just what Larry needed to hear. After all, if this crazy airline wanted to treat him to this fancy hotel room, then he might as well take the massage after all. He decided to let her in to the room. As she walked in she also looked around appreciatively.

So he allowed her to help him disrobe, although somewhat modestly. She then had him go into the oversized bathroom while she prepared herself. When Larry came out of the bathroom, he saw that she was in a beautiful silk robe, that she stood no more than 5' tall, with very long black hair and an interesting pair of glasses on her face.

"Lay down on the floor please."

Larry complied.

And for the next hour she walked all over Larry's back, neck, buttocks, arms, legs and feet. He crackled and popped like a bag of celery. At first it was very painful, but gradually he felt a releasing of year worth of tension. Then, after that hour was completed, she asked Larry to turn over. Turn over? He hadn't had a woman ask him that in, well, frankly, forever. What did this turn over thing mean?

Still, somewhat modestly, and with close attention paid to keeping the towel around his waist, Larry turned over. This beautiful woman, whose name he had since learned was Kim, began working on the muscles of his neck, face and scalp. Then she went to work on his chest muscles, such as they were, and on his stomach, more ample than it should be, the product of too many airplane and airport meals. All the while Larry kept his eyes pinched closed with no intention of making eye contact with this woman. Then she started working on his feet, cracking every toe and his ankles and his knees and then she began kneading his thighs.

Larry thought that was the end, except that just then, with a flourish, she yanked his towel off and said "Hmmm, so what have we here?"

"I, I, I'm sorry, it just all felt so good and I must have gotten carried away." Blushing now at the mild excitement evident below his navel.

"No, problem, honey, you certainly have more down there than I thought," she purred coming closer to him while she released the clasp in her hair and allowed it all to billow down around her shoulders. "That's also why I am here, Percy said you needed to relax and I can certainly help you relax."

"No, no, no, see I am a married man, and I don't do these sorts of things. I thought this was just a massage and I, uh, I've never done this" as he frantically scampered around the room and looked for clothing.

"Sir, I am here for you, no one will ever know, we are all grown ups here…"

Larry glanced up as she undid the front of her silk robe and allowed it to slide off his shoulders. Larry fell backwards on the bed and watched, helpless, as she climbed on top of the bed, and then, on top of him, dragging her beautiful hair up and down his body and then, as he murmured protestations, began doing something to him that his wife had never even considered doing in the marital bed.

Standby

Then, when he was finished, and she was dressed and ready to leave, she leaned over and kissed him on the ear and whispered, "Please consider me to help in your business…"

His business, thought Larry, what in god's name does an Angel like that need with hangars?

The door closed. Larry slept.

Chapter 6

Meanwhile, at 38,000 feet somewhere over the Gulf of Mexico, Edsel had just awoken from several hours of Valium induced sleep started with several stiff shots of brandy, strictly for medicinal purposes. He was thinking about that poor sot who got bounced out of his first class seat. My word, did such a man really think that he was entitled to a first class seat? "I paid for it", thought Edsel, "sure I was late for the plane and almost missed it but several well placed 100 dollar bills, which I am sure that pudgy guy didn't have, insured that I got my seat."

He now had time to think about his upcoming meeting with the Croatians.

As he thought, he realized that there were a few things he needed to write down lest he forget them in the midst of negotiating. Edsel reached under his seat for his "man purse", only it wasn't there. Hmm, he thought, that is strange, when I travel I always put it underneath me. Then he unbuckled, stood up and looked into the overhead, but it wasn't there either.

The first rivulets of anxiety sweat started to roll down his back. "Where is my bag?" he thought in a panic.

He opened every bin in first class, but it wasn't in any of them. Then, much to the annoyance of every passenger in first class, he began looking under every seat in first class, but he couldn't find it there either and all he was greeted with was a string of "Heys!" "What the hells" and profanities to make a sailor blush.

"May I help you sir?"

"Well, yes, you can, I've lost my, um, bag."

Standby

The flight attendant wrinkled her brow and said, "Well, did you check under and around your seat?"

"Sweetheart, I've checked every section of this first class cabin and I just can't find it. It's very important, you see, and it has everything in it, and I have to find it" he said with mounting anxiety and tension. In his mind's eye he could see it, sitting there on the ticket counter back in Los Angeles. He was sure he had taken it on the plane, hadn't he? Right after slipping that money to that ticket agent, what was his name anyhow? Royce! Yes, that was it, the name was Royce. He grabbed his boarding pass from Royce and then...

"Oh, Jesus", he thought, "I left it on the ticket counter in the airport in Los Angeles. It had everything in it. All of my contacts, numbers, schedules, credit cards, ID, and cash. My god, there was an exceptional amount of cash in that, that, bag."

"Where are we now?" Edsel shouted to the flight attendant closest to him, suddenly awakening all the passengers in first class.

"Sir, how can I help you?" asked the now perturbed flight attendant.

"Listen, missy, you can't help me and I am sick and goddammed tired of people asking how they can help me when helping me is the least of their concerns. All I want is an answer to my goddammed question!"

"Sir, if you would please calm down and we could talk about this rationally."

"How is this for rational you pinhead? My life is back in Los Angeles. My entire career, and everything I own and care about is sitting in Los Angeles. Now, if you want to help me, just answer my question. Where the hell are we?"

"Sir, if you would simply calm down and take your seat....

"Listen, bitch, you exist because of me. You have a job because of me. Everyone in this stinking lousy piece of crap airline has a job because of me. So, I am telling you now, I need this plane turned around and I need to get back to Los Angeles."

At this point, everyone who had been sleeping on the plane was awake due to Edsel's yelling and screaming. And all were watching were various degrees of apathy, concern, amusement, and chagrin.

"What seems to be the problem here?" announced a rather deep, gravelly voice.

Edsel turned and saw a grey haired gentleman, who he assumed must be the pilot. After all, who else would be wearing one of those short-sleeved shirts with those things on the shoulders? What were they called? Epaulets? Yeah, that's it. He reminded himself to make a mental note to talk to his design people about adding epaulets to the latest bachelor party dancer costumes for his spring catalogue. Of course, Edsel was never very good at mental notes. He always needed to write things down which is why he carried that bag with him. After all, one never could tell when one would have to write something down. I mean "hell", he thought, "I could do great things with epaulets if I only had a way to write things down".

"Sir, I said excuse me, is there a problem here?"

That broke him out of his epauletic revelry and back to the present somewhere over the Gulf of Mexico on an airplane that was moving some five hundred miles an hour away from his bag.

"Yeah, pally, you can help me" he said with each syllable punctuated with a poke to the pilot's chest. "My bag is still in the Los Angeles airport on your ticket counter. It holds my money, my ID, my credit cards, and some very important notes. It is critical to a deal that I am about to consummate tomorrow."

The pilot frowned.

"Sir, I must urge you to stop poking me in the chest. I am the pilot of this plane, and therefore in command of it, and every soul on board. No one is more important than anyone else. I urge you to cease and desist or I will have marshals waiting for you when we land."

Edsel fumed.

"Pally, I don't give a rat's ass if you have the Queen of England waiting for me when we land, just so long as you turn this damned airplane around first and get me my bag."

"I will not turn this plane around and you will take your seat."

"Listen, Captain Kangaroo, I need my bag. You people rushed me onto this plane without it and I need you to go back and get it. Please, I am begging you. I have to make a deal tomorrow and I need what is sitting there in LA"

"I'm sorry sir, but perhaps I could arrange for the airline to ship the bag to you to arrive later in the day tomorrow?"

He stood there for a moment, ruminating over his dilemma. The

Standby

problem was that Edsel was never very good at deep critical thinking. He was more of an impulse driven guy. Psychiatrists would say a "pure id" kind of guy. In business and in his personal life, Edsel Dodger just did whatever came naturally to his mind and since he was in the adult entertainment industry, he was servicing many people who thought just the same way. Always worked for him in the past, so why not now?

"What's it gonna cost?" he quietly said to the pilot.

"Are you attempting to bribe me?" responded the incredulous pilot.

"Pally, call if whatever you like, as long is it gets me back to LA tonight for that bag, we could call it a donation to your kid's college fund."

"Sir, it seems that we have a conundrum."

With that, something snapped in Edsel's infantile brain. It was like some synapse stopped working. This was the third time in one day that someone from this airline had told him there was a conundrum. He wasn't even sure what a conundrum was, only that every time someone told him there was one it cost him several hundred dollars which at this moment was sitting in Los Angeles at a ticket counter, probably being gone through with someone taking the cash, running up the credit cards, and trying to figure who the fuck the Croatians were? He just snapped, and without even realizing it, his fist shot out and struck that grandfatherly pilot right square in the nose.

Time stood still on the airplane. Passengers held their collective breath for a moment. No one could foresee what could happen next.

What happened next would be recorded in everyone's memory forever had things turned out differently.

What Edsel did not know was that the pilot who had just been punched in the nose was not just a pilot. In his younger days he had been a genuine United States Marine Corps golden gloves champion. And while he was carrying a few more pounds now than he had in his younger days, he still kept his hands quick with a speed bag at home. His training told him to avoid physical confrontation with a passenger. But his training also told him that self-defense was allowed and while he could have subdued this guy without a retaliation, he figured the humiliation of a punch to the nose warranted a couple of shots in return.

The pilot turned back to look at him with an even unwavering glance. At that moment, for the very first time in his life, Edsel Dodger felt fear. He knew he was about to take a beating and there was no amount of money that could stop it.

Wham.

The first punch caught him in the left cheek just below the eye. It rocked Edsel back for a moment. The pilot clearly knew how to punch. This first punch opened a nice neat gash on his cheek. Just as he felt himself going backwards, the second punch caught him in the solar plexus. All of the air in his body seemed to evaporate and he began to double over. Even while doing so he knew the beating wasn't over. As he doubled over trying to catch his breath, the third and final punch came. It was a wicked uppercut that caught Edsel squarely in the jaw, immediately knocking out several of his teeth and sending him into a delirious state of unconsciousness.

As he hit the floor, the entire planeload of passengers erupted in gleeful celebration. The pilot, normally a quiet reserved type, actually turned to the accolades and raised his arms in triumph. A three-punch knockout! Never in his life. What a blowhard this guy was.

Chapter 7

Edsel was in a happy place. He was in a large meadow surrounded by beautiful nymph-like women who wanted to serve his every whim and desire. Strangely though, every time he tried to have sex with one of them, they told him to speak to the Croatian. This didn't make any sense to him. No woman had ever turned him down. Not since high school when his mother made him join the marching band – not since he started working in that porn shop in college and made the decision to take his college degree and use it to peddle adult sex toys.

The meadow was a lovely place.

He woke up.

He awoke confused, like so many knock out victims do. He was in his first class seat but he couldn't move his hands. He also couldn't see very well out of his left eye that seemed to be swollen shut. And his stomach felt horrible and he had a strange coppery taste in his mouth, was that blood? And, for Christ sakes, where were his two front teeth? And, who the hell had handcuffed him to his chair?

He looked around the first class cabin and tried to get a better grip on his new circumstances. Everything was fuzzy in an uncomfortable disoriented sort of way. And then there were the glances. Everyone else in first class would look at him without really looking at him.

Why were they staring at him? Why was he handcuffed to the chair?

Then it all came flooding back to him. The punch he threw at the pilot. Boy, was that ever a bad idea. Then, the three, was it three? Punches that that pilot caught him with. Then, the greatest indignity --- waking up here in the first class section in handcuffs. And now he realized he still didn't have his bag.

"Hey, stewardeth" he lisped to the flight attendants through the gap where his two front teeth were missing. "Hey, take these damned cuffth off of me. I promith to behave."

"Sir, I cannot remove the cuffs. Only the pilot can remove the cuffs and he has advised us that you are under arrest and the air marshals will be waiting for you upon our arrival in Miami"

He considered his options. He could complain but it was clear that would get him nowhere. He couldn't offer this flight attendant any money because all of his money was apparently sitting on the ticket counter in Los Angeles. He certainly couldn't raise hell because he didn't want to deal with that pilot and his wicked uppercut. So, for the first time in his life he made the smart move. He shut up and did what he was told. He sat in the chair with his arms pinned down to his side and pondered what would happen when he got to Miami.

Chapter 8

Larry was in a quiet dreamy place. It was a Chinese restaurant and it was closed, except to him. He had an open buffet that was always refilled and no matter how much he ate he never felt full. And beautiful women who were all scantily clothed served the food. And one in particular came to him and said, "I was sent to you. Please lay down." So Larry lay down and she proceeded to walk all over his back.

Larry jumped awake with the sudden recollection of all that had happened the night before.

"Where am I?" he shouted to no one in particular. He looked around the room and tried to put all the events of the night before into perspective. He remembered the airport, to be sure. He certainly remembered the episode on the airplanes. Vague memories of a limousine ride to this hotel and a strange check in which all seem to have been handled in advance for him, an experience which he was definitely not used to after his history of discount motels.

Then the memories flooded back. That beautiful masseuse. "What was her name?" he thought, challenging his somewhat addled brain. "Kim. Yes, that was it, definitely Kim." A wonderful massage to be sure, so unlike anything he had ever experienced. To think, someone actually walked all over his back and cracked parts of his body he never knew existed. "But, what had happened after the massage?" he wondered.

That memory then came back with a flushing of Larry's cheeks. His guilt level rapidly began to rise. How could he ever explain all of this to his wife? He began to pace around the opulent hotel suite, his mind full of racing thoughts that changed between guilt over what had happened and pure elation and liberation over what had happened. But, how on earth could he ever tell his wife? Did he need to tell his wife? Should he tell his wife? Frankly, would his wife even give a shit? And then, even more frankly, should he give a shit about whether she gave a shit? Larry chuckled at that thought. No, this was one experience that he would definitely keep to himself. After all, who on earth would ever believe that he had done that with such an amazingly beautiful creature?

Larry mentally resigned himself to just accept the good fortune of the evening before. Just as he was willing to accept the good fortune of this incredible hotel suite.

For now, he needed a shower and a cup of coffee. First the coffee he thought. Larry began to search around the suite for one of those cheap coffee makers that he was accustomed to from his cheap hotel experiences. For years Larry had acclimated himself to cheap coffee in small pots that sometime required the wrists of a contortionist to make as they were often bolted towards the back of a TV cabinet. Then, to be filled with a powdered cream and some form of sweetener. For the life of him, no matter how much he checked around the suite, Larry just couldn't find the coffee maker.

Larry needed his coffee and his "grump" factor, as his wife referred to it, was rising with every wasted minute of not finding the maker.

Then, an epiphany. He wasn't paying for the room, the airline was. Did he dare? He stared at the phone like a child left alone with a full cookie jar. There it was, in all its glory, the room service button. In all his years of traveling, the thousands of miles flown, the nights spent on threadbare mattresses in rooms with cheap wallpaper that smelled of cigarettes even though he always requested a non-smoking room, in all those years, Larry never pressed the room service button. His cheap-budgeted boss wouldn't allow it. Larry lived by the per diem.

Now, he stared at the phone and pondered the call. Like a high school boy who couldn't work up the courage to call the captain of the cheerleaders for a date, Larry stared at the phone. Twenty-five years of conditioning hardens a man against this moment. And so, he swallowed, breathed deep, and picked up the phone, and, eureka,

Standby

pushed the button.

Seconds later a chipper voice answered and said, "Room service, May I help you?"

"Um, yes, can I, uh, order coffee from you."

"Of course, sir, regular or decaf…"

"Regular."

"And would you like cream or milk with that?"

Did Larry just hear correctly? You could really get actual cream with coffee.

"Cream."

"Certainly sir, and that coffee service, will it be just for yourself?"

Did this guy know about Larry's, um, companion from the evening before? No, that isn't it; this is simply him being polite. "Um, just for me." He stammered.

"Very well, sir, and would you like some breakfast with that?"

"Um, yes, why not, how about some bacon and eggs and toast?" Larry announced with the confidence of a room service veteran.

"Very well, sir, it will be up to your room within thirty minutes."

"Um, thanks"

"Enjoy your day, Mr. Dodger." The line went dead.

"Who was Mr. Dodger?" thought Larry as he headed for the bathroom for a shower.

Chapter 9

Felicity Jones was certainly aging poorly. She was the last daughter of a once successful banker. She had three older sisters who were all better looking than she. In fact, truth be told, the attractiveness of the daughters decreased from the oldest down to Felicity. That's not to say she didn't have her desirable qualities. She found as her older sisters drew further away from her in affection and came closer with their contempt for her, that she had certain, um, skills that got her the attention she desperately sought from her father but could never obtain as the ugly duckling of the family.

However, she couldn't get a man to marry her. Sure, they all wanted to date her. After all, her reputation did get around. But no one wanted to marry her.

Then she met Larry Jones and things began to change for her. At last she met a man who wasn't interested in her for sex. He actually seemed interested in her for her. They met at a church social. Felicity didn't have much use for organized religion; however, one of her older sisters suggested that Felicity might try the church as a way to meet a man. So she did. And in short order she hit the jackpot. On her very first church social, she met Larry. Turns out he was quite active in the local church and had been for many years. He used his free time to teach the children, repaint the social hall, play in the church band and otherwise generally made himself available to the preacher and the church.

On a lovely summer night, with a harvest moon shining overhead, Larry saw Felicity, sitting by herself and looking somewhat forlorn, and decided to show some Christian charity. He

Standby

walked over to Felicity and struck up a conversation.

"Hi, are you new here?" Larry somewhat sheepishly asked her.

"Hi, yes this is my first time here" Felicity responded and then more forwardly asked Larry "Is there someplace a girl can get something to spice up this fruit punch?"

"Um, well no, ma'am. There isn't anything like that here." He responded.

"Well, mores the pity. This girl sure could use something with a bit of a bite. Helps relax me you know. I mean, I find it hard to talk to people I know, much less strangers, you know. And here I am, new to town, and trying to find myself a church to worship in and so a friend recommends that I come here tonight, says I might meet some nice people, maybe even find a man that I have something in common with, who knows, make some new friends, some new acquaintances, and, well, um, you know…." She rambled to him.

In his life Larry had never had more than a cursory conversation with a woman. Now, Now here was this woman spilling her life story to him at a church social. A woman he had just met. Well, not really even met, yet.

"So, handsome, what about that punch?" Felicity asked him with as much brazen femininity as she could manage.

"Yes, ma'am" Larry replied awkwardly.

Not too bad on the eyes Felicity thought to herself. A little thick around the middle and a little thin up top, but, all in all a decent seeming man. And, at this point in her life Felicity was becoming less interested in the form, and more in the substance.

They had their punch in one-sided silence. Larry listened. Really he never had much of a chance to get a word in edgewise since Felicity could really take over a conversation. In fact, for the next several hours, as the crowd at the church social continued to thin, Larry sat next to Felicity on an old bench beneath an even older tree, and listened to Felicity tell him her life story. It was a useful conversational technique for Larry, really, since he had no idea what to say to a woman it was very helpful that she did all the talking.

They began to date, all at Felicity's direction, of course. She asked Larry out the first time, and the second time, and the third. She told him where to be, when to be there, what to wear, what to eat. Larry went along of course since he had never had a real date. In fact, his senior prom date gave new meaning to "kissing your sister". That one was too terrible to remember and had forced Larry to swear off cheap wine and nearly led him to the therapist's couch.

But back to Felicity.

There were times when Larry wished he could say something. But Felicity seemed content to handle both sides of the conversation.

"So Larry, what do you think we should do this weekend"?

"Well, um…"

"Yeah, I agree. I was thinking we should go to the coast, stay at a nice bed and breakfast, separate rooms of course, you aren't getting the milk for free from this girl, no sir."

"Ah."

"Oh, don't worry honey, your time will come with this girl, I just know it will," she said to him with a mouth full of pepperoni and olive oil running down her chin.

And thus they courted. Larry always obliging her whims.

"Let's go to the shore for the weekend."

"Ok, Felicity."

"Let's go see a ballgame this weekend."

"OK, Felicity."

"Take me to the church tea dance this weekend."

"OK."

Felicity always asking and Larry always obliging. No matter the expense, no matter the inconvenience, Larry obliged. Larry felt more and more sure that this strange, wonderful and beautiful woman liked him and was interested in him and as he had never had a serious girlfriend in his life, in fact, never had any sort of girlfriend come to think of it, he was content to oblige his Felicity.

After six months of this he still hadn't kissed her. Truth be told, at age thirty-five Larry hadn't done much of anything sexual with any woman.

They went to the church tea dance where the burgeoning love of Larry and Felicity nearly came to an end.

At the church tea dance Larry met Felicity's father for the first time. Basil Walters Jones, "B.W." to his friends, "Daddy" to his beloved girls. Felicity brought him along to the church tea dance.

"Daddy," said Felicity with innocence in her voice that only a youngest daughter can manage, "I'd like you to meet Larry Jones, no relation of course. This very nice young man has been courting me, and taking me to all sorts of wonderful places and...."

"Felicity, hush your mouth" boomed Basil, with a commanding baritone voice so unusual for a man of his meager height and slight build.

Amazingly, for the first time since he had known her, Larry saw Felicity shut her mouth. My word, she even talked when her mouth was full. Yet now, in the presence of her daddy, a man who hardly met the physical stature which Larry expected given the descriptions from Felicity, she went completely quiet, lowered her head and shot out her lower lip in a full pout which, to Larry's inexperienced eye, was the sexiest thing he had ever seen. It was at this moment that he realized he wanted to be with this woman, forever, to grow with her, have children with her, just . . . be with her."

"Felicity, why don't you run along and get us some food and drink, I'd like to have a few words with your young gentleman here."

"Yes, daddy."

Off she went.

Then Basil put his arm around Larry's shoulders, no small feat given that Larry was nearly a foot taller than Basil. In any event, Basil, who spent a lifetime intimidating larger and smaller men, began his intimidation of Larry.

"What are your designs on my daughter?"

"Ah, designs sir?"

"Yes, your intentions"

Larry knew what he was asking, and he wanted to shout at the top of his voice that he believed he loved Felicity, had never in his life met a woman like her, she made him happy, she made him feel complete, she excited him and made him feel manly. Instead, he meekly uttered

"I, uh, am not sure what you are saying, sir"

"Knock off the sir crap, boy, I want a simple answer to a simple question, are you sleeping with her?"

Larry immediately blushed. In fact, he turned so red that a person just coming upon him would think that he had spent too much time in the noonday sun. Larry didn't know how to respond. The simple truth was that he hadn't slept with Felicity, hell; he hadn't ever slept with anyone. In fact, all he had ever done was hold her hand, and that was only when she initiated that contact. As he tried to figure out how to explain that he had not slept with this man's daughter, that the relationship was chaste, and loving, and interesting, he looked around for Felicity for inspiration and managed to catch a glimpse of her with the preacher walking toward the rectory carrying empty tea glasses. Just seeing her calmed his nerves and he caught the inspiration to answer.

"No, sir."

"No?", responded Basil incredulously, "Aw bullshit boy! I don't know a single goddammed young man she ever went with who didn't pluck that goose!"

Larry just stared open mouthed.

"In fact, I do believe that that young lady has more experience in the sack that I do, and that's saying something" B.W. said as he broke into peals of bellowing laughter.

Again, Larry didn't know what to say or even if he was supposed to respond. He didn't know if he was distraught learning that the woman he loved had a sordid past or that her father could so freely talk about it to a man he had just met. He tried sorting out these thoughts in his mind.

Basil continued.

"Yeah, that girl is one little vixen. Not much to luck at I know, but like they say, what she lacks in looks she makes up for in sheer 'want to', if you know what I mean."

Larry was quite sure he had absolutely no idea what this man meant but he was also pretty darn sure that he was not prepared to ask for an explanation. Still, in this surreal place where his life had just taken him, Larry couldn't help but listen to Basil as he offered further unsolicited explanation.

"Well, boy, there was this one time when I was away for a day at a business trip and I left her at my office to do some filing in the filing room. Figured she just couldn't get herself in any trouble in there" Basil said, beginning to chuckle "well, wouldn't you know it, she did. With the file room boy, the mailroom boy, the janitor, and one of my partners, and then, to the delight of everyone who has seen the tape, I keep a copy myself --- makes great prison currency you know, my secretary, Lois. Now, Lois always was a fine looking woman and I tried to tap that myself on more than one occasion, but

Standby

never could seem to get her to respond. Now I know why. She played for the other team. Not my young girl, she played for both teams. Anyhow, suffice it to say, Felicity never came back to my office after that. Doctors said she was looking for attention and affection from me. Crap I say. Just a whore. Nothing more nothing less. It's okay though, always a place for the whore in every family."

Larry felt the urge to vomit coming on rather strongly so he excused himself as politely as he could manage and went running in search of a bathroom where he could relieve himself. As he ran he hear Basil shouting after him

"Listen here boy, I only tell you this so you know what you are buying! She loves you I tell you and tells me that you and she are gonna marry and have babies and..."

Larry threw up.

All over the table of tea cookies the women's auxiliary had so patiently baked and laid out for this event.

Not many things in a church like Larry's are a scandal. But vomiting on the tea cookies of the women's auxiliary certainly constitutes a scandal. When Larry finally composed himself to look up, he incurred the wrath of the three blue-haired women in polyester suits who each shouted at him that he must be a no good drunk, cause only a no good drunk would dare vomit on the tea cookies.

Larry supposed that what made it the most humiliating part of his life, to date, was that the lead blue hair was his own mother who explained to the others,

"Well, I told you that son of mine never knew how to talk to ladies, he must have been trying to get that young lady he has been courting to dance with him, made himself all nervous and upset, just like his father always was. Well, hell, his own damned father wasn't worth a lick, if you know what I mean," she tittered as her friends belly laughed their smokers laughs in full consent "in the bedroom until I taught him everything he needed to know. And I had to write away for a catalogue to get the materials we needed."

Larry suddenly felt the need to vomit again.

Going on mercilessly, his mother continued, "I mean, really, I don't think Larry has ever even kissed a girl, have you Larry? Much less touched or tasted the goodies. Gosh, he even tried to kiss his sister at his prom, can you imagine that?"

Larry vomited again, right into the punchbowl.

The three blue hairs were too wrapped up in their own laughter to even notice that the cookies and punch were all ruined. Larry went off in the direction of the bathroom to get himself cleaned up. As he walked away, he heard his mother tell one of the other ladies,

"I don't even think Larry knows that this girl of his has eyes for the preacher."

Larry stopped in his tracks.

What on earth could that possibly mean? Eyes for the preacher? The preacher? How could she have eyes for the preacher? Wasn't she his girl? Isn't that what she kept telling him, "Larry, I'm your girl, that's why we shouldn't do any of those grown up things together, not until our relationship is more, um, permanent." Of that, Larry was certainly not naïve. He knew that Felicity wanted a permanent relationship with him. Marriage. It was plain and obvious. The problem was that Larry was terrified of marriage. Not so much marriage as the consummation of the marriage. He had never consummated any relationship and, to be quite honest, he wasn't sure what to do, how to do it, when to do it, or, for that matter, how often.

Pondering those thoughts, Larry went in search of a quiet cool place to sit for a while and clear his body of these waves of nausea coursing through him from his conversation, as it were, with Felicity's father. He sat in the rectory and collected himself. Then he heard a bumping noise. Or, to be more accurate, the bump, bump, bump. Curious, Larry went in search of what was causing the noise.

There, in all her glory, was "his girl" Felicity, bare assed naked and using the preachers pelvis like a saddle in a rodeo. There she was, joined at the hips with the preacher, in the middle of the rectory. Larry simply was not equipped to stoically handle this. His equanimity rattled, Larry dropped his head to his chest and walked, alone, out of the rectory and back to his car.

Chapter 10

The right Reverend Franklin Thomas was a large man. To be accurate, he was a huge man. Six feet seven inches tall, 350 pounds, dark ebony skin, piercing white eyes which very few people could see as they were almost always covered in very dark wraparound sunglasses. But in spite of all of those imposing physical attributes, what really grabbed everyone's attention was his voice. A voice that thundered from the deepest part of his body.

An ex-football player who was about one collegiate play away from a promising and lucrative NFL contract, now had a severe limp and angled gait from a botched surgery to repair what little remained of his right knee after a rather unfair chop block. Having undergone the surgery to repair that knee and the surgery to repair the repair, Franklin Thomas needed to come to terms with two simple facts.

One, he would not be a football player.

And, two, he wasn't really equipped to be anything else.

Franklin Thomas had a personal conundrum. What to do with his life?

While lying there in the hospital bed after either the fourth, fifth, or sixth knee surgery, he met Ronnie James, hospital orderly.

"Hey man, ain't you Shadetree Jones, that football player?"

"I was."

"I knew it, just knew it, they always say the Weasel here ain't too pretty and I ain't too smart but I never forget me three things. That's right, three things in life that I never forget. Wanna know what they are Shadetree? Do ya?"

Franklin stared open mouthed at this pimply-faced skinny excuse for a human being and wondered who he must have pissed off in a prior life to end up with a torn up knee, in sheer agony, having to give an audience to this thing that calls himself "Weasel". Oh well, it was better than staring at soap operas and those damned Spanish novellas which was about all he could get on this hospital room TV.

"Sure man, what are they?"

Now, Ronnie James had never been this close to celebrity in his life. In fact, although the hospital had its fair share of celebrity athletes having their knees, hips, elbows, shoulders, hands, feet, and the occasional unspoken case of VD being cured or worked on, the hospital scheduling staff made sure that Ronnie was never assigned to the room of anyone famous, particularly because he had the annoying habit of never shutting up. Indeed, if it wasn't for the fact that the regular evening orderly was caught engaged in a somewhat compromising situation with a woman's soccer player, Ronnie wouldn't even be here. Franklin, however, since he had nothing better to do, figured he would listen to what this fella had to say. He nodded his head at Ronnie.

"Oh, man, Shadetree is talking to me!! The folks back at the trailer park would just never believe it. Man oh man, how incredible this is, the Shadetree talking to me. Who would have thought it?" As Ronnie continued to ramble on and on in this fashion, Franklin watched amazed as Ronnie's face became more and more animated, and the spittle began to fly from his mouth and the sweat began to pour from his body.

Franklin reached one of his meaty hands out of the bed and grabbed Ronnie by the chin and shook him back and forth and said, "My man, I would very much love to hear about those three things that get you through life, but, and I mean this with all due respect, if you don't shut up, I am going to squash your head like a grape."

That silenced the Weasel. He looked in Franklin's eyes and realized that what had just been said was not a threat but was meant with full sincerity. Then he cackled. His nervous reaction to most difficult situations. A cackle. Ronnie was one of those people who were truly meant to spend his life cleaning bedpans and urinals and mopping up after other people. Honest work, truly, but not the sort of job one has if one wants to get noticed by the likes of Shadetree Jones.

Standby

So, he cackled, and as he did the grip on his chin got stronger.

"Ouch, easy Shadetree, man, I was gonna get to it, but you gotta give a man the chance to build up a story, its what they call a prelude you know, I know you read them books in that fancy college of yours. Prelude is what it is. Like foreplay before fuckin'. You know all about that fuckin' stuff don't ya Shadetree? I hear you was quite the swordsman at that college of yours, weren't you"

"My man, do me a favor?"

"Shit, anything Shadetree"

"Actually, two favors"

Wow, two favors for Shadetree, a guy could do a lot worse than that, you know. He might even score an autographed football out of this. Well, seeing as how there weren't any footballs here in the hospital, maybe an autographed bedpan. Again he cackled. Wouldn't that be a hoot? An autographed bedpan!

"Sure, Shadetree, name it"

"Well, it's really three"

"Anything man, it could be a hundred and twenty-seven favors, anything for you."

"Alright then, listen carefully because I don't want you to mess any of these up."

"You got it, man!"

With that, Franklin "Shadetree" Thomas released his hand from Ronnie's chin.

"Ok, then, one, do not call me "Shadetree" anymore.

Ronnie nodded his head rapidly, thinking maybe he would be asked to call his new friend "Franklin", his first name, like proper friends do.

"Two, I want you to tell me those three things.

Again, Ronnie nodded rapidly and waited for the final instruction.

And he waited some more.

"Hey, um, Shadetree" he said, receiving a withering glance in return from the large man. "What's the third thing?"

"I'll tell you after you tell me your three."

"Ok, man, well, I am not usually in the habit of sharing these thoughts with just anyone you know, but seeing as how we are such fast friends, I will make an exception in your case. One, here it is man so you better be paying attention. One, if you can get a good piece of fish you are ahead of the game," he said with a smile and a knowing wink as if he had just shared some golden nugget of wisdom.

"What in the hell is that supposed to mean" roared Franklin "If I get a good piece of fish I am ahead of the game? Why that is simply the dumbest thing I have ever heard. I'm laying here in this hospital bed, don't waste my time, boy, get the hell outta here!!!"

"Okay, then, if you ain't interested in my three points, then I just ain't gonna bother telling ya! You can just lay there in that dirty bedpan too for all I care!" With that Ronnie began walking toward the door.

"Wait, wait, wait. Okay, all right, Damn but I sure am hungry for conversation. No one has come here to see me. It's like everyone loved me when I was tearing up offenses on the field, but now that I'm laying here all gimped up, no one could care less about me. So, why don't you go ahead and tell me the other two. Sheesh, a good piece of fish, who on this green earth gave you that nugget of information?"

Ronnie looked at him now with genuine hurt in his eyes. "My momma, afore she passed. And don't be thinking I ain't tough just cause I am smaller than you. I may be small, but I am wiry dammit. And, last time I checked, I was twenty-three and you are only twenty so that makes me older than you, and probably wiser too, and where I come from; you respect your damn elders! And, besides that, if I am good enough to clean up your shit and wipe your ass for you, than I am sure enough good enough for you to listen to!"

Well, in his life, no one, and he meant NO ONE, had ever had the nerve, the gumption, to speak to Franklin Thomas in that fashion. Anyone who ever had spoken to him like that usually received an "ass-whooping" and went home with a few less teeth than he had started the day with. But this little punk stood right up to Franklin and spoke his mind. Of course, it probably helped his nerve that Franklin was laying in a hospital bed in traction, but, who knew, maybe this guy was one of those "truth to power" guys that coach was always babbling on about. You know, guys who could speak their mind to anyone, regardless of that person's power. What could it hurt to let that man speak his piece? Sure beat lying in bed waiting

Standby

for the next meal service or those cute candy stripers that never stayed long enough.

"Alright, Ronnie, say your piece."

Ronnie stared at Franklin for a moment. He nodded his head. They had reached a moment of mutual agreement.

"Well, that's better then, even somewhat respectful as befits my mature years. Okay, so number one as you know is 'If you got a good piece of fish, you are ahead of the game,' okay, so are you ready for number two?"

"Like I said, I ain't got nowhere to go."

"Number two, the grass ain't always greener on the other side." Ronnie smiled proudly at this pronouncement.

Ronnie paused for effect to let that one sink in.

Franklin did, indeed, let it sink in. That actually may have been the most intelligent thing this fella had said since he came in to wipe his ass. He actually smiled at Ronnie and nodded his head, "Well, yes, I do believe that one is correct Ronnie, I really think you may be right, the grass definitely ain't always greener on the other side. So, now, what is the third one?"

Ronnie again stared at Franklin with his piercing eyes. Eyes that Franklin was now beginning to realize held considerably more intelligence than this man initially let on. Ronnie just stared at Franklin for what seemed like an eternity and then finally said, "I ain't ever told anyone the third one before. Always done kept it to myself ever since momma told it to me afore she died, you know. Never had no problem telling the first two, of course, as people sort of know those two anyhow." At this Franklin blinked, who the hell could possibly understand anything about having a good fish being ahead of the game? Still, he was deep into this life lesson now, and he figured, in for a penny…

"C'mon man, please tell me. I ain't gonna do nothing with it."

"No, you don't understand, if I tell you, you gotta do something with it! You can't just hear what I gotta say and then get better here and do nothing with this! This is important stuff. If I'm gonna tell you, you gotta promise me that you are gonna do something with your life more important that football! You gotta promise"

Franklin again searched for those eyes. They were glistening now with tears like a child who wanted to tell a deep dark secret but couldn't quite set it free. It was there, and Franklin knew that this one was important, if he could just get Ronnie to share it. Then, in a moment of intuitive revelation, like on the field when he could read the quarterback's eyes and know the play just a half second before it happened, he knew just what to say.

"I promise, my friend."

A lifetime of bottled up emotion released in Ronnie. A sob caught in his throat as he opened his mouth to speak.

"Number three," he paused, "Number three, in life there are three kinds of people. There are pilots, there are passengers, and there are standbys."

They again stared at each other and Franklin took Ronnie's hand and let his own tears mix with those falling from Ronnie's face.

Chapter 11

Clarence Darrow Sullivan always wanted to be a lawyer ever since he was a child, born with the heavy sobriquet "Louis Aloysius Ping-Smythe". He had few friends and his parents really didn't have the time for him. His father was the local town doctor and spent more time with his nurses than his mother. His mother was a crossword puzzle junkie who spent her days poring over the thesaurus trying to find the appropriate synonyms necessary to finish the daily puzzle. Clarence, a/k/a Louis, spent his days watching television and fell in love with the lawyer programs. He loved them and spent every night acting out the critical courtroom scenes. Then, when he was thirteen, he saw "Inherit the Wind" for the first time and it led him to actually go to the library where he learned all about the Scopes Monkey trial and its star, Clarence Darrow.

When he was old enough, he moved away from home. He not so humbly decided to change his name to match his hero, Clarence Darrow. As for the last name, Sullivan, he decided he wanted an Irish last name because he knew, hell, everyone knew, that the Irish were the toughest courtroom fighters. He picked Sullivan, not to honor a great Irish litigator, but because it was the only Irish name he saw when he was on the way to the courthouse to change his name. The fact that it was the name of the cab driver didn't really seem to bother young Louis, now a/k/a Clarence.

In fact, the chuckles of the judge who changed his name didn't bother him either. He knew that he was going to be famous.

The only wrench in his plans was learning the law. It was just too complicated for him. But now, burdened with his new legal sobriquet, he had to be a lawyer. So he altered his plans a bit.

He would still be a lawyer.

Not just a lawyer, a rich, very rich lawyer. And he always had a plan on how he was going to get there. Get the law degree, borrow some money, get his face on every phone book in Miami, get his mug on every billboard outside of every emergency room in Southern Florida, and on every billboard outside of every college football stadium in Florida, cause he knew, he just knew that those college kids were driving drunk when they left the stadiums. And there was his face, larger than life, telling the victims, the poor innocent victims, that he, the "Pit Bull", was there to bang home his message for them – "Have you been hurt? Well, if you have, I guarantee you it was someone else's fault and I will get you money. Call 1-999- PIT BULL. I am the super-lawyer! I am tenacious and when I get a hold of those insurance companies, I don't let go until I bring home your money!"

And, dammit, if it didn't work. The calls came in twenty-four hours a day, seven days a week. Hundreds of calls a week. New clients coming in all the time. So how exactly did Sullivan handle all this legal work? How did he manage the affairs and necessities of thousands of clients, many of whom couldn't speak a word of English?

Simple.

He didn't.

The truth of the matter is that he couldn't handle the cases even if he wanted to. The simple fact being that Sullivan's knowledge of the law was limited to what he learned from those lawyer programs he still watched.

He hired lawyers who could do the work. Lawyers who actually thought it was important to know something about the law. Lawyers who believed that the law was a noble calling where one could serve the least in society, those who couldn't speak for themselves and needed a lawyer to help them fight corporate greed and malfeasance.

How they worked. Hundreds of hours a month on Sullivan's cases, achieving settlements and verdicts for his firm, to fill his coffers. Sullivan couldn't afford to get his own hands dirty. No, he was certainly too busy advertising himself, pandering to the least common denominator of society. People just like himself who were

Standby

interested in one thing. That one great equalizer. That which simplified life for those who had it and troubled life for those who didn't. Money. Yes, money, moolah, dollars, samoleans, dinero. It was what drove Sullivan. It turned him on, made him moan and gave him the largest thrill in life. A larger thrill that even his young girlfriend with the fake breasts, ass and pin-sized brain, could give him.

But the question remained how to turn all of those little nuggets into miniature goldmines? The answer was really quite simple. Set up a mill. Mill the cases. Have lawyers of modest talent, little nerve, and no motivation sit at their desk for hours and settle small cases, sometimes fifteen or twenty on any given day. As Sullivan always said, "Ain't nothing quite like the sound of cases settling all day long!" So he did this, he hired individuals who were "lawyers" only in the broadest sense of the word. Indeed, individuals who really were nothing more than telemarketers. Young men and women who spent their days "Dialing for dollars".

Sullivan didn't stop there. If he had a particular genius, it was in marketing himself and his firm. He knew he needed a partner, if for no other reason that to make his firm look grander than it was. He found just the right man for the job. Jerry Gilbert. A capable trial attorney in his day, but his day was pretty darn far behind him at this point. Still, a noted name in the Miami legal community even if he was probably best remembered for being shot in the ass by the disgruntled male lover of an old client.

Jerry Gilbert now was a lawyer in title only. Since the shooting he had been on a drinking bender and hardly made it in to work anymore. Sullivan didn't care. All he needed was Gilbert's name.

The thing that Sullivan liked the best was the prestige of the new firm name. "Gilbert & Sullivan" a name with so much public recognition that Sullivan was able to see beyond his own massive ego just far enough to recognize that the marketing potential of that name was enormous. And so they joined, the new "Gilbert & Sullivan". The lawyers who made music with their greed. The lawyers who ran their TV commercials over and over again to the tune of "The Mikado".

The lawyers with enough marketing savvy to play the bulk of their ads during two time slots. The first, during the show of a female talk show host who made a habit out of blubbering incessantly over some new boy band, and during late night tele-evangelist shows. Those were the money makers.

That is where Felicity Jones saw them first. When the day came that she required the, um, ahem, services of a personal injury lawyer, she turned first to the Lord and watched that fine looking black preacher, Rev. Thomas, and then during commercial break, as if it was a missive from God, she saw Sullivan's latest commercial, played to the tune of the "Battle Hymn of the Republic,"

"You! Yes you! Have you been injured in an accident? Were you or someone you love injured in a collision? Have you had an accident with some big company's truck? If you answered 'yes' to any of those questions then you are entitled to compensation! I am Clarence Darrow Sullivan, I am the "Pit Bull", and I will get you your piece of the American Dream. Why, just the other day I got a migrant strawberry picker a million dollars when some piece of farming equipment fell on his head, and I say to you this <music gets louder and fireworks are seen in the distance> it is the right of every American to seek compensation from someone else if they've been hurt. I don't care whose fault it is, show me an injured American, show me a big corporation, and I will show you money. It is your god-given right as an American!!!"

And with that Sullivan turned and walked off into the sunset while dollar bills fired out of cannons to the tune of the 1812 Overture.

Chapter 12

On the other side of the continent, Larry was busy trying to figure out what he was doing in the fancy hotel room with the fancy fruit basket, and, more importantly the purple leather luggage and matching man-purse. As he toweled himself off from his second shower of the day, and it wasn't even nine am yet, having exited the luxurious marble tiled shower with four shower heads, he really began thinking about what he was doing here and how he ended up here.

He very definitely remembered the evening at the hotel, when Kim arrived, and the wonderful massage she gave him. Even now, he felt taller and more limber that he had just the day before, in large part due to Kim's ministrations with her feet on his spine. Then he remembered with just the hint of a smile, the other thing that Kim had done with him. Larry found it interesting that he had stopped feeling guilty about it and, indeed, allowed himself to revel in the moment that was the evening before. This was completely outside the character of Larry Jones, but it sure did feel good.

Now he sat himself down to his room service breakfast. He had never seen such an obscene amount of food for one person. There had to be a dozen eggs scrambled on his plate, along with enough bacon to feel an army, and probably a loaf of toast. Then again, Larry chuckled to himself; Felicity could really pack it away.

Larry ate with the appetite of the famished. Even though he was packing away a few too many pounds himself, he could not remember ever eating so much food with so much gusto. Before he knew it, he had cleared his plate and was on his fourth, or was it his fifth, cup of coffee. What Larry didn't realize was that this wasn't his wife's coffee, or the coffee those cheap motels provided in the ready made bags, this was hard core strong coffee which those coffee chains sold for four to five dollars a cup. Suddenly, and with very little warning, Larry developed palpitations, started sweating and began pacing the room. He kept looking for things to do but there was nothing he could do to diffuse the energy. So he paced the room, back and forth, and with the television remote in one hand, and a strip of bacon in the other. Larry dropped the bacon, picked up the television remote and began furiously and uncontrollably changing the channels.

He was looking for sports scores, anything really other than news and that tremendously large black televangelist who was cropping up on more and more networks, but all he could find was breaking news on every channel. Something that looked like a large fire in a swamp.

Larry couldn't focus on the TV long enough to hear what they were saying nor could he sit still long enough to watch the picture, so he just had no idea what was taking place.

Bang. Bang. Bang. Ring, ring, ring.

Larry looked around trying to figure out what the racket was.

Bang. Bang. Ring. Ring.

Larry thought it might be the door, but he had never heard of a hotel that had a doorbell on the guest rooms. It sort of took him off guard.

"Open the damn door!" shouted a female voice that sounded vaguely familiar.

Larry knew that he knew that voice, or a voice somewhat similar to that voice, although right now he couldn't place it.

"Open the goddammed door! Right now! I mean it"

Larry was frozen like a deer in the headlights. He simply had no idea what to do. He thought to himself "I am in a real conundrum". That made him giggle.

He finally walked over to the door and opened it.

In came a whirling fury of dark hair, olive skin and blazing brown eyes. She turned to him and Larry instantly recognized her from the night before.

"Kim?" he asked sheepishly.

"Actually, it's Sue, but I think the better and fairer question right

Standby

now is "Who the fuck are you?"

"I'm not sure I understand?"

"Don't be coy with me man, I have been in this game way too long. I've heard all kinds of stories from married guys trying to hide their identities, and I've always, and I mean always, maintained their confidentiality, but this one is just too over the top."

"Again, I am really not sure what you are talking about."

"Man, do you live on the moon? Did last night's blowjob destroy your sense of reality?

Larry blushed

Sue, aka Kim, stared at Larry for a moment and with a common sense wisdom developed after her time working as an escort, realized that this guy standing in front of her was probably more innocent and trusting than any of her johns, this guy probably had absolutely no idea what she was talking about.

"Honey, do you watch the news?" she asked him quietly.

With that Larry turned and looked at the large flat screened TV turned on at the foot of his bed and his mouth and jaw dropped wide open. On the screen the breaking news showed a plane crash in the Florida Everglades. The smoke, the fire and the grim faced recovery personnel bringing out bodies.

But that wasn't what dropped Larry back on his heels with the stunned look. And it was not even the revelation that the plane that crashed was Deacon Air 721, the plane he was to have taken.

No, what shook Larry to the core was seeing his picture in the upper right hand corner of the screen with the subtext:

Larry Jones

Sole Survivor

Larry began to sweat.

Sue turned to him and said as gently as the moment would allow, "Man, who the hell are you?"

Larry just blinked.

Chapter 13

Franklin "Shadetree" Thomas and Ronnie "The Weasel" James formed a fast, strong friendship. It was a friendship created by being two people who the rest of the world had left behind. Ronnie never was of much use to most people, and instead became the guy who wiped your ass when you were stuck in a hospital bed. The guy you knew was there but who you didn't want to acknowledge simply because there was something dirty, something unspoken, something rotten about having to have another human being clean your waste from your body.

Shadetree was left behind due to circumstance. His entire life he was a football hero. From a poor town where sharecroppers work was the only work to be had. Everyone in that town just knew Shadetree was going to make it out. Football would be his ticket. He played it like a man possessed. A man possessed to break away from his poor past and driven to achieve his ordained future. The colleges let him in even though his grades weren't that good because winning football games was so much more important than academics. After all, how many organic chemistry majors could help bring in five million dollar paydays from bowl games. But the Shadetree could deliver all of that and so much more. Not only could he play football, but also he was incredibly good-looking and well mannered. The product of a mother who took him to the Pentecostal church every week and a father who taught him respect at the end of the lash.

Shadetree got scholarship offers. Lots of them. Even from the Ivy Leagues. In the end he settled for the Central Florida A & T. Not because it was the best academic school, not because it was close to

Standby

home, and not because their football schedule routinely took on the likes of the University of Miami, the University of Florida, the University of Georgia and LSU. No, the plain reason that Shadetree Thomas went to CFA & T was that he wanted to learn farming. Real farming. Just in case football didn't pan out he could go back home and work the farm with his daddy.

Of course, all of that changed during Shadetree's junior year, the year he led the conference in tackles, sacks, and defensive touchdowns. The year everyone said he was a sure Heismann lock for the next year. One day, just after practice, Shadetree's coach pulled him aside and told him that his daddy was dead of a heart attack he suffered in the fields. The coach softly told Shadetree to take the next day and see to his father's burial but to be back the day after that for the Alabama game. After all, the boosters didn't lose a father, and they sure as hell weren't gonna tolerate losing Shadetree Jones for the most important game of the year, dead daddy or not.

Of course, Shadetree did what he was told, but his heart just wasn't in it. And when he went on the field to take on Alabama, his effort was listless and careless. He just wasn't Shadetree that day. He wasn't the human wrecking crew. And everyone knew it. Especially that fullback from Alabama who delivered the career-ending block to Shadetree's leg. The block that delivered him into the presence of Ronnie James.

Now here he was. Stuck in a hospital and no longer the hero of the Armadillos Football team. He knew he was a castoff. Just like that. "Hero to zero" in the time it took for his leg to get destroyed. From the super jock that the pretty coeds fawned over, to a hospital patient who had to suffer the indignity of having his ass wiped by a strange little man with his own "Zen-like" outlook on life.

"Hey, Weasel, what the hell we gonna do with our lives?" asked the large man.

Weasel looked back at him stunned. All of a sudden this football start, well, to be fair, ex-football star, was looking to him, the Weasel, for advice.

"I don't know Shadetree" he said, then blushed when Franklin fixed him with that glare which often caused opposing quarterbacks to, well, quite frankly, require the assistance of a man like the Weasel here. "Sorry, Franklin, um I mean Mr. Jones"

51

"Franklin will do just fine Mr. James", said Franklin.

"Oh, wow, but no sense getting all formal on me Mr. Jones, Ronnie or Weasel will do just fine" Ronnie squeaked out in admiration for his new friend.

"Well, one thing you need to understand there, Ronnie, is that for the remainder of what I hope will be our very long lives, and perhaps an equally long friendship, I know these two things. You will never again call me Shadetree and I will never, ever call you 'Weasel'."

"Well, um, I do appreciate that, and truly won't mind if you ever call me the Weasel, however, I do gotta tell you that I truly appreciate you treatin' me like a real human being. First time in my life and all" and the Weasel wept.

"Okay, then, so the question still stands, what exactly are we gonna do now"

"I don't know, Mr. Jones, but I do hope we do whatever it is we gonna do, that we do it together."

"That we will, Ronnie, that we will."

They sat there in silence. Two new friends, one whose road to stardom came to an abrupt and un-glorious end. The other who was a side-note in everyone else's life. They sat and looked at each other, then off into space, then back at each other. Two new friends, each perhaps the first real friend the other had ever had, trying to find their way in a world that they each realized was becoming more and more difficult and uncaring. Then, for maybe the first time in a long while, the big ex-football player did something that so few people had ever seen him do. He smiled. A broad, toothy grin that showed all of his very white teeth and let slide, even if just for a moment, the humor and good nature of the man within.

"Hey, Ronnie, do you believe the Lord?"

Chapter 14

Felicity somehow managed to convince Larry that it was just a brief, insignificant peccadillo. Larry, never one to hold a grudge, and now desperately lonely without the only companion he had ever really known, gave in and took her back. In response, probably for the first time in her life, Felicity showed loyalty to a man. She showered Larry with attention and affection. She even allowed him to touch her in what she called her "delicate" places. Actually, to be candid, she showed him where to touch and what to do.

Of course, trying to be coy, she never reciprocated for Larry. And while his sexual frustration mounted, he assumed that eventually he would get his turn and, to be sure, he was happy to finally be touching a woman. Sure, he had read about these things in books, but, wow, the real feel of a woman surely made him feel manly.

She promised "Larry, someday, when you and I are wed, I will most assuredly teach you everything there is to know and I will make such a good wife for you. I promise."

"I know Felicity. I know. And I will love you and will worship you and make you happy" All of these promises being made in the heat of the moment and in the desperate hope that Felicity would do something, anything, for him so that he wasn't just so damned sore.

Their courting period continued until that fateful day when Felicity's father called Larry into his office "Son, I'm a direct man, some would say blunt, to be sure, but I prefer direct, you know what I mean, don't you boy?"

"Yessir" Larry stammered, hoping that her father wouldn't rant on in another expose of Felicity's previous activities, and feeling the stirring of nausea in his stomach and the unsettling cramps from those two Danish he polished off along with some grape juice.

"So, I am going to ask you a very direct, brutal and forthright question, and if you want to continue working here after this meeting, you will give me a very direct, brutal and forthright answer."

That's it; Larry knew her father was about to ask him if he had had sexual relations with Felicity. The problem was that Larry didn't know what her father really wanted. The truth, which was that he had not had such relations, or a lie, that he and she had, what was the expression, "shagged like a couple of minxes" To be honest, Larry wasn't quite sure what that meant, but the thought of it made him giggle.

"You giggling boy? I asked you a very serious question, and I expected a very serious and direct, grown up answer to that question. Instead, you fucking giggle? Sheesh, are you a man or a little girl? Aw screw it all to hell, just answer my question. What are your intentions with my daughter?"

That one flummoxed Larry. He was sure that he was about to be asked about their sexual activities, such as they were, and instead he was being asked if he was going to marry Felicity.

"Intentions, sir?" Truth was Larry already knew the answer to that question. He wanted very much to marry Felicity, but he wasn't quite sure how to put that desire into words. So, for the first time in his life, Larry just trusted his instincts, closed his eyes and leapt into his answer

"Sir, I, um, I love your daughter. I have since this first time I met her. I love her now and will love her always and it would give me a great pleasure if you would, well, um, you know."

"Aw, hell, out with it boy!" Felicity's dad boomed with a growing smile on his face, because he actually was quite fond of Larry, saw a spirit of gentle kindness in him which was missing from most other people he met including his two deadbeat sons-in-law whose only skills seemed to be taking his money, and screwing around on his daughters. One with one of the bank secretaries. I mean how stupid could you be, one of his own secretaries? The other with the young boy in the mailroom. I mean, seriously, this was

Standby

beyond stupid and could seriously jeopardize the bank's standing in the community. "I said, out with it boy!!!" he boomed.

"I want to marry your daughter!" Larry boomed right back, in a voice considerably louder than he intended. Still, now that it was out, he felt enormous relief.

Felicity's father stared long and hard at Larry, who always tended to avert his gaze, and apprising himself of the situation finally said "Larry, look at me son."

Larry raised his eyes to meet those of his future father in law. A man who also happened to be his boss. "Yes, sir" he stammered.

"You have my blessing son."

Larry wept in response. He would no longer be alone. He had it all. A woman he loved, a great job, and an understanding boss who also happened to be his father in law.

"Thank you, sir"

"Larry, just one more thing" he paused, "get the hell out of my office and get to work!" he boomed with a wink and a smile. Larry left. His face held an even larger smile.

Once the door closed and Larry was safely out of earshot, he pressed the button on an intercom and said, "Felicity, you can come in now!"

Felicity came through the back door where she had been waiting in the private office. Larry never noticed the fact that the meeting took place in the outer secretarial office. She walked in, kissed her father on the cheek, and said "Thank you daddy."

"You're welcome kitten."

The wedding of Larry and Felicity Jones was quite an elaborate affair. Everyone who was anyone, and quite a few who were no ones, were in attendance. Everything was tastefully, if a tiny bit garishly, done in lace and taffeta, like all proper southern weddings. Felicity's family could trace its roots to a rather insignificant Captain in the Union Army whose only significant contribution to the war efforts was teaching army surgeons how to remove bullets from soldier's buttocks; his five buttock wounds coming from five separate engagements with Confederate soldiers, incurred while running away. These five wounds earned him three purple hearts. Even though a soldier normally received a separate purple heart for each war wound, this captain's commanding officer had to stop them at three, having been heard to say "If I gave a dammed purple heart to every cowardly ninny who soiled himself and ran in the face of combat, well, you know. So I'm cutting off Run Away Harry at three, and there it is."

Of course, the family wasn't that proud of having a coward in the family and so, as the years passed, the legend of Captain Harry evolved into a more civilized and sophisticated mantra. Run Away Harry became Rampaging Harry, or R.H., and, in point of fact, became the namesake for R.H. Savings and Loan, the bank which Felicity's father ran, a bank which could trace its roots all the way back to a cowardly Civil War Captain and, much more secretively, the chest of Confederate gold he was dragging away from the battlefield when he suffered his fifth, and most ignominious wound. A piece of confederate grapeshot, having already cut through the union lines and having shot the genitals off of a young Union private who, by coincidence, was a soprano singer in his church choir, and now would probably be the lead soprano in that choir, well, that piece of grapeshot, armed such as it was with that poor privates genitals, found its way right into the ass of Run Away Harry. Indeed, not just the buttocks, but right into his ass.

Such was the commotion at the field hospital that all available Union officers, and some lucky enlisted men, filled the field seating which was put into place so that people could view the extraction. In fact, a temporary battlefield truce was called so that some of the Rebel soldiers and their physicians could watch the extractions.

What made the moment even more priceless in history was that the piece of grapeshot which carried its genital load into Harry's ass, wasn't itself spent and traveled out through his own penis, leaving a shredded mess behind. So Harry lay on the surgeon's table, on his stomach so the world could view his ass and listened as the surgeons fretted over what to do.

Union Surgeon:"What do we do here?"

Rebel Surgeon:"Don't know"

Union Surgeon"Never seen a dick in the ass before. I mean I've heard of it, but I've just never seen it."

Rebel Surgeon:"Still though, do ya pull it out or do ya push it in and through"

Union:"Christ, Jaysus, but this surely is a conundrum."

Standby

Rebel:"Jesus, Mary and Joseph it is. And who would've thunk that the shot would go all the way through."

Union:"well, the question sort of remains, do you pull this dick out of his arse and try and stitch back on the poor choir boy screeching over there in the corner, or do you push it through to give our Run Away Captain here a second chance at manhood."

All that was left was legend. History would never tell which decision was made.

Run Away Harry kept the gold.

Back to the wedding.

It was a festive affair. Felicity chose as her wedding theme the Twelve Days Of Christmas. All was going beautifully until the wedding chef thought that the four calling birds, three French hens, two turtle doves and the partridge were all the birds for the main course and so slaughtered and butchered them for the dinner. All of this much to the chagrin and dismay of the little flower girl who instead of getting a basket of rose petals to drop on the linen walkway, was given a basket of calling bird feathers, still somewhat bloody from their recent demise, by a rather drunk leaping Lord who was actually a part time ballet dancer and the current paramour of the husband of Felicity's eldest sister.

Still, all of this would have been okay had the ring bearer, the son of Larry's sister, who still had eyes for him whenever their prom song, "My Sharona", came on at weddings, vomited all over Felicity as he reached the altar, out of shear anxiety brought on by seeing the birds slaughtered. Upon finishing his digestive misadventures, the young man held up his ring pillow and allowed Larry to pick one of the five different golden rings that lay on the pillow. Larry laid his hand upon the first one.

"Psst" Larry heard from behind him. Felicity, in her full linen and vomit regalia, was shaking her head.

Larry moved his hand to the second ring.

"Uh-Uh" she shook her head.

He touched the third ring and then glanced at her disapproving eyes.

Fearing he would get all the way to ring five, which was awfully small for his love's sausage like fingers, he gently touched ring number four, looked back at his puke-covered love, and was met with a smile.

They wed and became husband and wife, Larry & Felicity Jones. As Larry and Felicity walked down the aisle, it occurred to Larry that he had just been married to his wife by that same preacher who not so long ago was involved in a quite the indecent act in the rectory with Felicity. This struck Larry as quite wrong, quite wrong indeed. Then Larry did a most "un-Larry-like" thing. In one swift motion, he spun around and cold-cocked the preacher leaving him to be picked up by the other Lords who weren't leaping and who were, in fact, already engaged in trying to pull Felicity's sister off of the 6th Lord, now underneath the sister and getting his own clock cleaned.

Throughout the entire ceremony it was said that Felicity's father sat in a back corner and laughed the best belly laugh of his life.

The dinner?

Well, folks just said it tasted like chicken.

Chapter 15

Gilbert & Sullivan, PA was off and running. Suddenly, the one thing that Clarence Darrow Sullivan had always wanted, but had always been denied, was available to him. Respectability, clout, acceptance in the Miami legal establishment. Some form of societal acknowledgment that he was more than simply a hired gun, snake oil salesman, shyster out to make the quickest buck possible off of the sometimes made-up or falsified suffering of other people, with some real genuine catastrophic cases thrown in for good measure and to assuage whatever shred of conscience Sullivan had left. His mantra in the office, "the more they hurt, the more we make, so let's make sure they hurt", spoke volumes in regard to his love of the dollar over all else. When his moronic legion of associates settled cases they all did so with a notation in the case file that the case was "WGTM, TCMD". "We got the money, this case must die."

That was how he worked. The issue for Sullivan was never the client's best interests. The only interests that concerned him, that had ever concerned him, were his own interests. That is why cases were settled before the clients even knew a negotiation had taken place. Once the file was noted with that acronym, it was over, and everyone in the office knew it.

It often times happened that a client would hire Sullivan, then never see a lawyer nor speak to a lawyer again throughout the life of the case. In fact, watching Sullivan's commercials where he handed checks to satisfied clients who turned to the camera and smiled and said "I got hurt, I got Clarence Darrow Sullivan, and I got paid!" weren't really clients at all, but rather the very attractive women who worked in Sullivan's offices.

As for Gilbert, he had an office in the building but was generally never there. Rumor had it that Sullivan actually paid Gilbert to stay away. Sullivan had what he wanted, a recognizable name to gain him entry to the legal community. Gilbert was a liability. He had a drinking problem. Sullivan kept him in booze and golf course memberships and never had to worry about Gilbert showing up unexpectedly.

It was Sullivan's show to run.

There was, however, one decent, upstanding lawyer in Sullivan's gaggle of geese. Geoff Padua was a lawyer for whom money was never the issue. He was a trust fund baby who didn't really need the law for his livelihood but did it because he believed it was a proper calling. He worked hard for his clients, very hard and he accepted the difficult life that came with working for Sullivan and the disrepute that came with being associated with him. He did it because he got to try cases and because he loved the work. He did it because Sullivan gave him the most difficult cases.

So it was that Padua, a Midwesterner with a throaty lisp, took over all of the catastrophic cases and consistently brought home the big settlements and verdicts.

But it couldn't last, because in the end Sullivan couldn't handle anyone else in his office being a more shining star than himself. After Padua brought home his seventh consecutive sizeable verdict, he went to Sullivan to talk.

"Uh, sir, I would like to talk to you"

"What about, make it quick, I'm busy, very busy."

"Well, as you know, I've had quite a run of success lately and, in fact, the past three years you've seen your profits grown markedly."

Sullivan saw where this was going but he figured he would play it out for a while. After all, he always enjoyed watching the fish swim around with the hook firmly set. He knew he had what Padua wanted and he also knew Geoff would do anything to get it. So, ergo, Padua was hooked well and good, Sullivan was the fisherman, and he controlled the game for as long as it took to get things out of Padua. That is what this was about for Sullivan. Control. He was a control freak.

"Speak your mind Geoff, what do you need?"

Standby

Geoff answered in his typical blunt fashion.

"My name on the door, right after yours. Gilbert, Sullivan and Padua, PA. That's what I want, and what's more I think I've earned it."

Sullivan had never had one of his lawyers speak to him so directly. In fact, when Gilbert and he partnered up, it was Sullivan who drove the negotiations and it was Sullivan's proposal that eventually, and typically, held the day.

"Well, Geoffrey, that sure is an interesting sounding proposal. Why don't we think on it for awhile?"

Then Geoff did something that no one did to Sullivan. He looked Sullivan right in the eye and said,

"No."

To say Sullivan was taken aback would be a pure understatement. No one had ever said "No" to him. Everyone who worked for him was a "Yes" man or woman. No exceptions.

"Well, Geoffrey, I must say I am taken aback by your direct approach but I would remind you that this is my firm and I make the decisions in my own good time."

"Funny, I thought it was Gilbert's firm also."

"Gilbert?" Sullivan said with mounting incredulity, "Why he couldn't wipe my ass now could he?"

"Clarence, I am here. I have always been here and would like to always be here, if you understand what I am saying." Padua replied with just a hint of disdain in his voice. "But there is something which I think you will have to acknowledge."

Geoff pressed on while a flabbergasted Sullivan stared at him open-mouthed. He could not imagine how this punk could dare think of talking to him, Clarence Darrow Sullivan, like this. After all, he made and broke little punks like this everyday, didn't he?

"I know what you're thinking, Clarence. I truly do. You are thinking that I am a punk, that you cannot imagine how I could talk to you like this, and that you make and break guys like me every day. Well, let me tell you this. One, I am 36 years old, I am a trial lawyer, and I have been in the trenches my entire career. By any account I am not a punk. Two, I talk to you like this because no one else does nor ever has. And three, you haven't made or broken anyone in a very very long time. In fact, while by my calculations I do all of your trials, you can't find the courthouse. You are a joke in the legal community. You are the festering sore on the ass of the bar. And, deep down you know it; otherwise you wouldn't have made the desperate move of bringing that old drunk in as a name partner. Gilbert & Sullivan, really, honestly, can't you see how pathetic that is?"

Clarence stared open-mouthed.

Geoff continued with just the slightest hesitation.

"So, here is my proposal then. You have one week to accept it, in which case I stay and continue making you a lot of money. You can reject it, in which case I walk and take my talents elsewhere. I want my name on the door. That's right, Gilbert, Sullivan and Padua. And that will only be for one year, during which time you will buy out Gilbert and send him off to his alcohol addled bliss. That's right, he's done, he's through. I am your trial lawyer. He is just a name with a bar tab. Lastly, and this one ain't negotiable either. You give me twenty-five percent of the firm. I'm willing to give you majority control but I want a real partnership."

Sullivan just continued to stare like a deer in the headlights. He stammered out "W-Well, lets see what we can put together. Let's take a few days, Geoff, and see what you and I can work out when we aren't so tense."

Geoff just smiled because he knew that in just the last few moments he had completely broken the will of a man who was used to bending everyone to his will. Geoff had the power because he made Sullivan an extremely large amount of money and he knew that Sullivan could never give up that kind of revenue.

"Clarence, you have one week, seven days, and after that I walk."

During the next seven days hardly a word was spoken between Clarence and Geoff. Like a good employee Geoff continued to work hard. He knew he had played every card he had and yet he also knew that Sullivan held the aces. Geoff was bluffing now and it was a really high stakes game. He was all-in, had a smaller chip count, and Sullivan had "the nuts" as they said on the poker tour. Would his bluff hold?

Two days before the deadline was the office holiday party. It was held in a very upscale restaurant at which Sullivan had paid a considerable amount of money to insure that all the waiters acted like

Standby

they knew him by first name. As usual, the luncheon began tamely while Sullivan built up to the "question of the day". Gilbert, in the meantime, was passed out at the last chair with his sixth vodka gimlet in one hand, and the thigh of the pretty young receptionist in the other. He had promised her the position of being his secretary if she went home with him after lunch. She intended to keep the promise although it was certainly clear that Gilbert wouldn't be performing much short of a salute to the porcelain cheering section.

Geoff sat at the far end of the table with the two youngest associates, engaged in intense conversation on subjects beyond the pale of this holiday lunch of decadence.

Then, Sullivan asked the question that no one anticipated, one that no decent man would ask.

"Ok, folks, here it is, the question of the year. Let's take care of this business and then we will have the women's no hands cake-eating contest with the second place getting $100.00 and first prize being a night out on the town with me! How does that sound?"

The responses were mixed.

"Well, never mind that; let's get on with the question and answer. The question is: If you had to hire one lawyer in the firm to handle your case, who would it be, and why?" He said this with a degree of alcohol-emboldened contempt and stared right at Geoff while he said it. What Sullivan didn't know, and couldn't know since he only spent around two hours a day, maximum, in the office, was that while he was out cavorting with his young girlfriend with the fake boobs, ass, chin, nose, multiple piercings and tattoos which Clarence loved so much, that while that was happening, Geoff was making plans for his exit. Those plans included securing the loyalties of the best office staff and lawyers.

They glared at each other while the answers started to come in. To be fair, it was quite difficult for the staff to do this since they knew the answer Clarence always wanted to hear although usually to questions like "Who is the best looking?" was "Sullivan", of course.

The first staff member to get the question was a mailroom worker. Geoff hadn't spoken to her, but she had a raving crush on him. She said, naturally and honestly, "Geoff".

The next three staff secretaries all said "Geoff", and watched as Sullivan's face reddened.

And so it went on with alternating mentions of "Sullivan" or "Geoff".

Gilbert stirred just about the time the game came to his able and willing young assistant for answer. As his hand crept up to her breast, she blurted out "Mr. Gilbert!" much to the amusement of this audience of co-employees. A drunk Mr. Gilbert? Honestly…

Then, it came to Geoff. He said to Sullivan, "I'm pressing the deadline up to right now. Everything we talked about is decided right now!"

"Hold on a second, this is just a fun, innocent game" replied Sullivan.

"No, it's not, its mean-spirited and demeaning and debasing!" he paused and then said, "I don't need any more time. I'm leaving. Consider this my immediate notice." He tossed a hundred dollar bill on the table and said, "This is for my lunch." and he walked out of the room, trailed by the two young associates, half a dozen of the staff including the pretty girl from the mail room, and, running out behind them, the receptionist who managed to pry herself away from the drunk and drooling Gilbert.

Two days later, the Law Offices of Geoffrey Padua, PA opened right down the street from Gilbert & Sullivan, PA.

Geoff's first client was Deacon Air where his best friend from law school was the corporate counsel for the airline.

Chapter 16

Larry and Sue sat in uncomfortable silence. Kim, or Sue, or whatever her real name was, was trying to come to terms with the fact that the man she thought she was, well, servicing was not the man she was really was with. This guy, Larry something, was a nothing, a nobody, and she had just given him the proverbial good time, and hadn't even charged him extra for the extras she gave him. All because she thought he was Edsel Dodger, the adult toy guy, with links to the pornography industry. So she gave him the freebie just because she thought she could express her special talents to him in exchange for some introduction to the business. After all, all that strange little airport guy paid for was a massage; the rest had been her idea.

For his part, Larry was completely flustered and flabbergasted.

"Hey, you, 'Mr. guy with the phony name'!" she barked at him.

Larry stared at the floor.

"I'm talking to you, man. You ain't Edsel Dodger, I know that now and should have known it last night. Ain't no way a guy that looks like you could be in the adult toy business? Hell, I should've known about it last night, never would've given you a freebie. Way I see it; you owe me three hundred dollars. That's what I charge for what you got. And I don't take credit cards, so pony up mister."

Larry continued to stare at the floor.

"Hey, mister, I'm talking to you. You hear me? You gone stupid on me? You didn't have any problem last night while I was handling that needle dick of yours. Course it wasn't for very long, you must be really hard up. I mean, shit, can't you even last a minute? Damn, man, that wife of yours, and I know you got a wife, she must be one unsatisfied woman."

With that, the last insult, something snapped in Larry. Some wire that had always been set a little too tight in his head finally snapped and let go. Maybe it was the yapping in his ear from this woman, maybe it was the realization that his life was about to become the definition of chaos, or maybe, and most likely, it was the insult about not satisfying his wife, something he knew was true and something which he had tried for years to overcome but couldn't. Whatever it was, at this moment it snapped and for the first time in his life, Larry really lost his temper.

"Will you please shut the fuck up?" he yelled catching Sue, or Kim, depending on your mood and your pleasure, completely off guard and shutting her up immediately.

Larry continued yelling.

"Please, shut up, I cannot think with your incessant babbling. I mean, really, do you think that right now, at this moment, I care about your desire to be a porn star?"

Sue found her voice.

"It's adult film actress, sweetie, and you didn't seem to mind last night when I was…"

Larry interrupted her.

"Shut up! Please, will you shut up? Just shut the fuck up and let me think!" he yelled as began pacing the room. "Okay, just let me think out loud here, without being interrupted. All right, what do I do? I'm here in a hotel room in Los Angeles. I was almost on that plane and I guess I would've survived since whoever was sitting in my seat survived. And who the hell was in my seat? I mean there could've been anyone in my seat. Wait a second, why do they think it's me that survived when I'm here?" he asked of no one in particular.

Larry turned up the volume on the TV.

"…Repeating our top story, Deacon Air flight 721 crashed last night on approach into Miami International Airport. The cause of the crash is as yet unknown but it is believed that the plane encountered a flock of large white pelicans that were sucked into the one of the engines. There was one survivor. He is very badly injured and it is unclear whether he will survive the day as he sustained extensive

Standby

burns over his head and face, as well as the loss of both hands and his tongue, along with the traumatic ...."

Both Larry and Sue cringed.

"... The airline has, once again, identified this passenger as Larry Jones. Although all of his identification is missing and presumed lost, apparently Mr. Jones was handcuffed to his seat, and his entire seat broke loose carrying Mr. Jones clear of the burning wreckage but rather unfortunately landing him in a pile of manatee dung. Now, back to the Ophelia Show, her topic today, men who love men who love women who love chocolate."

The TV switched back to regularly scheduled program.

Sue spoke first after a long pause. "Well, honey, I know that guy from the crash ain't you."

Larry just lifted his head and looked at her blankly.

Strangely out of character, Sue walked behind Larry and began gently massaging his neck muscles. It was what the doctor ordered but Larry was feeling terribly about what Felicity must be going through. Ordinarily he wouldn't be all that concerned about her knowing something that came up on the news, but he knew there were two television programs that she never missed. One was the prayer hour with the Right Reverend Thomas. Felicity told Larry that the good reverend was a man of God and she surely loved the look of a strong black man. The other program that took on sort of a religious significance for Felicity was the Ophelia show. It didn't matter the topic, she never missed the program.

Larry knew that his wife saw the program and must now know that *he* was hospitalized with some pretty bad injuries. What could he do now?

What could he do?

Sue's work on his neck had its effect. Larry dozed.

There was another pounding on the door.

"Open the door Mr. Jones; I know that you are in there, open up!!!"

What the hell could this mean, he wondered, and who would know that he was here? Larry walked toward the door.

"Wait! Don't open that yet!" yelled Sue. Larry turned towards her voice and saw her coming out of the bathroom, in a hotel robe, and toweling off her head. "You don't know who it is or what he wants." Larry wasn't sure he had ever seen a more beautiful sight.

"I know," he replied, "but nothing about all of this makes any sense at all. I can't keep dealing with this roller coaster. All I know is that apparently I was injured very badly in the crash of a plane that I wasn't on, and apparently I'm locked up in a hospital room which can't be true because I'm right here with a beautiful woman who definitely isn't my wife while some strange man bangs on my door."

Sue blinked.

"You think I'm beautiful?" she said.

"What? Oh yes, sure, you are beautiful, but that's not the question on the table. It's really very simple. Do I open the door or not?"

She thought for a moment and then said, "Sure, open it, but give me a second." And before he could open the door, she was out of the robe; back in underwear and wearing a t-shirt she had picked up somewhere. She settled into some sort of martial arts ready position.

"What's that all about?" asked Larry.

"Girl's gotta take care of herself in this business you know."

She winked at Larry.

Larry felt a flutter in his chest, threw his shoulders back and reached for the door handle.

Before he could finish opening the door, a whirling dervish of red hair and cheap cologne came barreling through the door.

"Who the hell are you?!" yelled the redheaded intruder.

"I'm the guy in this room, who the hell are you?" Larry demanded. He was coming to enjoy this new confidence in himself.

The smaller man settled himself and combed his fingers through his hair. He looked around the room, at the room service trays, the television left on. Then he pulled himself up to his full, but still quite short, height.

"Percy, lighten up." Sue said to the whirling redheaded dervish.

"Sue, I will lighten up when I choose to. And, what the hell are you still doing here anyway."

"My business, not yours."

"You are my business. That pretty little Asian ass of yours is my business. And you better not have slept with him; all I paid for was a massage!"

"Fuck you Percy!"

Standby

Larry intervened.

"Percy, that is your name right? Percy? Do me a favor and shut the fuck up please!"

Percy responded in kind.

"Listen, Larry, or whatever the hell your name is, I know that you are not Mr. Dodger, I know this because I took you off of the plane. Mr. Dodger had your seat, and if he remained in that seat, then he is right now in a hospital bed in Miami, unable to speak or communicate in any fashion. And you are here with his boarding pass. As I see it neither of you had the appropriate identification, but I'm sure if you check out that man purse over there, you will find Mr. Dodger's identification, credit cards, and cash. As I see it you must contact the authorities right now and tell them you aren't on the plane and that you are, in fact, shacked up in a hotel room with a woman who most definitely is not your wife. How that plays out on the home front is not my concern."

"So, what is your concern?" asked Larry.

"Why don't both of you just sit down awhile and I will tell you my plan."

They sat.

Chapter 17

Felicity was just beside herself. Not with grief, as most wives would've responded, but with a controlled glee. She wasn't in love with Larry, hadn't been for a long while, and, truth be told, probably never was, although the wedding night brought out some considerable passion in her, due in large part to Larry's decking of the preacher who really wasn't a very good lay anyhow.

No, Felicity wasn't particularly broken up by the news of the crash, nor was she broken up at the apparent extent of her husband's injuries. Nope. Felicity's reaction was joy. Now she knew that her prayers, and donations, to the Right Reverend Thomas had been answered. Sure she had sent him thousands of dollars from her rapidly diminishing trust fund, and sure she never got an answer in return. But she just knew that the Lord worked in mysterious ways.

Felicity Jones was a woman in the midst of a dilemma. Her trust fund from her daddy was rapidly running out. Daddy was refusing to put any more money in the fund for her. Meanwhile, what she did have went into donations to Reverend Thomas and purchasing large quantities of whatever book Ophelia was telling people to buy, figuring that the least she could do was help get the book on the bestseller list because she knew, she just knew, that once that book was made into a movie, she would be the first one in line to see the movie. Otherwise, Felicity wouldn't know what the books were about because she never read a book in her life. Fact is, most people who knew her weren't sure if she could even read.

However, back to the main issue in her mind, what can she get out of her husband's apparent suffering? It was then, during the

Standby

Reverend Thomas' program that she saw the TV commercial for that lawyer, Clarence Darrow something or other, or whatever his name was. The problem was that his ad had already run and Felicity didn't know how to use a phone book. Instead, she just sat there watching the television and waiting for the advertisement to come on the air. Finally, several hours, and several boxes of chocolate later, the ad ran again and she called the number. She called Clarence Darrow Sullivan for his help. She did this before ever taking the time to go to the hospital. She definitely had her priorities in order.

Ordinarily Sullivan didn't take initial intake phone calls. Forgetting for a moment that many new clients were calling simply because the Pit Bull had told them he wanted to be their lawyer, the truth really was that the Hammer had no interest in ever meeting or speaking to a client. Indeed, he had been heard to murmur, "This law crap would be a great business if it weren't for the damn clients." In fact, the only time Clarence Darrow Sullivan ever met with a client was if the client refused to accept a settlement offer and that meeting was for the sole purpose of his actually hammering the client into submission and acceptance of the offer. This was happening more and more as Padua wasn't with his firm anymore and the litigation attorneys still with the firm lacked the intestinal fortitude for the courtroom. Since there was no one around to try the cases, the insurance industry started figuring out that they could settle cheap with Sullivan and made their offers accordingly.

However, this day wasn't like any other day. There had been a major plane crash just outside of downtown Miami. Right on the edge of that manatee farm. "Jesus", thought Sullivan, "I wish I had discovered that manatee crap was great fertilizer." But he hadn't and instead he was like so many other low-end advertising lawyers busily trying to pick up the scraps that the high-end reputable firms couldn't get. In other words, there was a feeding frenzy to sign up cases. Nothing quite like a major air disaster to bring out the better angels of the personal injury bar.

A plane crash had two things that other accidents did not. This was a simple fact that Sullivan held dear. Two things. Lots of victims and, even more importantly, lots of publicity. "If only I could get a damned client", he thought.

Sullivan needed a client, a real client. It was at this moment that the fates smiled down upon him. The phone rang and into Sullivan's office came running Ramon Scola, one of his two remaining trial lawyers.

"We got it boss," Ramon shouted, running through the office on his way to brown-nose Sullivan, tell him how wonderful he is, and show him what could be the mother lode. "We got the call!"

"Slow down Ramon, and tell me what you are talking about!"

Ramon Scola was a nice enough guy with average courtroom skills. But what made him valuable to Sullivan's firm was his willingness to kiss the ass of the boss at every opportunity. It always helped Sullivan feel better.

"The crash, Deacon Air 721, the crash, the guy who survived."

"What?" replied Sullivan, hardly believing his apparent good fortune.

"The real deal, boss. The wife of the guy who is in the burn unit at County General. You know, Larry Jones? Well his wife, Felicia or something like that is on the phone and wants to talk to you. This is it boss, I know it, and I can feel it." Ramon was now breathless.

"Alright", thought Sullivan, "take a deep breath. Get the call but act like you are busy and let her know you handle these type of cases all the time."

"She's on line 3, boss."

So Clarence Darrow Sullivan, king of the advertising lawyers, was about to enter the world of high end, big stakes aviation law. He pressed the blinking button, kept it on speaker so Ramon could listen in and admire him, and spoke in his deepest television voice

"Mrs. Jones, this is Clarence Darrow Sullivan." He slowly pronounced every part of his name, as if she had no idea to whom she was speaking. Ramon bounced in his seat and gave Sullivan two thumbs up.

You could feel the excitement on the other end of the phone. "My Lord, I never, well just never thought I would actually speak to you Clarence, um, I mean Mr. Sullivan."

"Take a breath ma'am, I know how difficult this must be." he spoke with a sense of sympathy that didn't exist in him but he knew it made good theater for Ramon. Ramon couldn't sit still.

"Well, as you know, my husband was on that Deacon Air plane that crashed in the shit farm, oh my, excuse me, the uh, um.."

Standby

"Ma'am, its okay, I know the crash. I've been busy talking to victim's families all day." Clarence winked at Ramon.

"Well, he is hurt real bad as you know and I suppose I need a lawyer and I always watch the Reverend Thomas and I always see your ad, and I say to myself, 'Felicity', that's my name by the way, Felicity Jones, oh my, but you must have already known that. Well, I says to myself, 'Felicity, if you ever need a lawyer and if the good Lord has seen fit to put your commercial right there in the Reverend Thomas' prayer hour, well, then, I guess that man is my lawyer'."

Sullivan had never heard so much driveling babble. But he knew what he had to do.

"Mrs., ah, Jones is it? I'm very busy here what with the Deacon Air 27 crash…"

"Don't you mean 721?"

"What? Oh yes, what did I say?" he blushed as he scribbled a note and slipped it to Ramon who grabbed it and ran out into the office.

"What did you say, ma'am, you will have to forgive me, my phones are ringing off he hook with people calling my office for legal representation. Just listen…." He said as he opened his office door. Just as he did so the entire staff began shouting back and forth as if the office was busy. He drew his fingers across his throat to stop the noise, which it did immediately, and left the door open for Ramon to run back in.

"I'm sorry ma'am, I closed my door for you, so how can I help?"

"Well, do you think I need a lawyer?"

This was the opening he was waiting for. Sullivan broke into his canned speech. "Mrs. Jones, I became a lawyer because I believe in America and because I believe in the Constitution of the United States of America. That Constitution guarantees you and all Americans the right to an attorney of your choosing. A lawyer to protect your interests against the government, against big companies that cut corners and take advantage of you, and against insurance companies that are only about profits. I believe this because I am about people, not profits. Ma'am, you need a lawyer because that is the American way."

"Why, thank you, but have you handled plane crash cases before?"

"Of course I have." Lie.

"And will you go to trial if necessary?"

"Of course." Bigger lie.

"And will you be my lawyer in the courtroom?"

Sullivan paused. He knew he was on the brink of something big and knew the next answer would decide whether or not he got the case. He paused only for a moment.

"Yes, ma'am, I will be honored to be your trial lawyer." Biggest Lie.

Even the normally kiss-ass prone Ramon blanched at this one. He knew Sullivan wouldn't know the courtroom from the bathroom.

"Then you are my lawyer." Felicity replied to the unseen Sullivan who was currently dancing around his office pumping his fist in the air while Ramon began weeping at the success of his idol.

"Mr. Sullivan, here is my address, I assume I will be seeing you soon."

Meanwhile, at the County general hospital, Edsel Dodger lay in a drug-induced haze, able to see only through slits of bandage that covered his damaged face. He tried to grab at the damages but realized that he had no fingers. Then he tried to speak and realized that he had no tongue and very few teeth. Every time he tried to speak it came out as "ah, ah, ah." He laid there listening to the doctors and nurses talk about him.

"Poor fella, no fingers, must've been torn off by the handcuffs he was in."

"Yes, doctor, and he also will have to learn how to speak without a tongue."

"You know, they said his tongue was right near him but when the paramedics came to retrieve it one of those big white pelicans that survived the crash had it in its beak. Who knew pelicans liked tongue?"

"Yeah, but I think the worst thing for this poor guy is the infection this guy is gonna develop after swallowing all that manatee shit. Imagine, landing face first in a pile of manatee crap."

Edsel felt himself getting dizzy and wanted to vomit but couldn't open his mouth enough due to the bandages all over him.

"Well, anyhow, we do the best we can, what's this fella's name anyhow? James?"

Standby

"No, it's Jones, Larry Jones."

At that Edsel let out the loudest cry, "MuaaaaH!"

The nurse, with the doctor's approval, turned up the pain medication and Edsel Dodger went to sleep.

Clarence Darrow Sullivan knew the benefit of a press conference. Fresh from his meeting with Felicity where she signed her contract with him, but in a new freshly pressed suit, Clarence held his first press conference about the crash and his new client...

"Ladies and gentlemen, if you will just wait a moment, we will answer your questions one at a time, but first I have some prepared remarks that I would like to address to you."

The press, to a man, rolled their eyes. They knew that Sullivan was just another egomaniacal plaintiff's lawyer, but they also knew that somehow he, over every other lawyer in the county, had the story. The one survivor of the crash now had this shyster as his lawyer. So, since they had stories to write, they had a press conference to handle and this meant they would each have to listen to his press conference and his statement.

Sullivan stared into the camera, put on his earnest television face, and began

"Ladies and gentlemen, ever since I was a young boy I have believed in the American dream and the American Way. I grew up in an America where if you built something it didn't break, and if it did break, you stood up and took responsibility for what you had done" he said this as he wore his smartest earth tones selected by a publicist who he retained earlier that day for a substantial amount of money. But when you had the homerun case, you paid the homerun costs.

One of the other things the publicist taught him earlier that day was to make his statements brief and to the point and get the victim out in front of the cameras as soon as possible.

"And so I finish with this. Deacon Air is responsible for this crash and my client's catastrophic, indeed, horrendous injuries. Felicity Jones, an honest God-fearing woman who loved, no, excuse me, loves her husband, and is entitled to compensation." Then, he stared right at the closest camera and said, "Deacon Air will pay."

Then, the questions.

"Mrs. Jones, why haven't you been to the hospital to see your husband?"

They had anticipated the question and the answer, practiced over and over in the car with the publicist before the press conference, came easily to her, "Because I have been so terribly stunned by what has happened. I will be going later today, right after I go to worship in my church."

"What was with the handcuffs on your husband?"

Sullivan knew this question would be coming so he intervened, "I think that's probably enough for now, my client is obviously shaken by these events and is quite emotional." She actually was not and in fact she was preening for the cameras. Clarence took her arm and loaded her into his car.

On the other side of town, in the corporate headquarters of Deacon Air, Geoff Padua, formerly of Gilbert & Sullivan, and now the attorney for the airline, watched the press conference on television and smiled as the first stages of a plan formed in his mind. He turned to his assistant.

"Marcia, I need to know everything there is to know about why this fella was in handcuffs. Get me the cockpit tapes."

Back at the office, Sullivan was telling Ramon to file a lawsuit immediately. Ramon actually drew together the nerve to protest.

"Boss, I tell you, this isn't how it's done. In these crash cases you usually get quick settlements. Wait a bit. See what happens."

Sullivan had another plan.

"Bullshit, this is the big one Ramon! You file suit first, get out in front of things, press them toward trial, then they pay the money."

"Boss, I appreciate that, but can't we negotiate outside of litigation?"

"Usually I would say yes. But this case is gonna change everything for us, Ramon." Sullivan placed special emphasis on the "us". "Besides, just think how big your one percent bonus is going to be on this one."

Ramon simply wasn't mentally equipped to disagree with his boss and so he turned to walk away.

"Ramon, sit please for a moment, I have another idea."

"Yes?"

"What if, and I'm just freewheeling here, what if you after you draft a lawsuit, for my signature of course, against Deacon Air alleging whatever you have to allege, and we file it first thing tomorrow with the appropriate press conference, of course. What if then we issue a statement? Something like, 'Crusading Attorney takes first step in bringing justice for clients against Deacon Air'!"

"I like it boss!" Ramon said grinning from ear to ear.

Sullivan sat quietly, rubbing his temples, savoring the moment, the drama. Then he spoke, "Ramon, draft the complaint, we file suit tomorrow as soon as the courthouse opens."

Ramon practically flew out of his chair and ran to the door without a word.

"Oh, Ramon," and Ramon turned, "Remember, make it for my signature."

Chapter 18

Larry, Sue and Percy sat looking at each other in the hotel room. The silence was deafening. Each of them with eyes glued to the large television that replayed graphic images of the crash scene over and over. Then, the image would fade to a picture of Larry, obtained from the Department of Motor Vehicles. An old picture of him, but a fairly decent likeness.

Sue broke the silence.

"Okay, guys, I don't mean to break up the quiet, but what in the hell are we going to do? I mean, sheesh, I just blew the sole survivor of the first plane crash in who knows how long, except I thought he was someone else, and now I'm not sure about anything. So, what in the hell are we going to do?"

Percy stared at her open-mouthed. He, too, was confused about what they were going to do. Something told him to distance himself from both of them but he had a nagging concern. As he was the one who arranged for this very opulent room for the man he thought was Edsel Dodger, only to now find out that the man occupying the room was actually the only survivor of a plane crash, but not really since he had been in the room all night. Well, Percy didn't know much but this much he did know. There was going to be hell to pay with the airline when the executives put two and two together.

"I don't know what to do but I think we all need to get the hell out of here as soon as possible" remarked Percy "cause I think there is going to be hell to pay when the airline starts putting this together. And even more when they find out that Larry Jones ain't in a hospital bed in Miami but is actually occupying the most expensive suite in a very expensive hotel in the company of a very expensive whore."

"Hey, asshole, I am not a whore!" yelled Sue. "And you know it!"

"Shut up bitch!" responded Percy

"There is only one bitch in this room. Shit, I bet you could give me blow job lessons."

With that, Percy stood up and in one motion slapped Sue across the mouth. The room went deathly silent and for the first time Larry actually lifted his head from his hands and turned to face the commotion.

Sue became very still and fixed Percy with an icy glare. All five feet of her stood right in front of Percy while he recognized the trouble he had just created. "Hey, I'm sorry, the stress of the moment and all" he stammered "I never hit a girl in my life, and well, I'm really very sorry."

"No problem" she said with a smile. "Its over and done with, and I probably deserved it just a little for what I said to you. Friends?" she said as she held out her hand.

Percy relaxed for a moment and smiled and said, "Deal. Friends" and he put out his hand to shake hers. At that moment he realized he had made an enormous mistake for just as his hand contacted hers she yanked him towards her while simultaneously delivering a vicious kick to his crotch. Percy yelled once and fell to the floor where he couldn't move, and eventually passed out from the pain.

"Nice kick." Larry said. It was actually the first thing he had said in a long time. "Well, one thing is for sure, we can't stay here. I need to get home. As much as the idea of leaving my wife forever appeals to me, we just cannot stay here."

"Why not?"

"Because while you guys were having your lovers quarrel, I was going though that damned purple suitcase. You know what's in there?"

"What?"

"About three million dollars if my math is right, and it usually is, and it surely isn't for some legitimate reason."

"Why do you say that?"

"Its simple, one, no one carries that much cash around for a good reason, two, the bills are all old bills with what I figure are no consecutive serial numbers, and three...."

"What's three?"

"Well, I went through than man purse thing of his. All the names in there are strange, sort of Slavic sounding names, along with a small handwritten note on one of those post-it things."

Sue was bouncing off walls with anticipation now. "Well, what the hell does the note say?"

"It says 'be gone by Friday or else, call Javis for problems, 16-2882, remember – out of L.A. by Friday'."

"Larry, what the hell does that mean? It makes no sense. Who is Javis? Those numbers aren't a telephone number, and why the hell get out of L.A. by Friday."

"I don't know. I only know that I need to get to Florida as soon as possible and I need to see my wife before she does something stupid. But, here is the problem, I have no wallet, no credit cards and no identification. So, I can't fly and I can't rent a car so I'm going to need your help" he said as he glanced out the hotel window at a dark Sedan which had pulled up and was presently unloading three very large men in sunglasses; none of whom looked like they were from AAA.

Larry was suddenly filled with a feeling of dread. He instinctively knew those men were here for the bag he held and they surely didn't look like the type of guys who would be interested in an explanation about mistaken identity.

"Do you have a car here?"

"Huh?" she replied.

"I said do you have a car here?" he replied with a greater sense of urgency.

"Yes, a convertible mustang, I've worked really hard for it."

"Grab your stuff, we are outta here."

"Larry, what is going on here? Where are we going? Why do I have to go?"

"Do me a favor, shut the hell up and get your shit. We are gone like right now."

At that, Percy started to gingerly stand up and ask, "What are you doing?"

Sue looked at Percy and then to Larry and said "Larry, what do

Standby

we do with him?"

Larry looked back and, for reasons he couldn't quite understand, said "Bring him."

So out the door they went, Larry carrying the large purple suitcase and the man purse, Sue carrying her small bag and helping Percy walk. They exited the room together and Sue began to turn right for the elevator.

"Not that way, we better take the stairs." said Percy.

They reached the exit at the bottom of the stairs. Larry peaked his head outside and whispered to Sue.

"Where is your car?"

"Right over there behind the pole," she replied and they headed off in that direction.

Sue jumped behind the wheel. Larry began to protest but she told him in no uncertain terms that this was her car, her pride and joy, and testosterone be damned, she was driving. Larry consented.

He tossed the luggage into the trunk and as he was helping Percy into the car, he looked up at his hotel room window and saw the three large dark suited men in his room, looking down at him and pointing and beginning to pull what looked like guns from their belts.

"Shit, we gotta go now, they're coming."

"Who is coming?" replied Sue

"Which car?" asked a noticeably uncomfortable Percy.

"What?" asked Larry.

"Which fucking car did they come in?!" yelled Percy.

"That big sedan over there," Larry pointed.

"Count to sixty and start driving whether I am in the car or not."

"Okay."

With that, Percy climbed out of the car, jogged painfully over to the sedan and climbed in. Larry stared in disbelief. Why on earth would Percy climb into that car? And about thirty seconds later, with around 10 seconds to spare, Percy jogged back to the car carrying the steering wheel of the sedan.

"Go!" He yelled.

Sue floored it and headed for the I-10 expressway, heading east at Larry's direction.

"Hey, Percy" said Sue quietly

"Yeah" he moaned back.

"How the hell did you learn to take out a steering wheel?"

"Product of a misspent youth. Remember, nothing worse than a bitchy bitch."

Larry and Sue smiled.

"Percy?"

"Yes, Sue?"

"I'm sorry I kicked you."

"And I'm sorry I slapped you."

"I love you Percy."

"You too, honey."

Larry looked at Sue for an explanation.

She shrugged. "Long story, for another time."

Larry looked in the back of the car. Percy had drifted off to sleep crying about needing an ice pack very badly.

Chapter 19

Franklin Thomas left the hospital on a Tuesday. Ronnie "Weasel" James left the hospital the next day. They sat together in a diner near the hospital, the Weasel only knowing a few places to eat, most were near the hospital and he liked the split pea soup at this particular diner. They sat together, looking at each other across a linoleum table with scratchy cracked faux leather red booths, and pondered their future. Weasel slurping up pea soup and Franklin diving into a very large cheeseburger with all the fixings.

"So, Ronnie, what are we gonna do?"

"Dunno Mr. Thomas."

"Well, son" Franklin had taken to calling the Weasel 'son' even though he was younger and had less world experience "well, we need to find ourselves a real career, a genuine form of employment, cause I ain't intending to be dining on diner food and living in a trailer park." These last words were said with increasing volume as a busload of churchgoers was entering the diner.

"Well, Mr. Thomas...."

"Call me Franklin, dammit!"

"Ok, Mr. Thomas, uh, Franklin, the only thing I can think of is to open some sort of cleaning company, I know all the ins and outs of cleaning, and might be able to arrange some, what you call it, independent contractor business." This was when Franklin noticed that Ronnie had a somewhat annoying, although probably not intentional, habit of whistling through his nose when he was excited or when he spoke more that seven or eight words at time. He looked at Ronnie and smiled, as if telling him to go on, he was listening.

"Well, see, here is the thing, we get a contract with a small nursing home, and take care of all the cleaning needs. Just you and me. We do it dirt cheap too, the first time that is. Show them how honorable and decent we are and what a great job we can do when we put our minds to it. Start out at 50% of whatever their in-house cleaning people are charging and then, real slow like, build up our prices until we are charging at least what their own people are charging and maybe, just maybe a tad bit more.

Franklin studied Ronnie with an inquisitive look. As he got to know this man he realized that while most people would just see the guy who cleaned their shit, if you got to know him, behind all the exterior nonsense was a brain that worked hard. Not an entirely blessed brain, but a working head nonetheless, and with proper guidance, perhaps even a degree of street-earned intelligence that most people lacked. He raised an eyebrow, uncrossed his arms, leaned forward and nodded his head to Ronnie to continue.

This encouragement was all Ronnie needed. For the next hour, while the church ladies devoured their ham and cheese sandwiches and "Lord, no, I just shouldn't" pieces of apple pie, Ronnie regaled Franklin with a very detailed explanation of the custodial business, how to get the supplies, some of which he was storing in his trailer, probably enough to get them started, and who the contacts were in the business. See, Ronnie was wired in to the local nursing home community as his sister, just a couple of years younger than he, managed a string of three or four nursing homes, and was an excellent contact for them if they chose to do this.

Franklin listened to him go on and on and realized that Ronnie was probably onto something, perhaps not something big, but something certainly something at which they could make a living. What was more amazing to Franklin was that while Ronnie was spouting on and on about solvents, and bleaches, and what rate of shit was produced at a nursing home – and, my oh my, how his nostrils whistled at that one, no, what amazed Franklin is that he could be paying attention to every word Ronnie was saying while at the same time thinking about something else. Formulating another plan. His entire life had been dedicated to football or studies, but never both at the same time. It was now like suddenly because football wasn't an option; his mind was free to explore other options.

Standby

He interrupted Ronnie.

"Ronnie, two things I wanna say to you and I want you to shut up just long enough to hear 'em both, okay?"

Ronnie nodded his head and took no offense at being told to "shut up", after all this was his new, and only, friend.

"One, I think your idea is fantastic, just great, and I think we should go into it full bore, but with some proper business planning. Sounds like your sister could be of some service."

Ronnie was just beaming now. He had an amazing new friend, and he wanted to involve his sister. Wouldn't she just be so proud that I was bringing her a great business idea?

"And two, I'm gonna be a preacher."

"Huh?" said Ronnie

"Yessir, a real fire and brimstone preacher. You know the kind that holds the rallies, but my rallies are gonna be for the older folks and the sick and injured folks. Then, after I get them all excited, I'm gonna recommend the nursing homes which you and your sister manage, and which I am part owner, with you of course, although my ownership is gonna be real quiet."

"Wow."

"Yup, that is the plan, and we are gonna make it happen, together." Then Franklin rose and walked outside, leaving the check for Ronnie to handle, which he did without blinking an eye.

They began by going to see Ronnie's sister.

Ronnie explained everything to her and when he was done she bit her lower lip for a moment and said, "Ronald Reagan James, that is about the gosh-darned dumbest thing I ever heard."

Franklin started laughing, first at hearing Ronnie's full name, and second, that Ronnie's sister was about four feet ten, and about 90 pounds, could hold such sway over him.

Ronnie looked back and forth between his sister and Franklin and became more and more upset. He chose the easier path. "Now, Dolly Madison James, just one second. This is a good plan!"

Franklin fell right out of his chair. The names were just too priceless. Both Ronnie and Dolly looked down at him, first in anger and then in growing amusement as this giant of a man rolled around on the floor laughing until tears came from his eyes. Dolly, primarily, was enjoying the show. In fact, truth be told, she was become mildly turned on by this man laying on her office floor, this man who was at least three times her size.

Then Franklin composed himself and sat back down and told both of them to take his hands and look into his eyes. "Dolly, Ronald, I will not fail. It will not happen. I will take to this business the same drive I too to the football field. I will succeed and you will succeed with me."

Ronnie's hand was cool and dry and he nodded his head in full acceptance of Franklin's message.

Dolly's hand was wet with sweat as she too nodded.

Their entry into the nursing home business was slow and difficult, primarily because Franklin was busy at work becoming ordained in the First Missionary Church of God, based on a website out of California. For one thousand dollars, Franklin Thomas became the Right Reverend Franklin Thomas. Then he set about to spread his gospel. And what better place to do so that in the nursing home his now girlfriend, Dolly, managed.

Reverend Franklin came in like Moses through the wilderness, spreading love, hugs and the gospel according to Franklin. And the residents of that nursing loved him and worshiped him, especially his massive frame and thundering baritone voice. And when, after an hour long sermon filed with brimstone and salvation, he quieted the burgeoning mass of residents by lowering his voice and raising his hands, he then asked them, asked them to give, ask them to dig deep into the pockets of their cloaks, and robes and day coats, to dig deep and give, give, give till it hurts for their Lord and for his ministry so that he could set forth to other nursing homes around this great land and spread his gospel.

It was a plan so magnificent in its complexity yet so stunning in its simplicity. Reverend Franklin visited that nursing home twelve times in the first six months of his ascendancy. Dolly made sure that each time he had an audience that had not heard him before, or at least didn't remember hearing him before, not too hard to do with the audience generally made up of Alzheimer's patients, all too happy to fill the collection plate over and over and over again. So their wallets got fatter and fatter with the collections they repeatedly raked in from those patients.

Before they knew it, Dolly and Ronnie James had quite the

Standby

sufficient bankroll to approach the bank about a loan to purchase another nursing home. That began the cycle again. Franklin came in and sermonized and the money was collected and then shifted to Ronnie, who was always labeled the Vice President in Charge of Custodial Engineering. Dolly really ran the homes. The banks where they went for their loans never asked the identity of the secret partner.

Soon they were the owners of twelve nursing homes and every one of those homes provided legitimate income for their branching out to other homes where Franklin could do his preaching and expand his ministry. And then one day Dolly called Franklin to her office. Ronnie was out checking on the properties. Their office was the penthouse suite of a new building in downtown Tampa. Their business, James Properties, LLC, was gradually becoming the major player in the nursing home business. But Dolly had unfinished business.

Franklin walked into her office in his typical daytime wardrobe, a magnificent tan suit, crisp white shirt and maroon tie. All solid colors that Franklin believed showed off his dark, angular features. He was thirty pounds lighter than he was in college and looked tremendous in the suit.

"Franklin, honey, thanks for coming."

"For you sugar, anytime." They had long ago taken to calling each other "sugar" and "honey". It offended neither of them although it was becoming readily apparent to them both that the words were taking on more meaning.

"Where's your brother?"

"Out and about, acting busy at the properties... I think he has eyes for April, that manager over at Glory Acres. He gets all red and blushy when he talks about her or when I tease him just a bit about her," she paused "Sure would be nice to feel that way about someone. Just not get any younger here you know," she laughed.

The pregnant pause. They looked at each other deeply and each waited for the chasm to be breached.

"Dolly, you know I love you like family. Hell, you and Ronnie are the only family I got."

"Yes, Franklin I do."

"And I would love to see what could happen between us if we

gave it a chance but I worry about your brother and the business and…"

She walked close to him and gently pushed him down into her leather office chair, that way should could look him in the eye.. "Shhh, Franklin, I'm here, always have been and always will be." She purred in this ear and gently sat herself in his lap. "I am in love you Franklin Thomas, I have been since the day I met you and I will be forever. And I would be honored to be your wife."

Franklin looked up in surprise and said "Wife? We've barely dated? Why, we haven't even, well, you know…. "

"And that is about to be remedied. As for dating, that's for people who don't know each other, you and I know all there is to know" again she paused, but this time responded in a deep throaty voice "as I see it, there is only one thing we need to know about each other that we don't already know" she said as she began loosening his tie and taking his hand to her breast, larger than he would have thought for a woman so small.

"What's that?"

"Let's find out right now" she whispered as she gently met his mouth with hers. The first kiss was delicate and gentle, but that didn't last long as clothes started flying off and they soon found out that their bodies were more than compatible.

They married three days later. The wedding was attended by Ronnie, as best man, April as the maid of honor, and the one remaining cousin of Franklin Thomas who expressed his disapproval of the pairing.

Chapter 20

Geoff Padua stood before the entire board of Deacon Air, all hastily assembled in their Miami offices to discuss the first airline crash in young history of the company. Geoff knew that unless he got a hold of the litigation situation, all bets were off on whether the company would survive.

"Alright everyone, if we could all please settle down and take our seats. Thank you. Many of you know me already and many of you don't so I will be brief with my introduction. My name is Geoff Padua. I am the attorney for Deacon Air. I appreciate the attention that I am sure you will each give me in this meeting. What I tell you now is frank, open, and direct. This airline may fail. The amount of the claims against the company, when you add in all surviving children, spouses and parents is astronomical. The CEO asked me to cover this meeting as what we are dealing with is a potential litigation explosion against the airline, not to mention the public relations fiasco. To be blunt, your livelihoods are in jeopardy." At this last remark there were murmurs of assent, disbelief and frank horror.

"However, if I may continue and if everyone will please quiet down, I promise to be brief. We have to get ahead of this, if for no other reason than we have to stop the public relations nightmare that this airline faces."

Now they were all quiet.

"What exactly are you suggesting?" drawled one of the directors from the Texas office, who had arrived late after having to catch a late flight to Miami for the meeting, a flight that he most certainly did not take on Deacon Air. A fact that he hoped to keep quiet from Deacon Air.

"A three pronged attack."

"Seems our new young lawyer is awfully big for those britches of his ain't he" remarked the Texan, "Boy, let me tell you something, each and every member of this here board came from another airline, and virtually all of us have been involved with resolving a crash, so I think we know a little bit about what we are doing, son."

Geoff paused to let the blood that had rushed to his face settle back to its normal course in his body. In addition, he didn't want to appear to be blushing, which the board might take as a sign of weakness but which Geoff knew was actually his terrible temper rising to the surface. He knew, instinctively knew, that the airline was on the brink of failure and bankruptcy, and it was his job to get this board to understand. The moment was right now. The place was right here. And to get there he had to put this stupid Texan right back in his chair.

"First of all, I am not your 'boy' and I am not your 'son'. I am actually your lawyer and I know quite a bit about what I am talking about."

The Texan was stunned. He started to rise from his seat.

"Sit down right now!" Geoff yelled, and the entire room was silent.

"I am very concerned about the public relations disaster that is looming, and, sir, if you aren't then perhaps you can explain why you chose to fly here on another airline when a first class ticket was waiting for you on a Deacon Air flight departing thirty minutes later? Can you? Can you possibly give a rational explanation to this board of why your face is all over the evening news coming out of that airplane with a caption 'Deacon director won't even fly the airline after crash'."

Now, the Texan was fuming. He jumped out of his chair and began stalking menacingly toward Geoff, who, although he was roughly one hundred pounds lighter than this gorilla held his ground.

"Douglas, sit down, right now or I will have you removed," said the CEO. He continued, "This young man is our lawyer, OUR lawyer, and I believe his plan is sound. Everyone will have a chance to be heard on the plan, but Douglas, and I say this with absolute sincerity, you are on this board out of the kindness of my heart, and you will respect my wishes. So either sit down and shut the fuck up, or I will personally kick you out on your ass." Many of the board members had known the CEO for thirty years or more. None of them had ever heard him use a curse word.

The Texan sat.

Geoff paused. Truth be told, he was enjoying the drama. He knew his plan was sound, and he knew this was his moment. He drew a long, deep breath.

"Step one, an immediate public relations blitz, nationally. Expressing our regret over the accident and, this is the really important part, admitting blame."

This was met with a chorus of yells, screams, and general angst.

"Hear me out please. This is a manageable situation if we can get out in front of it." They quieted down. "I know what you concern is. Your concern is a public admission of liability. It's a valid concern, it would be naive of me too assume that you weren't concerned about this issue. However, and when you think about this I am sure you will agree, we have no defense to this crash. Our plane crashed. That is it, that is the simple no bullshit fact."

This time he was met with a stunned silence. Even the big, dumb Texan was too stunned to say a word. They all just stared at him open-mouthed. Imagine the idea of a company admitting it had done something wrong.

At last one of them spoke. He was the least intelligent member of a family not known for intelligence that had somehow managed to produce three senators and a governor. "Why on earth would we ever admit fault? A defendant never admits fault. Besides that we would be caving in to that shyster lawyer, Darlow, or what ever his name is…"

Geoff just stared back at him in amazement. That may have been the most intelligent thing that man had ever said. "Please allow me to explain….

"While you are all correct that it is highly unusual step to publicly admit fault, we have no choice. Any battle that can be won in this matter will be won in the court of public opinion. That is where your jurors come from. And I want those potential jurors to remember our message. We are sorry. This is our responsibility and we will make it right. Each and every family that comes to us with their claim will be met with compassion and understanding and a fair settlement that addresses their needs will be reached. This we promise you. Our message has always been 'Deacon Air....where your safety comes first'. Well, we failed all of you. It will not happen again."

The room was quiet. A few heads began nodding in understanding and affirmation.

"And there is more to this message. Not only will we settle most of these claims early and for less money than long litigation would bring on, but, and our pollsters tell us this is true, people will want to travel with an airline which commits to making their safety a higher than normal priority. Thus, more revenue to the company."

All the heads were nodding. Geoff knew he had them, now it was time to close the deal.

"Part two. I have already secured confirmation from our insurance carriers that the one billion dollars in insurance we had for this airplane will be immediately deposited into the court registry for settlement of claims. After the one billion dollars, Deacon Air will have to pay the remaining claims. We are going to immediately offer the family of every victim the sum of $2.5 million dollars. Cash. There were two hundred fatalities on this flight. That amount is only half of our insurance reserve. It leaves us room to negotiate. The offer letters go out today. Many of these families don't have lawyers. The offers will remain open for thirty days. Oh, and by the way, we are paying for every single funeral, without exception."

Again the heads were nodding, all but the Texan who this time raised his hand. "Excuse me there, uh, Geoff. What about the shyster lawyer Freddy just mentioned. He already filed suit didn't he? What in the hell are you gonna do about that?" This question was immediately met with murmurs around the conference room table.

Jeff knew the moment had come to set the hook. "We pay him nothing. We alienate him from the rest of the families who will settle. Our analysts figure about half of them will accept the offer, as it is the largest amount of money many of them have ever seen. The rest will settle real close to that and the few hard cases we deal with as they come. But Sullivan? Nothing. Nada. Zero. We go to court against him and, what's more, we ask the judge for an expedited hearing."

Standby

"Wait just a second," cried the numbskull from Florida, "Didn't you just tell us that we were admitting liability?"

Jeff stared at him with a look of bemused grace. The man actually was capable of having a cogent, coherent thought.

"Yes, it will be a trial on damages. Only damages. But I want you all to think about something that none of us have discussed yet."

"The handcuffs!!!" yelled the Texan, excited by his own epiphany.

"Exactly. The handcuffs. Why on earth was this man handcuffed to his seat? And what jury is going to give him money when they find out why...." Again he paused for effect. "Gentlemen, I give you the CVR, the cockpit voice recorder"

They all now were giving Geoff their full attention. He had them, every one of them. The plan was his and the best part was he could do some good for the other victims, while at the same time taking down Sullivan in a very public forum.

Chapter 21

They rode into the morning sun. Heading east on I-10 and right now going through the desert. Sue had actually climbed into the back seat and was currently icing Percy's groin, the contents of which had swollen to grapefruit size. Their drive was a silent one to this point, but Percy, in a voice slightly above that of a tenor, opened the conversation with the most obvious question, "Where the hell are we going?"

Sue replied, "Shhhh, you were sleeping and we have been heading east on I-10 for a couple of hours now."

"That's fucking great. I had a date tonight with a very cute young baggage handler," At this Larry glanced over his shoulder with some dismay. "That's right, I'm gay. What the hell did you think? You weren't paying attention to the 'bitchy bitch' portion of the evening? Christ, you think just because I can pull out a steering wheel make me straight?"

Larry said nothing but just shrugged.

Percy continued. "Hey, straight guy, you like art?"

"What?"

"I said, do you like art?"

"Sure, I suppose so.

"Guess you're queer then, huh?"

"Point taken" and with that the matter of everyone's relative sexual preferences was settled.

Percy spoke again.

"Question still stands, where the hell are we going?"

Larry waited a moment before responding, "Florida".

Standby

"Why in the hell are we going to Florida? And, why are we doing it in a car. Shit I work for the damn airline and could get you a ticket."

"Sue, you wanna handle this one?"

Sue nodded her agreement and turned to Percy, "Can't fly, Larry has no identification, it was on the flight that crashed. Last I checked you can't get on a plane without identification. And, if he did have ID, don't you think the name "Larry Jones" would trigger some questions, some alarm bells?"

Percy nodded as he saw the logic of driving. "Okay, I got no problem with driving, but why are we driving to Florida?"

"Cause I gotta see my wife."

"Have you called her?"

"Nope."

"Why not?"

"Cause I'm still trying to figure out why those three goons with guns were breaking into the hotel room and I'm pretty damned sure that they are gonna be following up pretty soon."

"Hmm, that sort of makes sense, but I still don't understand why you don't call your wife?"

"Well, Percy, it's like this. My marriage sucks, and it has for a long long time. So I'm sitting here thinking that the entire world, with the exception of you, me and Sue, thinks that I'm lying in a hospital bed in Miami with major facial injuries, no tongue, and a mouthful of manatee shit. Seems to me this might be a golden opportunity to start a new life."

"Okay, makes sense, I'll bite, why Florida?"

"Cause there is this note in the man-purse about a meeting with Croatians, and a name, Javis and a number 16-2882, and I'm just curious about it."

They all say quietly for a moment. Sue and Percy had roughly the same thought, seems like Larry has gone a little off the deep end.

Larry continued, "Here is what we know. One, I am not in a hospital bed in Miami. Two, apparently I am in a hospital bed in Miami. Three, my wife hired the biggest ambulance chasing scumbag in the world to represent her and I would love to be there to see her face when it all blows open. Four, I hate my wife, and have ever since she banged the preacher at the damn tea dance! I hate her and her wretched manipulating family, especially her father! She hasn't cared for me in years yet now she is all over TV talking about how wonderful our relationship was. So, yeah, I'm pretty fucking well pissed and I would like to rain on her parade," he paused, "and I've got a bag with three million dollars in cash in it and I'd like to do a little shopping."

Sue smiled and chuckled a little at this out of character outburst.

Just then, a dark sedan came racing up from behind them and slammed into the rear end of the vehicle. They all craned their necks around to see what it was, and were met with a gunshot that took out the rear view mirror. The next thing they knew their car was spinning in a circle right off the road. Larry braked them to a stop.

Out of the sedan jumped the three men who they had seen earlier at the hotel. They were all very tall, with Slavic features, two of them were very heavy set and one was exceptionally tall, exceptionally thin and wore very small round sunglasses.

"You are okay, I trust" the tallest one said with a very thick Slavic accent.

"We're okay" Larry replied.

"We make bargain right now, yes?"

"Yes, what do you want? And can you ask your friends to put the gun down?"

He did and they did.

"Here is what I am proposing to you?"

"Wait a second," Sue said, "It's you, Javis, isn't it?"

The tall one nodded his head and one of his goons holstered his gun and moved on Sue. Before he could close the gap, she jumped in the air, spun around, and delivered a vicious kick to his temple. He staggered and dropped like a house of cards.

The other goon began moving toward Sue, pulling his gun out and wearing a vicious grin on his face. Sue, to her credit, did not back away and assumed the ready position that Percy had so unfortunately learned about just hours ago.

The goon also assumed a ready position, but in a more classic boxing style. He moved to Sue and, with no warning, swung a lethal looking uppercut at her chin. She dodged back but was a half a second slow and the blow clipped her chin, causing her to see stars, and stagger backwards. He pursued her, smelling blood and waiting

Standby

to avenge the humiliation of his partner who happened to be his brother.

This was more than Larry could bear, as although he was a meek man by nature, he did have a sense of chivalry that required action. He did the only thing he could think of. He quickly reached into the back of the car and grabbed the pilfered steering wheel and with all his might brought it down over the bigger man's head. That was all the chance Sue required and she delivered her patented coup de grace. A kick to the scrotum. The big man was staggered but wasn't down. Sue kicked him again, three times in rapid succession, one in the stomach and one in each knee. The goon dropped to his knees and began reaching for his shoulder holster. Sue began to reach back for her best punch. Larry reached for the steering wheel to try and pull the man back.

A gunshot rang out. Percy screamed. Everything stopped. Larry turned to the thin man and saw that he was holding a very small pistol and saw that it was smoking. Everything slowed down. Larry looked at himself and realized he was okay. He looked at Sue who had a bloody mouth but was otherwise okay, and then he looked at Percy.

Poor Percy.

Percy's face was a bloody mess. He had turned sideways to watch the fight and the thin man had shot off his nose. Larry swore, "You son of a bitch" and turned and charged at the thin man. Only Sue's quickness kept him alive as she bounded towards him and tackled him from behind. She had been a fighter all her life, and was obviously not averse to a physical altercation, but even she knew when the odds were dramatically against her.

Larry looked up and saw the barrel of the gun in his face, and an evil, twisted smile on the thin man's face.

"I am Javis." He said to a stunned Larry and Sue. "You have something I want." He then turned to his henchmen, "Misha, Milos, get off the damn ground." The one who was Misha removed the steering wheel from his head and just before he dropped it he slammed it into Larry's forehead. To his credit, although a nasty cut had opened, Larry didn't fall.

"Misha, enough, there is no time. Soon enough. But not now."

Misha went and assisted his very woozy brother to his feet. As they staggered back to Javis, Larry and Sue smiled at their handiwork.

"I repeat, you have something I want."

"What?"

"The bag."

"What bag?"

"I assure you I have no patience for games, and I can kill you both and take what I want."

"Fine," Larry said and opened the trunk. He began to reach in and as he did heard the man named Javis tell his friends "We get money and go. Throw the gay one in the car; ve will take him with us. Remember, ve must be in Miami by Thursday with this bag. This man vill be our collateral. After deal ve kill him."

Larry heard all of this.

He handed the large purple bag over to Javis who briefly opened it and then threw it in the trunk of the car along with Percy who was currently having the wound to his face duct-taped shut by Milos

"Now what?" said Larry.

"Nothing, we go, you stay, simple, very simple. If I do not make Miami with this bag by Thursday, he dies. If I make it by Thursday, he dies. Either way he dies. All same to me."

"So why are you taking him."

"Simple, so you, Mr. Dodger, also make it to Miami by Thursday. Deal cannot be finished without you there."

Larry had a revelation.

"So why not take me with you?" Larry asked.

"Simple. You and I can never be seen together. Too many eyes watch us. Also, I think it is more fun this way. I enjoy a challenge, don't you? Plus deal cannot happen without you there. If you don't make it, he dies very fast. If you make it, maybe I let him live after I get rest of product. You are a resourceful man. Goodbye."

With that the three of them jumped in their car and began to pull onto the highway. Javis stopped the car. "Just to make more exciting" he said and then shot out two tires on the driver's side. They drove away.

"Well, Larry, thanks for jumping in. I was about done. We gotta go after them and save Percy."

Larry thought for a moment. "Save Percy? Is that what you want?

Standby

Save Percy? He is obviously mixed up in some very bad shit here. They knew him and you and they wanted him. Think! You want us to chase off across the country, in a car missing two tires, and drive several days to a city with a million people in it and then find these clowns, who, I might add would probably love nothing more than a chance at a rematch with you."

"Larry, look at me and listen to me very carefully. Percy saved our lives back there in Los Angeles. Yes, he is an annoying foppish prick and clearly is tangled up in some major shit by the looks of it, but he saved our lives. Where I come from that amounts to something. I'm going after him, and so are you!"

"I am? Why?"

"For the same reasons I am. Loyalty to a friend. And I am gonna kick both of those big guys asses."

Larry stared at her in disbelief. In his life he had never met a woman like this. Hell, he had never met a man like this, but her beauty made it even more intriguing.

"Oh, Larry, and one more thing."

"What?"

"I like your company. You are a gentleman."

Larry smiled and, after the briefest hesitation, nodded his head.

"Okay, Sue, I'm in, but what are we doing about a car?"

"Easy, rent one, you have money right?"

At that Larry smiled. Because the Dodger's man purse was under the front seat and Larry knew there was around ten grand in there. But the smile got bigger when he reached under the spare tire in the trunk. In perhaps the most devious move of his life, while Javis and his strongarms were handling Percy, Larry snatched out of the bag two bundles of cash. Two bundles each worth around a hundred thousand dollars. Their bankroll for the trip was well in hand.

Now to get a car. But again Sue was ahead of him, standing on the side of the road showing off two of the nicest legs Larry had ever seen. In just five minutes a young college student pulled over and rolled down his window and said, "Hey gorgeous, need a ride?"

"You bet," said Larry as he threw open the door and jumped in right after Sue."

The kid drove off with a smile that had turned to a frown.

Chapter 22

Sullivan was in the midst of a dilemma. He had seen the news reports and the press conferences where Geoff Padua, of all people, stood there and on behalf of Deacon Air accepted blame for the crash of Deacon Air 721. Imagine that. Sullivan could think of no time in history when a corporation had so quickly given a public admission of liability.

In fact, the pundits were all hailing it as an absolutely brilliant public relations move. Letting the public know the company is tremendously sorry for the accident and going further and mailing out settlement offers to every single family involved as well as directly paying all funeral and internment costs.

In fact, only one passenger was being been treated differently. His client. Felicity Jones. She had not received an offer. Truth be told Sullivan would probably have jumped at the offer. Fortunately he had not been required to discuss such an offer with Felicity because the offer hadn't come. The real question was why? Why hadn't his client been made the same offer as all the other victims?

He assumed the answer would come quickly as he had received notice to appear in the courtroom of M. Ira Berger, Judge of the Circuit Court, Miami-Dade County, at 2:00 PM. As he knew the value of publicity, he elected to handle the hearing himself rather than having one of his younger, although considerably more seasoned, trial lawyers handle it. He would regret the decision.

He arrived at the courtroom ten minutes late banging open the doors and entering dressed flamboyantly in a white suit, with a checkered shirt and solid orange tie. An ensemble that would make

Standby

Tom Wolfe proud he thought. People who knew Sullivan would be amazed to find out that he read books. He did. He was an enormous fan of Tom Wolfe and always considered himself to have the "Right Stuff". He smiled to himself. He was now a chosen one, a trial lawyer. He could hear the cash register in his mind ringing and dinging.

In any event, he walked into the courtroom with the flashing bulbs, shouting reporters and whirring television cameras. He raised his hands like a priest seeking quiet and asked told everyone "I will speak to all of you after I finish this business." Then he took a seat in the front row of seats, behind the bar. Then he heard chuckling.

"Mr., ah, Sullivan, is it? The lawyers generally sit at counsel table."

Sullivan stood up with a blushing face and made his way to the table where Padua was sitting and sat down in the chair next to him, murmuring a hello. Geoff ignored him.

"Mr. Sullivan, your own table." said the judge as he pointed his gavel towards the open table.

Sullivan stood up and went to his table and sat down. The chuckles and murmurs gradually subsided.

"Who is responsible for these cameras and reporters?" barked the Judge.

"Well, I am." Sullivan replied.

"Stand up sir!" Sullivan jumped up. "When you address this court you do so on your feet! Now, in the future if you want the press you ask me, understood?"

"Yes, your honor."

"Good, now they can leave."

Geoff stood up and said, "If it pleases the court, the defendant has no objection to the press remaining in the courtroom."

The judge frowned.

"Alright then, they can stay."

Sullivan looked over to Geoff and mouthed a "thank you." Geoff winked in response.

Judge Berger continued, "We are here on case 2006-199-CA-02, Felicity Jones, et al. v. Deacon Airlines, Inc., counsel identify themselves."

"Clarence Darrow Sullivan of the firm Gilbert and Sullivan," more chuckles, "for Mrs. Jones and Mr. Jones"

"Geoff Padua for the Defendant, your Honor."

"This is a court ordered status conference," said the judge, "first question, who will be trying the case for each party?"

"I will your honor." Geoff said.

This was a telling moment. Sullivan wasn't a trial lawyer, but he was here and wanted to play to the cameras, "I will have the privilege of representing Mr. and Mrs. Jones."

Judge Berger peered at Sullivan over his glasses.

The Judge continued, "OK then, the record will reflect that Mr. Sullivan will try this matter for the plaintiff and Mr. Padua for the defense. That being said and pursuant to the rules, there will be no changes absent death or grave illness, you two are the trial lawyers."

"Your honor, if I may?" asked Padua.

"Yessir."

"We would seek to invoke Rule 66 of the Rules of Procedure, and, most specifically, once this hearing is ended, there shall be cameras at all hearings and depositions, and, furthermore, as Mr. Sullivan has announced sole responsibility for the trial, we would like to bind him for discovery as well. In addition, we ask that all trial counsel, that being Mr. Sullivan and myself, be barred from any public comment, outside this courtroom, of course, on this matter from this day forward."

"What say you Mr. Sullivan?"

Sullivan was stunned and at a loss for words. This was a pivotal moment; of that much he was sure. You needn't be a trial lawyer to recognize that some form of trap had been laid for him and his client. Problem was, even as quick as he could think, he was known as a backgammon master, he was now in a courtroom and outside his element. He knew he was stuck and he knew he must respond.

"We agree your Honor."

"Very well, Rule 66 is invoked. Is there anything further from either the plaintiff or the defense?"

Sullivan glanced over at Geoff who was looking back at him and gesturing that he should go first.

As he could think of nothing to say, Sullivan stood up, pushed his shoulders back and said, "Nothing from the plaintiff."

"From the defense?"

Standby

Geoff sprung his trap.

"Your honor, as the Defense has already admitted liability and that we are the cause of the injuries, and the only issue to be decided is the degree of damages sustained by the plaintiff, and as plaintiff's counsel failed to ask for a jury trial in their complaint, we ask that under the expedited trials provision of Rule 66, that trial be set within fourteen days before your honor."

Sullivan was absolutely dumfounded. First, his idiot associate failed to ask for a jury trial, but there was nothing he could say about it since he had signed the complaint, he knew he was stuck with a bench trial before this judge. Worse still, the defense was looking for a trial in two weeks. "Your honor, that is simply not feasible. The complaint was just filed and we haven't taken any discovery…"

The judge raised his voice and replied, "What discovery!! They have admitted liability and causation. The only thing to be done is damages. Just get your pictures and your doctors and be here in two weeks from today, no exceptions."

"But your honor…"

He was silenced with a banging gavel.

"Excuse me your honor but there is one more matter." Geoff said with a sideways glance at Sullivan.

"Yes, Mr. Padua, and what is that?"

Sullivan was rapidly developing sweat stains which were evident through his white suit. He knew he had been sucker punched over and over again in this courtroom. He knew he had agreed to the rulings, and he knew there was a haymaker being launched right now.

"Judge, I have here the original and two copies of the cockpit voice recorder tape. It sheds a great deal of light on why exactly this unfortunate gentleman was handcuffed to his chair before the crash occurred. Ordinarily I would not have brought this piece of evidence to the court's attention until the trial; however, I felt that in the spirit of fair play I would file the original with the court today so the clerk may deposit it for safe keeping, a copy for plaintiff's counsel."

"Well, Mr. Padua I certainly appreciate your graciousness in this regard."

"Thank you judge."

"But may I ask what this tape has to do with the damages in this case?"

"Everything your honor, for not only does it show what type of person was locked down to his seat, but, more importantly, we believe it calls into question the identity of the person in that chair." Sullivan sat down hard and swallowed even harder.

"Your honor," Geoff continued, "While we are willing to concede to liability in that it was our plane which crashed, there is one critical issue which we will not concede and we will demand that Mr. Sullivan prove. We are not willing to concede to the identity of this victim. Perhaps there was a seat switch or some other improper piece of identification, but we do not believe that the man in seat 1J was Larry Jones and we demand that the plaintiff prove the identity of their client!"

Sullivan could barely catch his breath.

"Mr. Sullivan?"

"Well, ah, your honor, this is most irregular and we will most certainly respond to these charges in an appropriate fashion."

"I'm sure you will. Trial in two weeks." He banged his gavel and walked off.

Geoff glanced at Clarence, shook his head and walked out, leaving a dazed and confused Clarence Darrow Sullivan to answer the questions of the throng of reporters who he had invited to the courtroom.

"Mr. Sullivan, why did you file a lawsuit without first being sure of the identity of your client?"

Geoff walked out wearing a forced smile as the television cameras whirred.

Chapter 23

Franklin Thomas became an empire unto himself. He had television shows, radio shows, and a station on satellite radio and still took the time to do the occasional devotional in the nursing home. Of course they were usually in nursing homes run by his wife. Franklin was happier than he had ever been in his life.

However, he did not yet feel professionally fulfilled. He wanted something that would bring him national notoriety. Some congregant or parishioner or, hell, some viewer for that matter for whom he could preach the gospel in a public setting. Bring their problems to light, while certainly, and somewhat greedily, bringing his name to light.

This desire plagued him and continuously kept him from feeling fulfilled. He ached for it to happen. Even Dolly, who always knew just what to do, just what to say, to still the ragings in his heart and mind, had no remedy for this desire. He was single minded. He yelled at his staff, he yelled at the old ladies in the nursing home who couldn't hear anyway, he even yelled at Ronnie, even though Ronnie had now reached a point where he didn't fear Franklin. In fact, just about the only person Franklin didn't yell at was his wife. Not because she wouldn't tolerate it, but because he just wouldn't do it. He simply would not, could not ever bring himself to raise his voice to his wife. She was his rock.

So he fussed and fumed when he was in the office and tried to find ways to secure such a voice. Then, the crash of Deacon Air 721 occurred and Franklin believed his prayers had been answered. He called Dolly and told her to buy airtime, just after the dinner hour, on every network in Miami. She did and he went on the air.

"My fellow believers. This is a much different prayer hour today. Much different indeed. I will not be asking for your aid in helping our organization of love and prayer to grow. I am only asking tonight for your love. My brothers and sisters, there are many many, too many sufferers out there tonight. Needless sufferers. And you all know what I mean. There are mothers who have lost sons, fathers who have lost daughters. Children without parents. There is much suffering."

Throughout this the steady baritone of his voice raised in pitch and tempo, just enough to hook the listeners that more was coming. Just be patient, there is more coming.

"I tell you that the highway to heaven is lined with angels, hundreds of souls who grant their mercy from the heavens. They look down on us and are not asking us to pray for them for their worldly suffering is over. They are not asking us to weep for them as their worldly crying is over. They are not asking us to grieve for them for the days of grieving are done. We will see that at the judgment day and we will know we have done right.

He paused, caught his breath, and then lowered his voice almost to a whisper.

"But they do want something from us. They want us to love each other as surely as they loved us and we loved them. They want us to care for each other as surely as they cared for us. They want us to pray for each other as surely as they prayed with us and for us.

Again he paused, and wiped his head with a very white handkerchief, drank from a glass of water, pushed his shoulders back and went in for the kill...

"But they do want something else from us. My brothers and sisters you have known me for a long long time and I know we will all walk together on the judgment day. I have never asked you to do anymore than give what you can. But today, for the first time I am asking something of you. Last night I heard a calling. As surely as I stand here I heard a calling. It was the voice of a child, lost on the plane, taken before her time, and she said 'Lead them'." That's all, just 'Lead them'."

The tears rolled down his cheeks.

"How can I refuse that calling? How? So I ask you now my

Standby

brothers and sisters, if you lost a loved one, if you are suffering, call me. Please. In the name of all that is good, right and holy, call me. Let me lead you through the wilderness to the salvation on the other side. Let me be your instrument of glory! Ask this of me, and you shall receive. I love you all."

The screen went blank.

The calls came in droves, mostly from victims wanting his assistance. Some from victims telling him they wished he had been on the plane to spare them the indignity of his solicitations.

Then one call came in which forever changed Franklin's life. He was in his wife's office, sitting in her chair without his shirt while she kneaded the very sore and stiff muscles in his neck.

The phone rang.

He answered it, it was Ronnie calling to tell him to expect a call in about two minutes. The call would be from Felicity Jones.

"Who on earth is Felicity Jones?" Franklin thought, "Why do I know that name?"

Ronnie told him. She was the wife of the man in seat 1J. He was the survivor. Franklin jumped out of the chair nearly knocking Dolly through the wall. He paced frantically waiting for the call. Once two minutes had passed, he was ready to strangle his brother-in-law. At last, after around five minutes the call came. Dolly answered. She smiled at Franklin and passed him the phone.

"Mrs. Jones, how are you?"

The next day Felicity walked into Franklin's office with her lawyer, Sullivan, in tow.

"Reverend Thomas, what an honor to meet you." she beamed.

"Sister Jones, why I believe that our faith forbears good tidings, don't you?"

"I do, I do, and can I please tell you that your ministry has provided much for the least among us and provides wonderful good spirit and prayers of awe for us poor weak sinners."

"Sister, calm yourself, in my chapel I am a man of prayer and of God, but in here, I am simply a man, God's humble servant just trying to make my way and the way of my brethren easier on the way to heaven."

Felicity practically swooned.

"And let's not forget pocketing millions of dollars in

contributions that the IRS just never finds out about, " Sullivan threw this into the mix and received a shocked look from his client and a withering look from the Reverend.

Sullivan continued, "Hey, I know you!" he exclaimed.

Felicity answered for him, "Of course you do, silly; he is the Reverend Franklin Thomas"

"I know that," he said just catching himself before he called her a dimwit, "I know that he is the Reverend Franklin Thomas, hell, I am his largest advertiser, isn't that right, Reverend?" The last word coming out with just a hint of contempt.

"I know that you are Brother Clarence, and I can only say that it is because of the good works of the faithful such as yourself, that I can operate and spread the gospel to all god's children."

"Spare me."

"Sir, I am afraid I do not like your tone. This is a house of God and while I don't know how you worship in your house, in my house, we treat each other with respect," he paused, before standing and stretching himself to his fully enormous height and girth, and said "and those who don't get escorted out by myself, personally."

"Shadetree, right? I knew it. I always wondered happened to Shadetree Thomas. Wow, who would've thought that he would be a two-bit televangelist? Will wonders never cease?"

Franklin stood.

"I will thank you to never again call me by that name, you two-bit shyster hack. I am a reverend, duly indoctrinated by the church, and I will receive your respect or, so help me, I will beat it out of you." These last words coming as Franklin lost his temper and his voice grew louder and louder.

Sullivan, to his credit, had not gotten to where he was in life simply by being a wilting flower. He stood right up, and took off his jacket and looked in the eyes of the bigger man, and called his bluff. Two tremendous egos staring at each other while an amazed Felicity Jones stammered and stumbled and look for a way to defuse the tension. "Boys, boys, boys, we are all here for me remember?" as if there were nothing going the world other that the needs of Felicity Jones for these men to attend.

"Boys, you must both just calm down and let us please get started on helping my poor Larry who is just laying there in that hospital and

Standby

wounded and broken up."

Franklin spoke first, as he quickly regained his composure, "My child, how right you are, we are all just soldiers in God's army, sent here to do his service in the most unusual ways."

Sullivan, too, sat down and answered, "Well, I am here to help secure a recovery for this nice lady. And, I should mention, I do believe that I am the single largest advertiser in your network of gospel shows. And I think that should account for a little bit of courtesy, don't you."

Felicity nodded her head.

Franklin didn't. "Listen, son, I am the leader of these ministries, and therefore am looked upon by millions of people for spiritual guidance. If I say it, it happens, if I will it, it happens, if I don't want it, it ain't gonna happen. Now, Clarence, as I see it, you done played your main card that is that you buy advertising time on my programs. Who cares," Sullivan blinked, literally blinked, as he knew that his bluff had been called. He swallowed and listened as the larger man continued, "So what you need to get your head around real quick is the idea that I don't need your advertising monies. I have a whole mess of shyster lawyers waiting to jump into the void you would leave if I call the networks and tell 'em to pull your ads. See, I can make up the revenue, can you?"

While Sullivan had earlier called the Reverend's bluff, he now realized that his cards had been played. He was beaten, he knew it, and what was worse is that Franklin knew that he knew it. As for Felicity, it was pretty clear that she didn't know anything although she was very aroused, like she hadn't been in years with Larry, like she used to get before her wedding. She became flushed and sat down, fanning herself with a ridiculous oversized pink purse ordained with a garish oversized pink poodle.

It was Sullivan who spoke first.

"Let me, ah, be very direct here."

"Please do so Clarence, for we all have such little time."

"Yes, well, ah, Mrs. Jones, that is to say, ah, Felicity, Felicity Jones, has, ah, retained my firm, and me, of course, to, ah, represent her interests against, ah, against Deacon Air in this matter, and, um, especially, ah, in the upcoming, judgment, excuse me, I mean trial, yes trial."

"Son, I sure ass shit hope that you talk better in a courtroom than you are doing right here and now, otherwise that savvy Padua boy is gonna eat your lunch."

"Well, I know Geoff quite well, ah, I trained him, you see, and I have a few, ah, tricks up my sleeve to handle young Mr. Padua, just you wait and see."

"Name one."

"Excuse me"

"Tell me one trick you have up your sleeve for Mr. Padua that you intend to spring on his unexpecting, but apparently well-seasoned, mind."

"I will not, that is my work product. Its privileged."

Franklin released a belly laugh the likes of which hadn't been heard from him since early in his college days. Sullivan squirmed in his chair knowing he was about to be made a fool of for the second time today, first by that insolent Padua and now by this huge, ex-football player turned preacher. He lifted his head and tried to hold his eyes steady. But this was one bluff he couldn't hold.

"Clarence, let's all just be honest shall we, you wouldn't have a trick for a courtroom if I handed you three of them and told you just to hold them until you walked back into that courtroom and hand them to the court officer and tell him just to lock 'em up for you until the trial began. And before you start protesting, just shut the hell up and let me speak, cause from where I am sitting, the only chance Miss Jones has to secure any form of recovery is if you do exactly what I say."

"But, but, I am her lawyer. She hired me." He whined.

"Pit Bull my ass. The only thing obvious here is you getting your ass handed to you by that lawyer for the airline. Man, I saw the whole damn thing on the TV. You looked like a serious jackass. First, who the hell wears a white suit into a courtroom? Second, you let that boy lead you right into agreeing to send your case to trial right in the middle of their damned public relations blitz. Your entire jury panel, you know what that is, right? It's the people who are gonna decide this case. And do you know where they live? Sullivan? That was a question?"

"Well, ah, ..."

"Oh, Jesus, were you even present when they taught law in law

Standby

school? Nah, you one of those boys who is pretty smart in business and who advertises so he can get thousands of cases that the real smart lawyers in the firm handle. Lawyers like Padua over at Deacon Air, who clearly has a hard-on for you, and means to make a statement with this case. Yessir, he is gonna eat your lunch; you could see it in his eyes. He has nothing but contempt and disdain for you. If I were you I would not mess with that one. Be like climbing into a potato sack with a cobra and rolling down a hill. There just ain't nothing good can come of it."

Sullivan tried to find his spine.

"Listen here, Reverend, I know your game. You're a big guy with a big voice and you look fine in a suit. I know about your little nursing home games and how you bankrolled your start. Don't go getting all high and uppity with me. I may be a shyster. But I am the shyster who made Geoff Padua and I am gonna kick his ungrateful ass all over the courtroom. And, what's more, neither my client nor I needs to take advise from an uppity Negro half-wit reject preacher with a gimpy knee, who wasn't gonna make it in football anyway."

The room went silent. The only sound was Felicity's fanning herself in the corner chair and moaning. She appeared on the brink of orgasmic bliss.

Reverend Thomas stood up and came around the desk and did something unusual. He actually kneeled. He kneeled right in front of Sullivan. Then, with remarkable swiftness for a man his size, he poked Sullivan right in the sternum.

"Listen here, I am going to let the racial epithets slide because I believe you are nervous about the trial and what happened today."

Sullivan held his chest right where he had been poked.

"But make no mistake, if you get uppity with me, you will see the dark side of the Shadetree and I will make you suffer," and with that he poked Sullivan again, and as Sullivan leaned backwards Franklin grabbed the leg of the chair and yanked it up sending him crashing to the floor.

Franklin moved back around behind his desk and turned to Felicity.

"Sister Jones, please forgive these childish remonstrations. Two very large egos, two bulls in the same cow pen. Sometimes we just have to establish the alpha male." This last remark was made with a sidelong glance at Sullivan, who was too busy resetting his hairpiece to hear what was being said.

"If I may continue, I know you are probably thinking to yourself that you should change lawyers. Don't." Sullivan breathed a sigh of relief. Franklin continued, "You are too far into it now to make a change and you have too little time to do so. Your trial approaches rapidly. I can help and I will do so, for the proper compensation of course.

Both Felicity and Clarence stared at him and waited for him to continue.

"You will win or lose this case in the court of public opinion. I cannot for the life of me understand why you haven't yet been to the hospital to see your husband. There is not a juror in the world who would give a penny to a woman for her injured husband, if he was in a hospital, any kind of hospital, I don't care if it was drug rehab, a knee surgery, or a mental hospital, no juror is giving money to a wife who doesn't visit her husband. The Husband is fifteen hundred miles away? Who cares? Get on a plane and be at his bedside, every minute of the day. Mortgage the house, sell the art, do whatever it takes to be there."

They were both nodding now and they could sense Franklin's momentum building.

"You need to be at that hospital as much as possible now, especially at peak news hours," he said with a smile that showed a mouthful of pearly white teeth. "You must be there soothing him, whispering him, loving him. I don't care if what you are whispering is that you hate him or that you've been banging the neighbor's pet iguana instead of him, just be there. The news will cover it."

Sullivan jumped in. "Perfect, I will arrange a press conference at the hospital just after she leaves, and there will be press there for when she arrives."

Franklin drummed his fingers on the table, looking at Sullivan like he was an insolent child who required direction. He took a deep breath, pinched his nose and closed his eyes, then let the breath out, opened his eyes to stare at Sullivan and continued,

"Clarence, if you come anywhere within one mile of that hospital, I will kick your skinny white ass."

Sullivan was, quite frankly, stunned. Not that he had been talked

Standby

to that way. He chalked that up to what was rapidly turning into the worst day of his life. No, he was stunned that a client of his would be having a press conference and he would not be there. What television-advertising lawyer had ever done such a thing?

Franklin continued. "I will handle the press conferences with Felicity. I will speak for her and be her liaison. You will work. You will be getting ready for trial, and that is what we will say, 'Mr. Sullivan wishes he could be here but he is at his office diligently preparing for trial'. It's not negotiable Clarence."

Sullivan knew he was beat. He simply nodded his head. Again Franklin spoke,

"There is one thing concerning me. Why isn't Deacon offering you the 2.5 million that everyone else is getting? What does he have?"

"The tape?"

"Shit, yes, the tape, have you listened to it?"

"Not yet, it's in a format that requires some special equipment, I will have the machine tonight."

"Perfect, I guess its all settled then?" he said as he shook Felicity's hand. She gushed and hugged him.

Sullivan replied, "All settled but your fee…."

"Brother Clarence," he said as he shook Sullivan's hand in a gradually tightening grip, "I am here to do God's work. You pay me what you think is fair. Of course, I would probably think anything less than 50% of your fee as an insult." He then released Sullivan's hand that had turned purple from the handshake. "I know a gentleman of your caliber would never, ever want to insult me."

Franklin escorted Sullivan to the door. "Now, Clarence, if you would kindly leave Mrs. Jones with me, we can get to work on her, uh, compassion skills."

Chapter 24

Percy was in a dark place when he awoke. He wasn't sure where he was and wasn't sure how he had gotten here. He had the sensation of motion but since everything was so dark he couldn't tell how fast or in what direction. He also wasn't too sure about his method of conveyance since he wasn't on a seat and there certainly weren't any windows. There was, however, a faint smell of oil and another of leather. Not just leather, expensive leather. Then he realized that his head was lying on the expensive leather and the memories began flooding back.

Larry and Sue.

The side of the road.

Those big goons with the funny accents.

Sue kicking the ass of one of them before the other one got in a lucky punch.

A gunshot.

His nose.

My god, he thought, my nose. I was shot in the nose. Well, not really in the nose, which to Percy meant being shot from the front and into the nose. That, of course, would probably have meant no more Percy. This shot was from the side and went through his nose. He remembered the pain and gingerly lifted his hand to his face and began slowly lowering his hand to touch his nose and try and get a sense of the damage. He made contact with the wounded flesh and felt knives of pain shooting through his face. So he quickly removed his hand.

Just then, the car he was riding in hit a bump, or a pothole, whatever, and it bounced into the air and back down again causing Percy's still suspended hand to crash back into his face, most particularly, directly into the remnants of his nose. He screamed. Not a muffled, semi-silent scream, but a full-blown wounded animal scream. Then he passed out again.

Inside the car, Milos, sitting in the back seat, was still nursing his various wounds courtesy of the girl. As he rubbed his sore face with his two oversized paws, he thought of ways to inflict pain upon her. Her pain. His pleasure. What a round, round world. Then the car bounced causing him to bump his bruises with his over-sized gold ring and let out a scream of his own. His brother, Misha, sitting in the front passenger seat, turned to look at him and smiled.

Javis, driving the sedan, wasn't smiling at either of them. In fact he was quite annoyed that the silence he had previously asked for was being disturbed by these two large goons. Didn't they understand that genius sometimes requires absolute silence? Then he hit another bump and heard a much louder, although somewhat muffled scream, it appeared to be coming from the trunk. Javis jerked the steering wheel to the right and slammed on the brakes to bring the car to a rapid stop. He spun around and glared at Milos, who raised his hands and said, "it wasn't me, boss."

"I know that you idiot. I wasn't concerned with the scream, per se, I was concerned that our friend in the trunk could scream at all. Didn't you muzzle him?"

"Um, no boss, I didn't."

"And why the fuck not?" asked a progressively more agitated Javis.

"I, ah, thought that he was hurt bad enough and wouldn't cry out."

Javis was enraged and was tempted to shoot Milos right then and there. The problem with that strategy was that although it would temporarily satisfy his sadistic control issues, it would not help in the long run. He knew that if Milos died then his brother, the second half of his own private tweedle-dee and tweedle-dum, would be of no use as he would be grieving such was their degree of brotherly closeness. Once again, Javis realized the benefits of growing up in an orphanage. Since he never developed close bonds with anyone, he lacked the impulse control that ordinarily prevented one from hurting a friend. Simply put, Javis had no friends. He was a pure machine.

He stared at the two giants and his face reddened considerably. Another thing he knew was that neither of them would intervene if he disciplined the other. So, that is what he decided to do. But he was going to put a twist on it.

"Milos! You failed me again!"

"Yes, boss, I am sorry."

"And it will never happen again will it?"

"No, boss, you have my word."

"Good, now tape him up properly." Javis stopped the car and Milos jumped out.

Milos went to the trunk, opened, lifted Percy partially out of the well and used duct tape to cover Percy's mouth and eyes, leave air holes to breathe and a hole through which to drink, then cuffing his hands behind his back with the tape and lastly securing his feet together and linking them to his hands. Once he was done, he lifted a weeping and visibly hurting Percy into the trunk, and slammed the trunk lid down.

As Milos turned around he heard a gunshot and then a scream. He finished his turn and saw his brother writhing on the ground holding a bloody hand. Around ten feel away stood a sadistically grinning Javis, still aiming that ridiculously small pistol in his hand, watching the smoke rise up to the sky.

Milos spoke, "Why did you do that boss?"

"To teach you a lesson."

"Yes, boss, I learned the lesson already. I won't fail you again." As he said this, his brother was quite unsteadily rising to his feet holding up his left hand, that was now missing its pinkie finger.

"I know you won't Milos. And do you know how I know that you know? It's very simple really. You love your brother and he loves you. Every time you screw up, I hurt him, and every time he screws up, I hurt you."

Javis glanced at them both as they all climbed into the car. He saw them look at each other and knew that needed to be nipped in the bud. As Milos helped Misha into the front seat, Javis quickly drew his pistol and a shot cracked out and Milos jumped back in pain. His left hand was now also missing a pinkie.

Once he settled down, Milos joined his brother in the car. Javis

Standby

turned to face them and held his pistol and leveled it at their eyes.

"And lest either of you think I am kidding, I vill kill you both if there is another foul up."

He threw the car in gear and pulled onto the highway.

Meanwhile, back in the trunk, Percy was again trying to get a gauge on where he was. All that he knew to this point was that the two big goons had now put him in the trunk twice, only this time was worse than the last due to his inability to move around thanks to the duct tape wardrobe he was now wearing. And, worse still, he needed to urinate in the worst way possible but was afraid to make any noise about it lest he incur the wrath of the thin man who seemed to take great pleasure in shooting off body parts with that strange small pistol.

So, Percy did the one remaining thing that he clearly had plenty of time for. He thought. He thought about how he could get out of this mess and, more specifically, he thought about how he got into this mess.

Percy's story went back just two years to the time Deacon Airways was just getting started. It was a true start-up airline. The type made possible by the deregulation in the aviation business. Low fares all over the country with limited amenities for its passengers and two classes of service. It was, really, the dream story. Based on its business model, no one familiar with the industry thought they had any chance of getting out of the starting blocks. But the airlines succeeded beyond the pale. Deacon Airways was a force to be reckoned with and it was now challenging the big boy airlines for routes and passengers.

Percy was there from the beginning. He started as a ticket agent, and through hard work, as well as working the beds of some higher executives who had some tendencies that they would rather not be made public, he became the gate supervisor in Los Angeles, a real plum job.

Percy was the man who could solve problems for passengers or, if they were nasty, he could create problems. Problems like a suddenly unavailable seat, or a suddenly lost upgrade on a trans-continental flight, my, oh my, how those first class travelers would gripe when faced with the idea of having to fly coach on a cross country redeye. Percy could work the system. He knew it inside and out. He knew which palms to grease, as well as from what palms he should expect grease. He had become very successful. Not bad for the son of a grease monkey from Camden.

This particular problem began for Percy one day as he walked out of the baggage handling area where he had been admiring the posterior of a young man upon whom he was intent on lavishing affection. Two large men who spoke in an accent he couldn't place, not then and not now, approached him,

"We vuld like to speak vit you about business proposition." The larger of the two said quite matter of factly.

"About?"

The two men chuckled, in laughs somewhat higher than their size belied.

"About assisting us vit a problem ve are having."

Percy paused. Not only because he was having trouble making out what they were saying due to the heavy accents, but also because, notwithstanding his sexual proclivities, he still maintained a healthy street sense. He really wasn't sure what he was dealing with here.

"Fellas, I don't know who you are or what you want. But I have things to do and I cannot dawdle here with you." He began trying to push his way between them.

They, of course, each grabbed him under an arm and lifted him off his feet and back into the baggage area. He was roughly dropped on the only available chair and was rapidly silenced by both the gun placed on his temple and the duct tape strapped across his mouth. Percy didn't want to be here, but he knew he was stuck, so he calmed himself down and looked directly at them.

The talker of the two then slapped him hard across the face. Percy bit back a cry, which would've been useless anyway given the current condition of his mouth. The tears, however, he could not stop. This time he sagged his head.

Again the talker chose the violent route, grabbing Percy's hair and yanking it back thereby forcing Percy's head up. The tears running down his face were unstoppable and his thoughts were filled with one question, who are these men and what the hell do they want from him?

"As I vas saying, ve require assistance for a business proposal. Ve believe you are best suited employee to assist."

Standby

Percy stared at him blankly.

"Ah, yes, is clear you have no idea vat I am talking about. Correct?"

Percy stared. He did not acknowledge the question.

Slap. Again Percy felt the sting of the large man's blow. Each time he was hit the other man giggled.

"I ask question again. If you don't respond, I slap again. I am not angry. Please do not make me so."

Percy stared.

The big man raised his hand.

Percy nodded rapidly.

"Ha, yes, good, very good. Now we are friends yes?" the big man said as he laughed and bent over to pinch Percy's cheek.

Percy nodded through the pain.

"Now, here is our business proposition. Ve have certain business interests in California and in Florida. And ve require assistance to deliver certain products in a timely manner. I know that you are not following, so I vill tell you directly. But you must understand. If you tell anyone about this plan, ve vill kill you. There vill be no second chances. Do you understand?"

Percy nodded his head rapidly, tears running down his checks. Working very hard to breathe through his nose as his anxiety and sense of panic rose.

A thin man appeared and began speaking.

"Very good, very good. Now, you understand that you vill accept our offer. It is not, um, how you say, optional. It is very very mandatory. You vork for airline, yes, but you also vork for us." He paused and smiled at Percy and said "You must have questions, yes?" and with that he ripped the duck tape off of Percy's face.

"Yahhh" Percy screamed. His mouth was instantly muzzled by the big man's face.

"Shhh, my little cupcake, yes, I know your proclivities. You vant to know the job?"

Percy nodded.

"Simple, you vill insure that certain luggage gets on your planes regardless of the contents. No, it vill not be bomb, ve are not terrorists. Let me just say that they vill contain things you should not look at. Agreed?"

Again, he nodded.

"Do you have questions?"

"Yes, two questions"

"Yes."

"One, how will I know the bag?"

"Easy, it vill be purple."

"Okay, two, what am I being paid? See, I mean no disrespect, but I gonna have to get someone inside the baggage area and that will require greasing some palms."

"Do not worry about it, you will get more than you need."

Again, Percy nodded. He knew this was not time to negotiate.

"Thank you for your understanding Percy, you are a good boy, now close your eyes."

"Why?"

Percy never saw the punch that struck him in the back of the head sending him into a blissful state of unconsciousness.

When he awoke, in a back corner of the baggage area, his head was propped up on a stack of money that added up to ten thousand dollars. He knew he was in it now.

Over the next two years Percy recruited two baggage workers, one from the morning and one from the evening shift. A few bags were missed and, of course, never made it on the planes. The authorities properly disposed of their contents. A few properly greased palms and all was well. After a couple of months, the purple bags made the flights consistently.

Percy knew that he was engaged in something that, if caught, would put him away for many many years. He also knew that accepting the risk of incarceration was worth it since the alternative was another beating by those sadistic men. No sir, he was definitely in for a penny, in for a pound. Besides, the money was good. Deliveries to his car or his apartment of cash in various sized bundles. Sometimes a thousand and sometimes ten thousand dollars. He loved the lavish lifestyle that these risks allowed.

Chapter 25

Larry and Sue continued their drive to the east. They had splurged with the cash and rented a convertible Corvette. Larry had never driven anything so powerful although he certainly felt like he was warming to the task. Sue, for her part, had slept much of the last few hours and Larry hadn't minded at all. He kept sneaking glances at her sleeping next to him and he liked what he saw, especially the beautiful legs that she had kicked up on the dashboard. What Larry didn't know is that Sue had sort of an inner sense that allowed her to know when someone was looking at her. She didn't mind. She thought he was a nice enough fella and he seemed to be rising to the challenge that this day had brought about.

When she woke up she broke the ice.

"Where are we going?"

"East", Larry mumbled with an overtone in his voice that let Sue know, in no uncertain terms, that he did not want to be bothered right now.

Sue did what most passengers in cars did when the driver was otherwise occupied. She stared out the window. Several hours ago they had stopped and put the roof back up because Larry was starting to develop quite a nasty sunburn on his forehead and while they had taken the time to stock up on snacks and drinks, sunscreen wasn't on the purchase list.

She stared at the window and the endless desert that ran past the car and began to consider what in her life had led her on this course, to this desert, in this car, with this man she hardly knew but to whom she was strangely attached, going Lord knows where and to accomplish Lord knows what.

She closed her eyes and with the rhythmic rolling of the wills, allowed herself again to drift off to sleep.

Sue was born Susan O'Reilly in Brooklyn, NY, just enough years before to be in her early twenties. Her father was a drunk who, when sober enough, was a cop, and her mother was the manager of a dry cleaner and worked nights gutting ducks in Chinatown so there would be enough money for food and clothing as they had purchased their home in a more affluent suburb which had a better school district. Sue mused that her parents were, in essence, the ultimate cliché. Daddy was a drunken Irish Cop; Mommy running a dry cleaner and skinning ducks, sneaking the best cuts of meat out for Sue and her brother to eat.

Both of the O'Reilly children did well in school. Her brother was a couple of years older and he was a street fighter by nature. He honed his skills in the Chinatown area where he would come with his little sister in tow to help his mother clean up duck parts after the long evening of work. Sue and her brother always took the early morning train down to Chinatown, helped their mother for a couple of hours, and then jumped on another train to go back to the suburbs go to school.

But it was for the Saturdays and Sundays that Sue and her brother lived. Her mother worked both of those days in Chinatown and her two children would spend the entire weekend there with her, helping in the store, cleaning up as needed, practicing their Chinese – and the customers loved the beautiful little girl in pigtails who could speak fluent Mandarin with a lilting Irish brogue – and sleeping upstairs above the store on small mats placed on the floor. It was always very hot in the summer but since they were so young, heat didn't seem to be a concern and since their mother never complained, not once in her life, the children didn't complain either. In the winter, it was always warm and snug as their room was right above the ovens where the duck was cooked, every day, twenty four hours a day. When she was an adult, nothing would bring her back to her childhood faster than the smell of duck, and she would never eat it again.

For the two of them the greatest part about being in Chinatown was the freedom to explore lower Manhattan and all of its wonderful

Standby

neighborhoods, Little Italy, Soho, the Lower East Side, Tribeca, the city was always in such flux, always in such change that Sue was never sure from one weekend to the next if the neighborhoods she had seen were now just neighborhoods she would have to remember.

Her brother got in his fair share of fights. He was always quick to the fist and slow of the head, as his mother said on those occasions when she was tending to a gashed brow or ministering to a black eye, always ready to fight, anyone, any size, anytime, especially if any of them dared impugn the integrity of his baby sister.

To his credit, while he had a ferocious temper, his sister, four years his junior, never experienced the wrath of it. While he had absolutely no patience for the rest of the world and was desperately seeking a way out of New York, Sue could do no wrong in his eyes. She was his beautiful flower, his light. As she reached her teen years he saw in her that her beauty was transcendent, and that she was becoming the object of many eyes in the neighborhood. This he never tolerated and even though Sue may have wanted a date that would not happen with her brother around.

Her brother also demanded that she learn self-defense. While most of Sue's friends from school, fresh from just having entered puberty, were busy buying training bras and giggling about the cute quarterback and his cute butt, more giggles, Sue was taking self-defense courses from her brother. After around six months, she was more than able to give her brother a run for his money in the training room. He only hoped she would never have to use those skills in the real world, and since their father had all but abdicated responsibility to her brother, she followed his instructions. There was one instruction he stressed to her above all others, the most important rule of self-defense, when in doubt, run!

Sue fixed him with her most beautiful smile and said "Never worry, older brother, I will honor you with my speed" in fluent Mandarin.

One weekend, after Sue had turned fourteen, she went to her mother and told her that a very nice, well behaved Irish boy wanted to take her to a movie, and would her mother consent? Her mother immediately refused telling her that one Chinese woman in the family marrying a drunk Irishman was enough of a mistake for the family.

Sue's brother laughed behind them but quickly stopped when his sister's beautiful eyes implored him to help her. There was an unspoken communication between them and he knew he would assist. He too spoke in Mandarin. It was their mother's preferred way to communicate.

"Mama, I will take her with me."

"No!"

"And I will sit close to her and make sure this drunk Irish boy minds his hands."

Sue pinched his arm.

"No." Their mother paused just long enough to see the tears welling up in her daughter's eyes. She looked her up and down. A face of pure innocence yet with a body nearly that of a woman. Of course she will be asked on dates. Of course she should go just as she herself had wanted to go so many years ago. How she had resented her mother all those years ago for not allowing her to go on the dates, and now, looking at her daughter's beauty, she knew, deep inside, that she must let her daughter go.

"Ay, she can go, but you must sit right next to her."

"Mom!"

"Ok, right behind her."

And that ended the discussion. Sue could go on her first date with her brother as chaperone.

That weekend Sue and her date, a sixteen-year-old Irish boy, went to a movie. Sue's brother and his girlfriend, a beautiful Chinese girl who Sue admired tremendously, chaperoned them pursuant to their mother's orders. Sue's brother could see right away that these two were quite smitten with each other. They had seen each other grow up. His name was Paul and he was a fine young man. His sister had chosen well.

Sue's brother did his sister a favor and moved several rows away from her so she could have some privacy. She thanked him with her eyes. About halfway though the movie he looked over and saw his baby sister receive her first kiss. He thought he would be filled with rage but he wasn't. Paul was as innocent as Sue and the kiss lasted just seconds, and wasn't repeated.

The movie ended and they all walked out and Sue was like a woman who was walking on air. For his part, Paul looked sheepishly

Standby

at his shoes.

Sue's brother suggested ice cream and the four of them walked, as two couples hand in hand down the street for ice cream. They stood outside on a cool fall evening and laughed together as they ate the cones.

Then it happened.

"Hey, Paulie, pissin' Paulie, what you got there?" yelled a kid from across the street.

"Yeah, pissin' Paulie, what you got, a nice young chink piece of ass?"

Sue's brother dropped his cone and Sue stopped in front of him and asked him, in rapid fire Mandarin, to walk away.

"Pansy ass pissin' Paulie, got himself a chink!"

The crowd across the street increased to six or seven toughs.

Sue's brother quietly said, "You should leave right now."

"Fuck off chink, we stay as long as we want. And now we want to stay until pissin' Paulie pisses his pants."

Paulie did the one thing Sue's brother wanted her to do, he ran leaving them all behind.

Sue and her brother turned in disbelief to watch him take off. He was shocked that a young man he had thought so deserving of his sister had turned into a coward. She was shocked that the man she had shared her first kiss with was a coward. He rapidly turned to his girlfriend and whispered to her in Mandarin to go into the store and call the cops and to take Sue with him. She attempted to do so but Sue pulled away and shouted that she was staying with her brother. He yelled at her to go, she yelled back she was staying, the girlfriend ran into the store. A crowd had gathered around them and was soon cheering and jeering and actually laying bets.

The issue was decided as the group of thugs, seven of them to be precise, had encircled Sue and her brother. He was still imploring her in Chinese to follow him and bust through the hole he would try and create. She refused.

The other boys attacked. They made a classic error. They attacked one by one and Sue's brother repelled every attack. Soon the attackers appreciated their mistakes and moved as a pack on her brother yet he continued to fight them off. Then two of them jumped at Sue and she began to fight with a fury beyond her fourteen years.

She rapidly dispatched two of them and then when she turned to help her brother someone in the crowd threw a bottle and it struck Kim in the temple, she went down like a stone. She tried to get up but one of the men began kicking her fracturing several ribs. Her brother saw this happening and leapt up like a crazed animal. He threw his sister's assailants off of her and spun to meet them. Unfortunately, as he did so, one of them stuck a knife into his belly, pulled it out and stuck it into his throat.

Just then the sirens started and the group of thugs ran away dragging their wounded friends with them.

Sue sat in the street, holding her brother's head in her lap as he whispered to her that she was his little flower, and she wept because she was powerless to help him. She wept because she realized he would never know how much she loved and admired him. He hushed her and told her not to cry, and that he knew how much she loved and admired him. They both hushed and stared at each other and spoke the unspoken language of siblings who understand each other as much as they understand themselves. A gentle stranger took off his coat and placed it over Sue's brother and he tried to hold the wound closed until the police arrived. She looked at him and thanked him. He told her he was sorry he couldn't help more and he was praying for her and her fallen brother. Through her tears she told him that her name was Sue and asked him his name. He told her his name was Percy.

On that dark, cold evening, just after sharing ice cream with their dates, Sue held her brother while he died quietly in the her arms.

Percy and Sue became friends, of a sort. He was at her side all the way through the funeral of her brother. Sue's mother would not speak to her at the funeral, nor for a long time afterwards. It was as if she had decided that both of her children died that night. The only conversation took place at the police station the night her brother died.

"Mama, oh, Mama, I'm so sorry, I tried to help him, he died in my arms, in my lap," she said, sobbing.

"Get your things, we are leaving."

"Yes, mama."

They walked into the night, to catch a cab, a true extravagance for her mother, to go back home to Brooklyn. In the cab, her mother

Standby

at last spoke.

"I never wanted you to go on this date. If you not go, your brother he still alive."

"Mama, it is not my fault, I tried to get him out, but there were too many, he was my brother and I loved him."

"Not matter, you have disgraced us."

"Mama, no!"

"Yes, you go on date with Irish boy, everyone knows those Irish boys, I bet he touch you all over, your brother try to stop him, because you don't, and other Irish boys jump your brother and he die, simple as that."

Tears were welling up in Sue's eyes. She always knew that her brother was her mother's favorite and there was a time in her life when it didn't really matter, but those were the days when her father wasn't drunk all the time. Before that she was her father's favorite. None of that mattered now. Sue and her brother were each other's favorite. They were best friends. Now he was gone, another loss to senseless street violence, and she was being blamed for it by a mother who still ran her life according to the rules of the old country. It was all too much for Sue to bear.

"No, mama, that was not how it was at all. They jumped us for no reason and Chris and I had to fight back and we, we, oh god, we were winning, and then Chris had to help me because I got knocked down and he came to help me and then he got stabbed. You see, Mama, he tried to help me, and he got stabbed, and he died, and I have to live with that forever, and I don't know how I can live with that, with knowing that he died coming to save me."

Her mother stared at Sue. For just a moment Sue thought her mother would hug her, and love her and talk to her, and tell her it would all be okay, that her Mama would make it all okay. Sue looked at her mother through red eyes swollen with tears. Then, with no warning, her mother slapped her across the face with a viciousness Sue could not imagine. Even the taxi driver jumped at the sound.

"You are a whore!"

"Mama!"

"A filthy, Irish loving whore. And because you needed to be a whore with that boy, your brother is dead. His blood is on your hands! You live with that my filthy little whore!"

The remainder of the cab ride home was silent. They walked into the front door of their Brooklyn Heights home, which was rent controlled and therefore manageable in cost on the joint salaries of her mother and father. Her mother placed her coat on the coat rack and immediately went to the kitchen to make some form of foul-smelling, but supposedly therapeutic, tea. Sue walked into her father's study. He was sitting in his leather chair, clearly drunk, but also clearly overcome with grief, and his eyes were red-rimmed and swollen.

Sue walked to him and placed her hand on his shoulder.

"Daddy..."

He looked at her, and for the first time in many years she believed he was connecting to her.

"Daddy, I'm so sorry. I didn't want him to die."

She dropped to her knees and began quietly sobbing.

"Daddy, he was trying to help me, you see? He jumped in to help me. And he got stabbed and he died."

He put his hand on her head and began playing with her hair, just like he had done when she was a child. Then, just like she had done when she was a child, she laid her head his lap, and he stroked her head and hummed an old Irish lullaby to her. She soon fell asleep safe in the knowledge that her father was going to make it all okay; he was there to protect her and would help her through his grief.

The day for the funeral arrived. The weather suited the mood of that fall day. It was cold and rainy outside. Percy had come to Sue's house everyday and, even though her mother would not allow Percy in the house, explaining that as her son had died at the hands of an Irish boy, she was not going to let any Irish boys in her home. So Percy sat on the stoop. Percy knew from an early age that he wasn't interested in girls and made that clear to Sue, not so that she would be guarded about being his friend, but simply as a statement of fact, so that the tension in her could dissipate rapidly.

They would sit on the stoop for hours on end, sometimes talking about what happened and sometimes doing nothing more that hold hands chastely and listen to the rain. They would talk about the funeral. Percy was at her side for the burial of her brother on a day even colder and more damp that those which came before. It was to

Standby

Sue as if the heavens wept for her brother and her pain. Throughout the funeral Sue and Percy held hands and they both wept, she for the pain of her loss, he for the pain of his new friend. Sue's father sobbed and wailed like a wounded animal while her mother stood rock still and shed not a tear. Once the coffin was in the ground, they turned and left the cemetery and Sue knew, in her heart, that she would be the only member of the family to visit her brother's grave. For her mother it was over and would not be spoken of again, for her father to come back would tear open an emotional scar best left alone.

There was no Irish wake. Two days after the funeral, after the mourners had all left, Sue's father walked into the basement of the family home with a bottle of Jamison's whiskey. He turned on a record of old Gaelic tunes and sat in the dark and wept. He wept the tears of a father who has failed his children, of a husband who has failed his wife, and, for him the most difficult, the tears of a man who has failed himself. He finally stopped crying, and listened for a moment to the sounds of his wife upstairs putting together some sort of dinner, and he wondered why he had ever married such a woman. Then he stopped himself because he knew that his two wonderful children would never have come without her. How he loved his children. If only he could have saved them from all of this misery. This was all too much for him to bear. He only hoped that Sue would be strong enough to stand alone. He believed she would. He believed her brother had taught her well. It was this thought he carried into eternity as he placed the barrel of his service revolver into his mouth and pulled the trigger.

Sue's mother jumped at the explosion downstairs. She paused for a moment and then went back to preparing dinner.

An hour later Sue came home. She has been at her school picking up her missed assignments. Percy had taken her. He was old enough to drive. As always though, in respect for the wishes of Sue's mother, he stood outside on the front stoop while Sue went inside. They had plans to go into the city today to see an art exhibition of a hot new artist. Percy loved art and knew quite a bit about it, and he hoped that such a day might help settle his new friend. Sue went into the house.

"Hello, mother."

"Ay."
"I am going to the city with Percy."
"Why?"
"To see some art exhibit. He is my friend."
"Ay."
"Okay then, I am going."
"Ay, you do what you want, then."
"Goodbye mother."
"Sue?"
"Yes mother?"
"Can you check on your father, I think he went down to the basement? Haven't heard from him for a while." There was a shrill harsh tone in her voice.

Sue thought absolutely nothing of it. "Sure." And so she went down stairs.

From his place on the front stoop Percy heard the worst screams of his life. Disregarding the explicit rules of the house, Percy barged through the front door and followed the ongoing screams down into the basement. There he saw Sue in an all too familiar position. She sat on the floor, covered in blood, clutching her clearly dead father's head in her lap, and sobbing terribly. He immediately sat next to her and placed his arm around her and began humming in her ear. Strangely Sue found that he was humming the very same Irish lullaby that her father used to hum to her. She laid her head on Percy's shoulder while he held her and while she held her father, as he grew colder. They had no idea how long it took until the police arrive. Sue's mother never came into the basement.

Shortly after her father was buried, right next to her brother's still fresh grave, her mother called Sue into the kitchen of their home and told her that she was leaving for Seattle to live with her sister. Sue said she didn't want to leave New York, that this was where her school was and where her friends were. Her mother replied the decision was made and that she was flying out that evening. If Sue wanted to stay that was up to her, but the apartment was not theirs anymore and all of their belongings were going to be moved out that afternoon. If she chose to stay she had until the afternoon to clear out her belongings. That afternoon Sue and Percy packed up her clothes and a few of her personal items and loaded them into her car. They drove off to Percy's

Standby

home where his mother took her in like one of her own, even moving three of her eleven children out of their room so Sue would have some privacy. Sue and her mother would never again speak to eachother. She was just fourteen years old.

Over the ensuing years she grew more and more beautiful. So beautiful in fact that it was not unusual for one or more of Percy's brothers to try and sneak glances of her while she was changing or in the shower. They never were quite able to do so and almost every time that they tried Percy would come charging at them and break off their pursuits violently. Invariably Percy got the worst end of the bargain but such was the degree of familial love in their household that no one ever took too much of a beating. Additionally, Sue had a thing for Percy, after all he had been such a rock for her the last couple of years, it was expected that she might develop romantic feelings for him.

Such was the situation one night when Sue and Percy went with a couple of friends to a high school party. They danced with everyone else and each snuck a drink when they could. By the later part of the evening all of the couples had found quiet corners throughout the house to engage in various forms of teenage lust. Sue and Percy sat out front.

"Percy, can I ask you a question?"

"Sure, anything, you know that."

"Well, it's sort of embarrassing, but how come you've never kissed me? I mean don't you think I'm pretty?"

He turned to her rapidly.

"Oh, no, you are beautiful; you are the most beautiful person I have ever known, but…."

She kissed him; she kissed him hard and deep. She pressed her body against him and waited for the hardening that the magazines all talked about, the things she had seen when she peeked in on Percy's brothers in the shower, and what they had done there. Yes, she peeked too. But nothing was happening with Percy and his kiss felt so mechanical. She finally pulled away and began sobbing.

"You don't like me, all you do is pity me."

"Sweetheart of course I like you, I've liked you since I met you, in fact I love you."

"Then why won't you touch me? I would do anything, anything for you."

"Because I'm gay, Sue," he whispered.

She looked at him with startled eyes and then they both simultaneously broke into peals of laughter.

Percy went to work after graduating high school. He became a stagehand for the City Ballet. It was where he came into his own and also allowed him to bring his pay home to help his mother and to be there for Sue who was coming up on her own graduation. She had found plenty of ways to keep herself busy, from helping care for all of the younger brothers and sisters, to her school work, to her Tai kwon do classes, to her job at the corner grocery so she could also bring money home to help out; she was a very busy young lady. Still, she found time for a boyfriend. Fred was a basketball jock and he was taken with her the moment he saw her. Percy wasn't particularly crazy about him for Sue. Oh, he was nice enough and seemed to treat her very well, but Percy was jealous. It was an emotion he was not used to and he didn't take to it very well.

But, to his credit, Fred knew the special place that Percy held in Sue's heart and he never tried to interfere.

Then, as will happen with all teenage romances, Sue and Fred were coming close to a decision on whether to take their relationship to that last level. Sue was lost and didn't know where to turn. Certainly she couldn't turn to Percy's mother; however, when left with no alternative, she turned to Percy.

"Percy, Fred and I are talking about something and I want your advice."

"Sex?" he said in a matter of fact way.

She blushed.

"Yes, how did you know?"

"Sweetie, I'm gay, not stupid. Do you love him?"

"Yes, I think so."

"Love isn't a 'think so' proposition sweetheart, it's a yes or no, it's an absolute. Now, don't get me wrong, I'm not a prude, if it's not love and it's just lust and you just wanna sow your oats, then do it, but go into it with your eyes wide open about what it is."

"I'm not sure I understand."

"Baby, I love you, you are family to me. You are my sister. You don't need my blessing or my counsel. All you need is what is in your heart, you will know whether it is right for you, I promise. Just go in with your eyes wide open."

"Okay, I understand."

"Good, and Sue, one more thing."

"Yes?"

"Please use a condom."

She blushed again.

Two nights later Sue and Fred were at his parents' house while they were away. Their passion intensified and she lost herself in the moment and before she knew it he was inside her and it hurt and felt wonderful all at the same moment, and she felt joy, and fear, and love, or perhaps lust and it was wonderful, and then it was over and they clung to each other with him whispering words of love to her while she shed tears of joy and pain.

Later that evening Fred took Sue home and as she walked in the door her surrogate mother looked at her, smiled, and said, "Oh, my darling, you're pregnant. Now what are we gonna do about this?"

Sue ran up to her room and wept into her pillow. She wept at her lost innocence, she wept because she knew Percy's mother must be right, but mostly she wept because Percy was not here to share this moment, in all its complexity, with her.

A few days later Sue confirmed the pregnancy. Percy took her downtown to a clinic and with the money he had been saving to buy a car, he paid for an abortion. Sue wept the entire way there because Fred had stopped returning her calls. Her innocence was lost to a man who had so little to really offer.

Sue graduated high school as the school's salutatorian. She would have made valedictorian but for her being so ill after the abortion. It was okay though. Percy's entire family was there for the graduation and they all cheered when Sue's name was called and then they all wept the day that she and Percy loaded up his new car, well, actually an old car but all he could afford, and left for San Francisco, she to attend Stanford on a scholarship and he to find work and experience a more open lifestyle. His family all knew and all accepted him.

Just before she got in the car, Percy's mother walked over to Sue and said, "I wish you all the very best, I love you like my own child."

Sue's tears flowed and she replied, "I love you mom."

Chapter 26

When Sue awoke in the car she had tears pouring down her face. She sat up and turned to Larry and said, "We have to get to Percy. It doesn't matter how we do it or how hard it is to get there, we have to find him. I owe him everything. I owe him my life."

Larry nodded his head. He didn't speak, just simply nodded his head and recommenced his driving. He had been lost in his own thoughts.

Larry Jones was born, interestingly enough, Larry Jones. He was the son of a lay preacher and a church pianist. The area where he grew up was entirely too poor to have an organ, so his mother's piano would have to suffice. It was a loving home, poor in money and material goods, but rich in caring, trust and devotion. It was the sort of home Norman Rockwell must have been thinking about when he painted all of those magazine covers so many years ago.

Larry had a stepbrother and a stepsister. The oldest was his stepsister, Eve, and the next was his brother, Jeremiah, or Jed, as his friends and family called him. The first two children had been named after important biblical persona, strangely, however, Larry had been named just plain Larry. He never quite understood why and as he got older the only thought which made any sense to him was that he was, perhaps, nor a planned pregnancy, so his parents hadn't really thought out his name. That, combined with the fact that the old doctor who delivered him was Dr. Horace Larry, the man who became Larry's stepfather, seemed to make the most sense.

Regardless of the history of his name, Larry was well loved and

Standby

certainly doted upon by the women in his family. He certainly worshipped Jed, like younger brothers will do, although Jed, as he got older had less and less time for Larry. Larry's adoration for his brother never wavered.

His stepfather died soon after he and Larry's mother wed. Larry was just eight years old when it happened. The entire congregation wept for days and went through writhing adoration for their dear doctor, so soon departed. Larry and his brother and sister attended the funeral and acted the appropriate roles of grieving children.

The funeral ended soon enough. Larry dutifully saw his mother home and then dutifully collected all of the pies and cakes and stews which the ladies of the church had prepared for them. It struck Larry as somewhat nutty that there was just so much food for so few people, especially since Eve and Jed spent less and less time at home now. But he also knew that he needed to be gracious about accepting the food because the food was as much about the grieving of the person bringing it as it was about the person delivering it. So he stacked the pies and the cakes and he put out the food, and all the while his mother sat on the porch swing, chain smoking cigarettes, and telling everyone what a good boy Larry was to his momma.

Soon they were alone. Jed and Eve had come home and the visitors had all gone their separate ways. Jed spoke first

"Momma, I need to tell you something."

"Yes" she answered through the visual haze of cigarette smoke and the non-visual haze of bourbon.

"Momma, as you know there is a war going on over in Vietnam, and I ain't been drafted but some of my friends have, and I think I'm gonna enlist, seeing as how there ain't no jobs here and all. There will be money for college then."

"And you?" she said to Eve.

"I'm gonna be a nurse for the Army."

"Well, then I guess you both better be getting on your way."

And that was it. No protestations. No argument. Their mother had just sent Larry's older sister and older brother packing for Vietnam. It was 1969 and the country was in chaos and even Cronkite said the war was lost, but their mother sent them both packing. What the hell was going on here? But Larry was too young and too compliant a son to argue. So off they both went to Vietnam.

Three months later they got a telegram. No letter. No honor guard. No Marine chaplain to deliver the bad news accompanied by a marine surgeon to administer sedatives if necessary. The telegram came. Larry's mother wasn't home from work, yet, and his curiosity wouldn't be quelled. He opened the telegram. He read and re-read the contents of the telegram a hundred times, each in a rapid succession. It never changed. Larry dropped the telegram and fainted.

Sometime later Larry came to due to the smell of ammonia wafting up his nose. His brother was dead.

They stood with two dozen other military families at the airbase in Dover, Delaware, waiting to welcome home his brother, Jeb. But Jeb didn't walk off the plane. Instead, an honor guard escorted his shining aluminum coffin off the plan and to the hearse that would drive him to the family plot outside of Allentown, Pennsylvania. The Lehigh Valley was bringing home another of its honored dead. Like most spring days in the "Leakey Valley", it was raining. Larry's mother stood under an umbrella, sobbing quietly, mumbling, "My son, my son..." over and over again. Larry and his sister, given emergency leave and resplendent in her Navy Nurse's uniform, stood quietly in the rain and watched their brother, older for him, baby for her, lowered quietly into the ground.

Two days later his sister left to return to Vietnam.

After that he didn't see very much of his mother. She was out enjoying what was left of the late 1960's as they rolled into the '70's. His mother voted for Nixon, not once, but twice, while at the same time experimenting with free love and drugs. She definitely "tuned out". Larry continued with his schoolwork and hit his teen years without much incident. He kept up a regular correspondence with his sister, and had learned recently that she extended her term for another term due, in large part, to the fact that she had fallen for a Captain who was swearing to her that he was going to leave his wife for her. Larry doubted that this last part would ever come to fruition, but he loved his sister very much, notwithstanding that unsettling prom thing, so he disregarded he transgressions and praised her accomplishments.

The next fall as Larry came home from college, he had enrolled in a local school to be close to home, he saw an envelope lying

Standby

against the front door of the house. It was, as usual, raining outside. The envelope was yellow. Larry picked it up and immediately recognized it as a telegram from the Defense Department. Larry looked at it and then quietly laid it on the table. He never opened it; instead he picked up the phone and called the funeral home.

Larry's sister was buried next to her father and brother on the first sunny day they could all remember in the Valley. As soon as the coffin was covered his mother turned to him and said, "Pack your things, were moving to Florida." Larry simply nodded his head. The few friends he had all lived there in Allentown, and he would have to leave them. He supposed it was okay. Still, that wasn't the part that bothered him. What bothered him is he didn't know how long it would be until she was able to come back and visit his brother and sister again.

He took a few moments to linger by the graves of his father, brother and sister. He wept. For the first time in his life, he truly wept. And when he was done he joined his mother, walked to the car, and began the migration to Florida.

Larry and his mother moved in with an aunt on Miami Beach. This was the Miami Beach of the 1970's, before the glamour and glitz of the late 1990's. Many of the hotels which would ultimately become the destinations for the hip and famous were now nothing more than holding grounds for the elderly relatives of the financially well to do in the Northeast, the place where they sent their old to wait and die. That is the environment that Larry entered for his college years.

He applied late to the University of Miami and was admitted largely due to an excellent high school transcript and an admissions advisor who was sympathetic to his loss of a parent and two siblings in short order. He worked throughout college. There was nothing he wouldn't do, but at the same time none of the jobs he selected allowed him to stand out. He cooked the pizza, but never worked the register. He made the hotel beds and cleaned the sheets, but never delivered the bags. He polished the football helmets, but never got to stand on the sideline.

Larry was always there, but never seen. He was the employee you always took for granted.

But he did well in school, and he was devoted to the church that his mother had joined. He was indulgent of her odd behaviors as well as her particularly poor taste in men. All she asked was that he tell her he loved her, which he did, always ending their visits with "I love you, Mama."

He graduated college in three years with a degree in civil engineering, whatever that was, and set out to work in some obscure government division. His life became his work and his church. He did not date. He did not socialize, and with the exception of his ordering of his meals from the local diner, he hardly spoke a word all day, content to simply work with his slide rules and charts.

The only change to this tedium was the two days a week that he was at his church. Sunday for prayer and Wednesday for meetings and whatever social or philanthropic events were occurring.

It was on one of those Wednesday tea socials that he met Felicity.

Chapter 27

Several days later, although Edsel had no concept of time, a rather frumpy looking woman came in and sat down in his room. There was also a considerable amount of light and commotion as well as some cheesy looking guy in a mauve colored suit. The suit had a shine to it, like it was either over worn, or purchased from a store that tended to provide clothing to gangster wannabes. All in all, there was just a great deal of commotion in the room. He could hear what was being said but he couldn't engage in the conversation, for reasons he still couldn't fathom.

The guy in the mauve suit spoke first.

"Ladies and gentlemen, as you know my name is Clarence Darrow Sullivan, and I have been given the sacred responsibility of representing Mrs. Jones on behalf of her husband, Larry. As the court has ordered that I not speak to the press, I turn this over to the Reverend Thomas," he said.

"Who the hell was Mrs. Jones?," Edsel thought. "And who the hell was Larry Jones?"

Then the largest black man he had ever seen in his life walked into his room. The man was just plain huge. He spoke and his voice filled the small room like he was talking to a church full of parishioners.

"Ladies and Gentlemen, I am the Reverend Franklin Thomas."

Oh, shit, it was the Shadetree. "Jesus", he thought, "the friggin' Shadetree is here in my hospital room."

"This man has suffered devastating injuries. His life is forever and irrevocably altered. He has lost his hands, his tongue, and his face has been burned apart."

"Holy shit", Edsel thought, "is he talking about me?"

"I am the spiritual advisor to Mrs. Jones, who is seated here behind me as you can see. I am here to offer her guidance on her difficult journey. She is here to support her husband. That is all we can do for him now. That, and pray."

With that, the big man turned to Felicity and gave the slightest nod of the head. She stood and walked over to the bed and leaned over and whispered something in his ear. Something that she would never disclose to the press but if they had asked Edsel he would've told them was pure gibberish. Then she tried to hold his hand. But there was no hand to hold. So she looked him up and down and finally settled on holding his foot. Then she sobbed and turned away.

The press ate it up. Imagine the headlines. "Wife holds foot of poor suffering husband" "Wife vows husband will not be de-feet-ed" The story had everything, a victim with catastrophic injuries, a reasonable photogenic spouse, a well-known spiritual advisor, and a shyster-advertising lawyer. This story had everything!

Later that day, the Reverend Franklin Thomas stood at the podium and surveyed the masses in front of him. The location for the press conference was selected to suit the needs of both him and Sullivan. Right in front of the offices of Gilbert and Sullivan and just a short distance from the hospital where their "client" lay in the hospital trying to recover from his grievous wounds. Sullivan began the press conference,

"Ladies and Gentlemen, I would love to be able to address you on behalf of my clients, but as you know, the Judge has issued an Order restricting my ability to exercise the First Amendment rights of myself and my client, and I therefore cannot speak to you. I will turn over the press conference to Reverend Thomas and Mrs. Jones."

Franklin began.

"Members of the press and assorted dignitaries. You all know me. You have all heard me worship with my congregation and bring joy to the masses. You all know me. You also all know Clarence Darrow Sullivan. You have heard him on the TV, you know his successes for his clients and the efforts you put forth for him. What you don't know, however, is anything about Felicity and Larry Jones. And that is what I wish to tell you about today.

Standby

"Felicity Jones is the youngest daughter of a stalwart in the community. A banking legend. But now, my ward, dear dear Felicity is burdened with the heaviest weight imaginable, a husband so grievously injured, so catastrophically hurt by the negligence of this airline, Deacon Air, an airline which is blitzing the airways trying to make themselves look good with cheap settlements sent to suffering widows and widowers, suffering children and parents.

"But Mrs. Jones intends to hold Deacon Air accountable. She intends, with the help of Mr. Sullivan, her able bodied attorney, to walk into that courtroom, that sanctuary of justice, and ask a jury of her peers to award her an amount of money appropriate for her pain and suffering. When that happens, justice will be done. When that happens, justice will prevail. When that happens, justice will carry the day!!!

"That, and nothing more, my brothers and sisters. And now, if you will excuse us, we will not be taking any questions, as we are on our way to church to pray for Larry. And we ask that all of you keep him and Felicity, and all of the victims of this catastrophe in your prayers. God bless you."

Franklin was walking off the dais toward his car when his wife swiftly took Felicity away and Ronnie grabbed him by the arm with an urgent gesture that indicated to him that the Weasel had secured some piece of important piece of information that he wouldn't trust to the cell phone.

"What is it Ronald?"

"Judge wants to see you and Sullivan in his chambers."

"When?"

"Right now."

"Okay."

"Oh, and Reverend ..."

"Yes"

"He's pissed. He said bring bail money."

The judge thundered from the moment he walked into the courtroom, "Mr. Sullivan, what exactly did you not understand about my order regarding appearing in public to discuss the case?"

"Uh, Judge, I assumed that your Order applied only to discussing the merits of the case."

Padua couldn't suppress a smile. This was all turning out so wonderfully.

"Mr. Sullivan, this is not a bullshit whiplash case, nor a slip and fall, it is a complex case involving the crash of an aircraft with complicated damages. In short, Mr. Sullivan, this case requires the services of a trial lawyer, a real trial lawyer, which, much to my chagrin, you have not yet turned out to be."

At this, everyone in the courtroom began laughing audibly. Most, in fact, had given up trying to suppress the laughter. Sullivan reddened noticeably.

He attempted to rise to the challenge.

"Your Honor, I must protest. I am a duly licensed member of the Bar and therefore qualify to serve as Mrs. Jones trial counsel. What's more, the 6th amendment to the Constitution guarantees her the right to counsel." Sullivan was particularly pleased with this last argument.

"Did you just quote the 6th Amendment to me? Did you?" thundered the judge.

"Yes, I did, your honor."

The judge's expression softened for just a moment, a moment that Sullivan mistook for a weakening in his position, but if he had known the judge, he would have realized it was actually the closest the judge actually came to pity. Pity at what he was about to do to this poor excuse for a lawyer in front of him.

"Five thousand dollars."

"Excuse me?"

"Ten thousand dollars"

"Your honor, I'm not sure I follow?"

"Fifteen thousand dollars."

"Your Honor, I don't follow, I apologize."

"Twenty five thousand dollars." This last amount was bellowed from the bench. Even Padua couldn't swallow this much abuse. He whispered to Sullivan,

"He is sanctioning you, Clarence, he is fining you until you shut up and sit down."

Contrary to his instincts, Sullivan sat down and shut up.

The judge again broke the silence.

"Now, let me be perfectly clear. No one talks to the press. Not the plaintiff's attorney, not Mr. Sullivan, nor anyone from his office. And, as I don't at present have jurisdiction over Reverend Jones, I

Standby

will not order him to stay quiet, but if he crosses me, I sure as hell will get that jurisdiction. Understood?"

"Yes, your Honor," they both replied, simultaneously.

"And one more thing" the judge continued "Mr. Sullivan, if I see you at one of the Reverend's press conferences or if I see your commercials timed so that they appear right after a news segment on the crash, I will assume that you have breached my order and I will sanction you accordingly. Do not tempt me sir!"

"Yes, Judge."

"Any further matters to be taken up before I adjourn?"

Padua weighed this moment carefully. Up until know he had a judge who was certainly against plaintiff's counsel, if not swayed towards the defendant's position. All of that could be ruined and the judge could rapidly swing against him if he felt that Geoff was taking advantage of the situation. Still, this had to be balanced against the knowledge that the judge would certainly come down on him very hard if her felt that Geoff had been sandbagging and delaying what he knew he should disclose.

He closed his eyes and leaped.

"Your honor, one more matter from the defense."

Sullivan felt his stomach dropped. What else could possibly go wrong now?

"Yes, Mr. Padua, what is it?"

Geoff paused, fully aware of the cameras whirring behind him. He knew this was a critical moment in his planned dismantling of Sullivan. If he succeeded, Sullivan's credibility would be forever undermined. However, if he failed, it would be his credibility that would be dashed.

"Your honor, as we previously advised the Court, the defense plans to file a Motion to Dismiss later today, but wished to notify the court and plaintiff's counsel at the same time as we believe it will require an immediate evidentiary hearing."

Sullivan was noticeably sweating now.

"Alright, Mr. Padua, I'll bite, what's this all about?"

Geoff paused. This was his moment and he dragged out for all the drama the moment could muster. "Your honor, as you know we believe that the man lying in the hospital is not Larry Jones, but some as yet unidentified passenger, and since it is not Larry Jones, then

Mrs. Jones has no standing to bring this claim and it should be dismissed before the trial."

Notwithstanding his fear of the judge, Sullivan dropped heavily into his chair and sighed audibly. His surefire winner was rapidly becoming a three-dollar nag.

Chapter 28

Edsel Dodger was born with no name in a small suburb of Topeka, Kansas. His mother was an itinerant farm worker and his father was a traveling preacher, the type of guy who rolls into town on a Wednesday preaching hell fire and damnation, and promising the good neighbors that they will all be saved if they simply attend his church revival that following Sunday. Then he and his small army of assistants, his able apostles, attend to the needs of the local population and gradually, in small numbers, beginning in the ones and two and gradually continuing to the threes and fours, and soon by the scores, the entire town populus is whipped to frenzy. A frenzy that can only be satisfied by attending the Reverend's revival and, most certainly, being generous at the collection plate. It was a formula that had worked since the beginnings of organized religion and it was a formula surely followed by Reverend Thomas today although his methods were a bit more organized.

Into that town, on that sleepy Wednesday, rolled Edsel's father, spouting venom against sin and promising salvation through sacrifice. Edsel's mother, a rather plain sort but with a true heart of gold, fell prey to his promises as time went on. In fact, in a manner most unlike her she took it upon herself to organize the local ladies' constabulary to perform works of good deeds on behalf of the good Reverend. They organized a bake sale and a barbeque with all of the proceeds going into a small cigar box. The proceeds of these donations were to help the good reverend build a church in their little community and provide them with a regular dose of spiritual salvation.

Kenneth S. Spiegelman

Every night as the blessed event of the revival approached the reverend would appear at Edsel's mother's home and share dinner with her family and sit ever so closer to her on the porch swing. In fact, on the night before the revival, she even allowed herself a chaste, if rather long, kiss good night. He was, after all, such a sweet young man, and was so handsome, and she had never really had a man pay such attention to her.

The day of the revival came and Edsel's mother worked hard all day assembling the local lades into work crews necessary for the handling of the bake sale and the Barbeque. For her part, Edsel's mother was devoting all of her time to the Reverend, and in helping him prepare himself for the evening's devotions. It was a night alive with electricity, rocking with a thunderstorm.

He preached that night and those who remembered him fondly would recall that they had never, in their lives, heard such true notes of salvation and redemption from the pulpit. Their own regular preacher felt that he was in the presence of a messenger of God. And when the thunderstorm hit and the bolts of lightning hit and the thunder roared, that cacophony of sounds seemed only to underscore the power of his sermon. His voice rose in fury and passion as the sounds of the storm rose higher and higher. The tears that flowed in the congregation were as real as the raindrops that poured off of the revival tent.

Throughout the sermon, Edsel's mother watched this man, so clearly a messenger of her Lord that she knew, in her heart, that she was born to be in this moment, sharing her love of God with this man, and, if the chance should arise, praise be, her flesh with this man who she hardly knew yet so clearly loved.

Then it was over. As the lights failed from the storm and as the Reverend raced off the stage, pulling Edsel's mother behind him, the crowds pulsed back and forth with a fury all their own, still entranced at the preaching they had witnessed and the love they each felt they had shared.

"My darling, did you feel the power of the Lord tonight?"

"I did, my love." She blushed.

Then they were in his car, driving away, her with her head nestled on his right shoulder, his arm around her, the cash box from all the donations resting on her lap.

Standby

"How much?"

"Excuse me, my love?"

"How much did we raise?"

"I, I, don't know. I haven't counted." Again she blushed and then continued, "I was overwhelmed tonight. I haven't felt that way, ever"

The next thing she knew he had pulled the car over and he was kissing her and she was kissing back furiously, all the while professing her love for him. And she was only fifteen years old, and he was much older, and wiser and he guided her, rapidly, into womanhood, there in the ragged back seat of an old car on the side of a rain-soaked road. Then he delivered the cruelest blow of her life.

"Get out."

"What?"

"Get out of my car!"

"Why?"

"It wouldn't be seemly for me to be seen in my car with a woman so young. Might even get me in trouble. You just wait here, and tell whoever comes along that you were walking home and got lost, whatever, just get out."

"But my love," she said as she kissed him and tried to hold him, "I don't understand."

"Get the fuck out of my car!" He roared and she obeyed.

She turned back to the car to grab the box while the vicious rainstorm pelted her with hail.

"Leave the box." It was the last thing he ever said to her as he drove off with an evil wink.

She stood there on the side of the road weeping more furiously that the rain that was coming down. Eventually, a farmer and his wife stopped and without a word, loaded her into the car and took her back home.

Later that night the reverend was shot to death after trying to cheat in a local card game. He had already lost all of the donations made to his revival. Nine months later, Edsel was born. He was born to a mother who the town had ostracized, holding her responsible for the lost money.

He grew up alone and without any friends. He also had a lisp that ostracized him more than having an unwed teenage mother ever would. She regretted having him and even found him burdensome as he became older. He was a burden to her social life. She was, after all, a very young mother and had never really dated. Edsel's father was, in fact, her first and only boyfriend, if such a coupling could really be called a relationship.

She reached her early twenties with a son she didn't know how to raise, no education to speak of and few redeeming qualities short of a generous spirit for strangers and a figure that a young childbirth had done little to diminish.

Unfortunately for Edsel, she utilized the second attribute much more frequently than the first and she led a progression of boyfriends brought back to the trailer she shared with Edsel. He was actually much more likely to be found occupying the trailer than his mother as it was equally likely that she would not be coming home for the evening. He learned how to fend for himself at an early age. He taught himself to read from cereal boxes and educational television as the only network that came through on their small television was the local public broadcasting station. He taught himself to cook by heating cans of spaghetti and soup over a sterno stove, the tricks of which were taught to him by the kindly trailer park managers who took pity on his poor lost soul always wearing yesterday's rags and always trying to make his old sneakers look new with white paint and chalk.

The difficulty for Edsel was three-fold, really. One, he had a lisp and a mother who didn't care enough about it to seek help. He taught himself to control it through shear force of will and found that it only came out in moments of true stress. Two, he received a sex education at much too young of an age from seeing the parade of suitors his mother brought back to the trailer. The walls, after all, were particularly thin. By the age of ten, when other boys his age were just reaching the age when a woman's breasts were still giggle material, Edsel had a vocabulary rich with words to eloquently describe all the different parts of the female anatomy as well as the various positions of the human coupling experience.

It was the third part of his problem that was the real problem for Edsel. He had no last name. After his mother had delivered him, a hospital social worker came to visit with her to fill out the paperwork the State required for the preparation of the birth certificate. The conversation went something like this,

Standby

"Ma'am, we need some information for the birth certificate."

"Okay."

"Alright, what is your full name?"

His mother gave her the information.

"Okay and what is the father's full name?"

"I don't know and I don't care. Besides, he is dead anyhow."

"Still, ma'am, this is most, ah, unusual. We really do need a father's name or the certificate won't be completed, you see."

His mom thought for a moment before responding.

"Let me asking you something, what if I really don't know the father's name. What if, say, I got real drunk at a church social and, oh, I don't know, took on the whole high school football team in the back of the school bus, and let them each have their way with me, you know, a real life experience. Taking one, or two, or, oh, I don't know, thirty for the team. What happens then?"

His mother obviously was in a foul mood, brought on, no doubt, by the recent conduct and subsequent death of the "reverend".

The hospital social worker was even more set off – honestly, she had never in her life heard anyone speak in such a fashion. Still, she was much too professional to allow this moment pass without some addressing of the fact.

"Ahem, well, I suppose, under those circumstances, an exception would have to be made for a lady of such, um, ah, repute, and we would have to leave the father's name blank. It would be most unusual but I suppose I could understand how such a 'lady' would want to leave the father, or should I say 'fathers' names off the birth certificate." Clearly, the social worker was finding her groove.

Edsel's mother rose to the moment.

"Then if the whore in the back of the bus has the right to leave the father's name off of the birth certificate, why don't I have the same right? After all, it was just one man?"

The social worker was stumped.

"Well, you see, rules are rules, and the state does like all the lines filled in, and…"

"Fuck your lines woman!" His mother screamed in return. "I've had just about all I can take with the rules. I've lived my whole entire life by the rules and where has it gotten me? Here, in this hospital bed. I'm fifteen years old. I have no job, no boyfriend, and hell, no friends for that matter. And now I have a son and all your stupid head seems to want is to know the father's name. Well, he is dead, and rightly so. He was a thief and a scoundrel and an evil man, and he took my virginity and left me here. So his name just won't be on that certificate. Do you get it?"

"Yes, ma'am."

With that, the issue of whether Edsel's father would appear on the birth certificate was resolved. The line, much to the chagrin of the state and the social worker would be left blank. His mother had won her victory. There was only one battle left to fight.

"Ma'am, I don't mean to belabor you anymore, but could you please tell me the boy's name?"

Truth be told, his mother had never even thought about a name for her child, much less be concerned about whether she was having a boy or a girl. And now, she was being told that she needed to give the baby a name, right here and right now. She thought, and nothing was coming to her, at all.

"I'm sorry, I have no idea."

"Well, this is most irregular, most irregular indeed. Child needs a name, you see, must have a name. And he is such a strong looking boy, as well, he deserves a strong name, don't you think?"

Again, his mother had not even held him yet much less looked at him, so the social worker was probably in a much better position to tell whether he was strong looking or not, or, for that matter, what sort of name he needed or deserved.

"Ma'am, I'm very tired, can we just work on a name later?"

"Well, sure honey, I will just come back in a couple of hours, how does that sound?"

"Fine, just fine."

The social worker began to depart the room. As she was walking out, his mother's thought back to the night in the car. An evil smile crossed her lips. She called to the hospital employee,

"Ma'am?"

"Yes, dear?"

"Edsel."

The employee stared at her, confused. She eventually replied,

"A fine strong name. And the last name?"

"None, just Edsel. Just Edsel."

Standby

"Okay, Edsel it is."

Edsel, no last name, began his life.

It was a very simple life with very few, if any friends. A psychologist who studied his life would likely view his upbringing as one equally likely to produce a hermit as a serial killer. In his own unique way, Edsel, no last name, proved them all wrong.

School was always an adventure. As he had no last name, lining up in alphabetical order always proved difficult. To Edsel it seemed an obvious answer, he should simply line up with the "e's", right there between the "d's" and "f's". His teachers ultimately agreed.

He never found himself picked on any sports teams and was content to idle away his free time with works of literature. People who met him later in life would have been stunned to learn that he was a very well read man, having devoured most of the literary classics while the other students were busy with kickball, or, as they grew older with spin the bottle or seven minutes in heaven, a strange game that seemed to require two oddly suited youngsters sneaking into the custodians closet for some unknown reason. As if anyone would have any reason to spend any time in the custodians' closet.

Edsel found his passion in books. He lived them and consumed them with the only passion in his life. He had no one with whom to share his interest. The real shame of this was that behind the bookworm like appearance lay a rather handsome young man. Even his mother noticed that as Edsel grew older, he took on more and more of the physical qualities that had so attracted her to his father. Unfortunately, however, those physical similarities did very little to assuage his mother's dislike for him and as he grew to look more and more like his father his relationship, such as it was, with his mother grew worse and worse.

Then he hit puberty.

And everything for him changed rather rapidly.

Now, many of the writers who had so intrigued him in his pre-pubescent days, attracted him for a whole new reason. Of particular interest to him were James Joyce and D.H. Lawrence. To him, these authors brought out a rapture that had previously been unknown. They were more erotic for him that any pornographic magazine could ever be and, what's more, he found that he finally had a voice that the other students would listen to.

Everyone was at the age of burgeoning sexuality. Edsel gave them an outlet, and it was an outlet that channeled their curiosity into literature, real literature. Not the type of dime store paperbacks you could buy for a dime and which didn't last through a summer of self-adventure, no, real, recognized, gosh-honest literature. How could a teacher honestly get upset at you for reading D.H. Lawrence? It just was not possible and, what's more, allowed him a foot in the door with the teachers. Now, for the first time his life, Edsel had clout. He achieved that clout by introducing students to a legitimate outlet for their sexual instincts and urges.

However, there was one thing that he lacked. He wanted it desperately and often tried to engage his mother in conversation on the subject but found that he got nowhere whenever he raised the subject.

"Mom, I need to talk with you about something."

"What now?"

"Well, we've talked about it before but I still haven't been able to get an answer from you and I think that I'm reaching the age where I'm sort of entitled to an answer, don't you think?"

"Listen, you're only ten, I decide when you've reached the age."

He paused.

"Mom, I'm fourteen,"

"What?!"

"I'm fourteen, only you've been too liquored up to notice my last four birthdays."

"Watch your tongue young man."

"Yes, ma'am, only I feel like I have a right to know is all." He said sheepishly.

"What is it you wanna know? The name of your daddy? Some asshole only gave me a moment or two in the back of a beat up pickup truck. Hell, and he was my first time too. I can't even get a good story out of it. So, I'll bite, you tell me, what would your fancy author boys say about that sorta romance? Young virgin girl gets knocked up by a bullshit traveling evangelist? That's you're daddy. A bullshit con artist. Same as you're gonna be, I bet. So, now what you wanna know?"

"Mom," he wept, "I don't care about him. I love you. I just want a name. Like everyone else."

Standby

She paused now and considered him. Unfortunately, her heart was hardened by a love scorned at a young age and hardened even more by too much liquor. She had no love to give him back. Instead, she reached into the last vestiges of her soul and responded.

"You pick yourself a last name, and I will go with you to see the judge and make it so, on your next birthday."

Now he wept, in actual joy. It was the first and only gift he could ever remember his mother giving him.

He spent the next year in a desperate search for a last name. Should he go common like a Smith or Jones? Should he go ethnic like a Schwartz, a Khan, an O'Reilly? How about Lawrence or Joyce?

Nothing sufficed.

For the first time in his school career, his grades actually suffered, just a bit, not so much as you would notice, and, after all, the teachers were all aware that he was a good kid on a quest that rivaled the Knights of the Round Table.

In the end, it was Dickens who provided the name for him. Oliver Twist. No, not Oliver, Not Twist. In the end it was the strength of the character that provided the last name. The Artful Dodger.

And his mother was, for the first time in his young life, good to his word. On his fifteenth birthday, the heretofore Edsel, no last name, became Edsel Dodger.

He graduated high school a year early and immediately left home. From that point until this moment, lying in this hospital bed, he had never seen nor spoken to his mother again. The last he had heard she was dealing "pai gow" poker at one of those riverboat casinos on the Mississippi River. She was considerably overweight, favored tacky polyester pantsuits and wore her hair garishly high. Some would call it New Jersey girl high, but his mother hardly had the figure of a young New Jersey girl.

He put himself through the local state university on the strength of academic scholarships, grants, financial aid and his jobs. He worked two or three jobs at a time. He did all of this while maintaining near perfect grades in a business curriculum that, while not necessarily the best in the county, certainly was not an easy program. It was while he was working one of these jobs that he stumbled upon a new job. He answered an ad in the local student rag:

"Seeking. Student. Flexible hours. Work at an all night business establishment. Mostly quiet location. Free reading material."

That was it. He found the perfect job. He could work all evening, hopefully in a relatively quiet environment, carry on his studies while he was there, and get in some reading. Of course, when he went for the job interview, such as it was, he found that what he was interviewing for was a position with an all-night adult bookstore. He stood outside of the store for almost an hour, before finally gathering the courage to go inside for his interview. At last, however, it was his desire and need to make money along with the promise of a quiet location, and not really the free reading material, that caused him to walk inside.

The jangling bells on the doors rang much more loudly than he would have thought possible. It was as if the owners of the store wanted to announce to the denizens of the world that someone was actually entering the sanctum sanctorum of the pornography world. Sort of like the cute girl at the check out counter yelling out for a price check on condoms.

The pimply-faced teenager at the checkout counter lifted his head ever so slightly from the magazine he was staring at and nodded his head at him. Edsel stood and stared back at him.

"Something I can help you with?" said the younger man in the most grown up voice he could muster. He continued his stare, not quite sure how to handle this kid.

"Whatever you need, it's on the shelves. Just help yourself. And limit your browsing time to less than five minutes, if you please, I don't want you messing up the merchandise."

Edsel spoke. "I'm here about the job, who do I speak to?"

"That would be me. Name's Ronnie James. But everyone here calls me "Weasel". Don't know why; only know that the name stuck. My uncle owns this place. I work here for some spending money and he lets me take home two or three mag's a week, if you know what I mean. Not that I really need the mag's, if you know what I mean, I have no problem, no problem at all with the ladies. Aw hell, but you don't care about that, you don't care at all do ya'? No, I think you probably just want the old Weasel to shut up an tell you about the job. Well, it pays five bucks an hour plus you can pick one or two mag's a week to keep, not any of the richy rich stuff, just the

Standby

standard stuff. Plus, you are allowed to read whatever you want so long as you don't mess it up, if you know what I mean, and you're gonna wanna keep that conduct to a minimum, if you know what I mean, cameras al over the place." This he announced with a wink and a nod, pointing to the ceiling.

"So, got any questions?"

"Uh, no, I don't, well, maybe just one I suppose, anything you wanna know about me?"

"Nope, you want the job you got it. Hours are 8 pm to 7 am. Store never closes. Six days a week, you get Sundays off if you want, if you wanna work then you can on Sundays too, same hours, pays eight bucks an hour on those days. Not too much of a crowd on Sundays, even the perv's take a day off I suppose. Gotta really watch the shoplifters though, real important cause you gotta pay for any merchandise stolen on your shift."

Edsel thought about the offer for a moment. His budget being as tight as it was, he could really use the money. He knew he would be giving up his sleep time to take this job but he figured he might get by with some cat naps during the nights, once he figured out when the quieter times were.

"I'll take it."

"It's yours. Paperwork you gotta fill in is in the desk drawer. Know how to work the cash register?" Edsel nodded. "Good, cause we are a cash only business. No credit here. No returns, no lay aways." With that one Ronnie broke into a fit of laughter as if he had just said about the funniest thing in the history of the world.

"Let me give you the tour. Wanna start tonight?" Edsel nodded. "Good. You understand there ain't no benefits package." And again, another fit of laughter, along with a strange whistling noise from his nose.

Edsel genuinely took to his new job. Not the source material so much. He really didn't have much time or need for those pursuits. No. What first drew him to the position and what he found very much to his liking was the solitude of the work. He realized as he sat behind the counter, with its filthy bullet proofed glass, that he was completely isolated, completely alone, and the experience, while initially unsettling, was really rather cathartic and enjoyable.

He relished being alone. His studies improved, he found his time to catnap after discovering the pattern of customer activity ran in direct relation to the business hours of the strip club on the adjacent corner. He discovered that once the dinner hour began and until the strip club closed, his store would be quiet. Then, once the strip club's customer's spilled into the street and needed ways to fulfill their prurient interests, his sales picked up. He even took it upon himself to go to the owner of the store, Uncle Eddie, and suggest to him that he work out a business relationship whereby customers of the gentleman's club could use their leftover strip club dollars as cash at Uncle Eddie's Adult Book Emporium and Coffee Shop.

To his great pleasure, Uncle Eddie was right on board with the idea. It wasn't until later, much much later, that Edsel discovered that the reason why Uncle Eddie was so on board with the idea was because he was actually one of the owners of the strip club and therefore where the money was spent was far less important than whether it was spent at all. Edsel, however, to his credit, would not be swayed from his interest in improving the business of Uncle Eddie's. In fact, upon graduating from college, in three years no less, he approached Uncle Eddie with a request for a full time position; one with more managerial responsibility.

Uncle Eddie was happy to oblige. His sales during the dead hours were dramatically improving and with the Weasel and his sister having taken off for parts unknown, Eddie was willing to turn over the reigns of control to his young upstart. Eddie preferred spending his time at the strip club instead of the bookstore. Eddie was not much of a reader anyhow.

Edsel took over. He changed the layout of the store and with the increased profits rapidly convinced Uncle Eddie to broaden the scope of the stores in both their size and location. Soon he was adding stores near every airport, bus and train depot and sports venue in town, not to mention every gentleman's club and emergency room. His own research having taught him that patients in emergency rooms didn't really want to read the three year old gospel magazines that were laying around the waiting rooms while they waited to get a hangnail pulled. Edsel still cared enough not to put the stores outside of any emergency centers that catered to cardiac patients, after all, a dead patient was a sealed wallet, like Uncle Eddie liked to say, "excite 'em, but don't kill em'." Another one of Uncle Eddie's

Standby

slogans. It always made Edsel chuckle.

Before too long Edsel was managing over a dozen adult entertainment and paraphernalia stores around town and had, in fact, saved up enough money to actually purchase an ownership interest in no less than a half dozen of them. In fact, as he began to save more and more money, he found that he could actually just take on sort of a supervisory role and could, in fact, hire more local students to manage the various stores and would, in that fashion, maximize the efficiency of the stores.

By the end of the first full year in the business, Edsel Dodger owned more adult stores than Uncle Eddie had ever dreamed possible. He had also brought into his business model the concept of mail order adult magazines and videos and was starting to seriously consider the possibility of producing adult videos under his own production company name – Happy Juice Videos. He knew the name was sort of trite but he found the concept worthwhile and certainly worth looking into.

Edsel rented some office space from which he could manage the day-to-day affairs of the business he was developing. He was spending less and less time actually at the stores and more and more time in his management endeavors. He was so busy managing that he decided to enroll in a local night school to obtain an MBA. He was just twenty years old.

One day as he sat at this desk marveling at the week's receipts, there came a knock on the door of his private office. There was only himself in there along with a young buxom blonde who had managed to make herself his personal assistant. Aside from the daily roll in the hay, Edsel wasn't sure what she did for him; however, given his dismal history with women, he felt it prudent at that juncture to keep her around.

"Come in!" he shouted to the door.

In walked a short, but gangly, acne scarred and greasy haired young man. Edsel stared at him trying to make a mental connection about who it was.

"Hello, Edsel, remember me?" the intruder asked innocently enough.

"You sure look familiar, are you in the industry?"

The young man smiled, whistled through his nose, and then

cackled an odd little laugh.

"Of course you don't remember me. Too much trouble for a guy like you, as successful as you, to remember a guy like me."

"What can I do for you, stranger?"

"Stranger, huh? You surely don't remember me, do ya? Well, I suppose that is to be expected, no one ever remembers the …"

Edsel interrupted

"The Weasel, right?" Edsel said with an enormous smile that evaporated the tension in the room.

"Right, old man, its me and I've come to offer you a proposition." Ronnie James said with his own enormous smile.

Several hours later, after the beers had been drunk and the blonde had left for home, after servicing Edsel just one more time in the bathroom, and after the Weasel, himself, declined her services although he certainly, and effusively, appreciated the offer from Dodger, he just wasn't into the sort of thing. Truth be told, no one was really sure of what the Weasel was into, and no one particularly cared to find out.

Ronnie filled him in on where and what he had been doing for the last couple of years. He had some college time, found it not to be his liking, got busted on a couple of minor possession charges, he wasn't a user and only kept enough to keep the good looking girls in marijuana. He thought it would be his "in" to meet good looking girls, and he surely met them, although they just as surely found that they could manipulate him into giving them the best weed, gratis, just by showing him a little attention.

The marijuana business wasn't very profitable for him and he didn't score any dates either from it. He graduated into cocaine and heroin, and of course, one of those good looking girls who seemed to show the most interest in him turned out to be a cop. He got busted with a ridiculous amount of heroin and, thanks to a liberal judge and an overworked prosecutor, only went to jail for eleven months. He used that time to educate himself, found religion and learned the three rules to life that he would later spend so much time ingraining into Shadetree Jones while he worked in the hospital.

Ronnie James was one of those rare prison success stories. He came out of the jail system a true changed man. He no longer drank, completely foreswore drugs, and found it much to his liking to secure

Standby

an honest days' pay for an honest days work. The task he performed was hardly the issue, what mattered to him was that he worked. Hard. Every day. His only derisive humor was that he would tell the few friends that he had that he worked more jobs than a Jamaican housewife. Then he would cackle his very strange little laugh and let out his odd nasal whistle.

He even worked at educating himself. He took typing classes, some business classes, and, much to his enjoyment, classes toward obtaining a private investigator's license. This was his goal, his dream. He wanted to be a private investigator. "A private dick", he thought, again with the cackling little laugh. But he knew it would have to be informal, as no state would ever issue him a license with his criminal record. He loved learning about eavesdropping, both personal and electronic, tailing a car, and surveillance. He figured these courses would really come in handy.

Then, one night at the local college he saw a familiar face. As he was exiting one of his investigation classes he saw a face he knew he recognized. It was Edsel, the guy who took over for his at Uncle Eddie's. He tried to get his attention but he couldn't. For the next few weeks he would see him in passing and say "hello" but Edsel didn't respond. He always seemed deep in thought with his nose buried in a book.

Ronnie grabbed the bull by the horns and followed him one night, all the way back to the adult book store where their "friendship" began all those years ago.

"So, I'm back, and here to save your sorry ass."

"Ronnie James, the Weasel, as I live and breathe. How are you?"

"Well," he cackled and gave off a short nose whistle, "quite well, actually, I been seeing you up at that fancy college with your nose deep in the books. Been trying to catch your attention but you are so deep in those books I ain't sure that the grim reaper could get your attention, you know what I mean…"

"Funny, I kept thinking someone was calling my name but I was always thinking. Been really busy around here. I really never was trying to ignore you, I hope you know that. Hell, if I had known it was you I definitely would've stopped. Hope you know that compadre."

"I do, I do, and don't you worry. Cup a coffee would've been nice though. Hell, you can buy it tonight. We're friends. Always have been, always will be."

They went for coffee and caught up on old times although neither of them was really genuinely interested in what the other had been doing during the past several years. Both had been too busy, entirely too busy, to even give any thought to the other and what they had been doing. Still, both were somewhat intrigued by certain lessons, certain truths, that the other had acquired during the past couple of years. For Ronnie it had to do with learning the three truths he shared with very few others on the outside world. For Edsel, it had to do with one specific truth. Sex sells. That was it. Two words which became his business mantra throughout the remainder of his career. Sex sells. Everyone has it. And those who might not be having it certainly wanted to have it. Soon. Very soon. And if there was no possibility that they were going to have it then they all needed some outlet for themselves. He certainly provided that outlet. His growing number of Adult Emporiums demonstrated not only the truism that "sex sells" but also his growing business acumen.

Then the Weasel threw him a curve ball.

"I'd like to offer you some work."

Edsel thought for a moment before responding, a habit he had developed as a child when he knew that the wrong answer to a question could lead to a violent physical response.

"What's on your mind, Weasel?"

"A business offer, is all."

"I'm listening, not necessarily agreeing you understand, but I am certainly listening."

"Well, I've led not such a good life. Made some bad mistakes and gotten involved with some bad people. People who don't care that I want out of the business, they want me in, and if not me then I gotta find someone to take over. You know, do my job. Take care of things. Find a place....." He hesitated. Edsel responded.

"For?"

"Storage."

He instantly knew what Ronnie was talking about, and while he thought the idea should repulse him, he instead found himself excited. He was too hungry for money not to hear out a potential business opportunity. He knew that the adult entertainment industry

Standby

already worked on the fringes of the law.

"I'm still listening."

This actually caught Ronnie off guard. He shook his head just to be sure that he had heard clearly Edsel's response. He was convinced that Edsel would've booted him out of the office already.

"Well, ah," Ronnie said, trying to get his mind to catch up with his mouth, "I've got certain contacts, you see, who can bring good product into the country, only the thing is they sometimes need places to store that product until they can move it to the street."

"Yeah, and…?"

"Well, I'm figuring we can use, maybe, your stores, not Uncle Eddie's, he can't know about this, you know, to store the products and get a storage fee and maybe some other money."

"What's your cut?"

"No cut, I want out. Free and clear. Turn it all over to you. Gratis, like."

"Fuck off, Weasel, I am not jeopardizing my stores for a storage fee. You understand? So, what is your cut? And before you answer, don't waste anymore of my time, get it?"

Ronnie stared at his friend, amazed by the change that seemed to be occurring in his face, just before his eyes.

"No cut, I swear it."

Edsel sat silently for several minutes. He knew he was about to cross a line into uncharted, but very dangerous waters. He knew, in his heart, that while boats may be safe in a harbor, that is not what a boat is made for, and that whoever coined that sentiment, probably some nobody copywriter for a greeting card business, he or she probably wasn't thinking about the drug trade at the time. He also thought that additional capital would allow him to further his adult bookstores openings, and might even allow him to get into the lucrative Los Angeles market, and move away from the lousy East Coast. So, with all those thoughts, and his own desire not to be a standby to life anymore, he made the mistake that so many have made upon entering the drug business. The mistaken belief that they could get in for a short time, make money, and get out when they pleased. They would all ultimately learn that it just didn't happen that way, except at the end of a gun.

"Ok, Weasel, I'm in."

He and Ronnie shook hands to seal the bargain. Deals like this were never reduced to writing.

"Good luck Edsel."

He nodded. Then he continued.

"Only thing left for you is to meet your, uh, partners."

"Okay. But one thing, Edsel, behave, he is a peculiar sort of guy."

"Why do you say that?"

"I dunno, but I think he is Croatian or something like that."

Edsel and Javis met several days later at one of the outdoor cafes which had become so popular on Miami Beach. It was August, the mean season for Florida weather and Edsel was sweating before he met Javis, a fact that became much worse after he met the man who would play such a large role in his life over the next several years.

Javis wore all black, and was watched over by two very large, and quite efficient looking bodyguards whose names didn't registered with Edsel, although he was sure they rhymed.

"Veasel tells me that you vish to assume his business obligations?"

It took Edsel a moment to adjust to the curious accent.

"Yes."

He knew this was a situation that called for nothing more nor less than one word answers. Yes or No. Nothing longer. If this was a police setup, then he was already on the hook, and the devil be damned.

"So, ve must talk percentages."

"Yes."

Javis stared at him for a long while. Edsel found it particularly unsettling as Javis was partial to mirror-front sunglasses and it was impossible to know what was going on behind the lenses. Then, Javis did something Edsel had not expected. He suddenly removed the sunglasses and grasped both of Edsel's wrists, squeezing subtly but definitely causing extreme discomfort.

"You vill listen to me very carefully, now, yes?"

He winced. "Yes. Yes."

"Excellent, shut up now and listen."

He nodded.

"You vill be paid in accordance with what is written on that piece

Standby

of paper. No more, no less. From time to time, ve may modify your compensation, completely at our discretion. Bonuses are at our discretion. I love this vord, discretion, yes?"

Edsel sat silent.

Javis squeezed his wrists again to the point where Edsel was sure he heard something crack. Javis stared at him and waited for a reply.

"Yes. I understand."

"Good." Javis released the wrists.

"Now, do you accept the terms on the paper? If so, you vill be rich, but you vill also be ours. Ve know you wish to go to Los Angeles. Ve think this is good, very good. Ve vant to be in Los Angeles as well. As a token of our good faith, in this bag you will find start up funds. It is a loan, you understand, but a loan you do not have the luxury of turning down. You vill accept it, yes?"

He nodded. Again, the subtle pressure on the wrists. "Ahhh, yes, yes."

"Good, the terms of the loan are on the paper as well. Oh, and by the way, that paper is made from the skin of the last moron who turned me down. His ass in fact. Think about that before you make a copy or go to the police, yes?"

This time Edsel needed no encouragement or negative reinforcement. "Yes, I understand."

Javis smiled, dropped money for the check, left the bag and walked away.

A devil's bargain. Done and made.

Chapter 29

Larry and Sue stopped at a truck stop somewhere deep in the Texas panhandle. It was the first real time that they had stopped. The place was enormous, with full service bathing facilities and a full restaurant and, much to their mutual amusement, a fully stocked bar, as if that was just what the long haul trucker needed.

They sat together at a small corner table and checked out the menus. Larry ordered soup and a tuna sandwich, Sue, with her considerable appetite, ordered a loaded cheeseburger, French fries and a milkshake, all of which she polished off with considerable relish.

Larry chucked as he watched her eat.

"What's funny?"

"Watching you eat."

She smiled at him. Much time had passed since their sexual encounter back in Los Angeles, and they had each moved away from it in their own ways. Their relationship, such as it was, was perhaps now even more intimate after having shared a near death experience, watching Percy get his nose shot off, and driving for a full day and night through the country's southwestern desert. It was a bond of the road.

Again he smiled.

She smiled back and spoke, "What now, Larry?"

"I could really stand for a shower, I think, how about you?"

"Done. Let me just finish up here first."

She did, she polished off every last morsel of food and even belched loudly enough that a couple of truckers at a nearby table

Standby

applauded, causing Sue to blush for perhaps the first time since Larry had met her.

Thirty minutes later they were back in the car, gassed up and bellies full. Larry was clean although in the same shirt. Sue was clean and radiant and was sporting a T-Shirt for some sort of loading equipment, and a pair of work shorts she purchased inside which she was hemming in the back of the car, sitting in her underwear while Larry tried to stare straight ahead at the road.

His eyes wandered.

She smiled. "Larry, its okay if you wanna look. Not touch, mind you, but every now and then a girl likes to be noticed, you know?"

He smiled back.

Sue sat quietly for a moment and then turned back to Larry. "Can I ask you a question?"

Larry sat even more quietly before responding, "Sure."

Sue measured her words carefully.

"Larry, I mean no offense by what I'm asking, but I'm very curious."

"Yes"

"Why are we going back?"

"Excuse me?"

"To Miami, why are we going there? I mean I understand that part of what we need to do is try and get Percy out of that position he is in and all, but maybe we could just call the cops about that? Don't you think?"

Larry sat quietly for a moment and considered the passing miles in this bleakest part of the Texas landscape. Sue's question was fair and merited a response.

"I have to go to her."

Sue looked at him. She was becoming more and more impressed with his quiet dignity.

"Why?"

"Well, she's my wife, you see, and she is entitled to know that I am really still alive and not laying in a hospital bed all beaten and burned."

Sue turned fully in her passenger seat and began nervously chewing her lower lip. It was a habit she had had since childhood and showed itself when she was in a difficult situation or, more particularly, in the difficult part of a conversation.

"Larry, do you love her?"

He responded quickly.

"No."

There it was, simple as pie. A one-word answer to the most complicated question a spouse could face. For Larry, it carried with it the full redemptive power of absolution from his preacher.

"No, Sue, I don't love her. Probably never have, and definately never will. But, see, Sue, here's the thing, she is my wife, for better or worse, and because of that I have to, need to, see this through."

Again silence passed between them. The miles ticked by like the steady beat of a metronome playing a slow rhythm on top of a piano. Larry broke the silence again.

"That's not the question you wanted to ask me, though, is it?"

"Excuse me?"

"You asked me before, 'why am I going back?', but I think that is probably not the question you wanted to ask me."

Sue paused and thought before answering.

"No, Larry, I don't suppose it was the question."

"So?"

"So, why her? Why now? What do you want to get out of this? Why don't you just call her?"

Larry smiled. "Which of the questions do you want me to answer?"

"All of them," she answered tersely. She wasn't smiling anymore.

"Why her? I don't know and never will know. I never had a girlfriend before her, and sure haven't had one since her. I know she has had her dalliances and I've put up with them. Suffered in silence you might even say. But why her? It just happened and even after I knew it was bad I just sort of figured bad was better than alone."

"You really never had a girlfriend other than her?"

"Nope, imagine this, I took my sister to the prom."

At this, Sue burst out laughing. She didn't even try to stop. She laughed for their strange pairing and the drive ahead of them and what was past, and for Percy and the shooting and the three goons and their strange mission, but mostly she laughed at the sheer absurdity of hearing Larry tell her that he took his sister to the prom.

Standby

As if people actually did that, She thought it was just an urban myth. Generally speaking she had always been correct, but in a country of something like a quarter of a billion people she had met the one guy who had actually gone to the prom with his sister. And, what's more, he was willing to admit it.

Larry laughed as well. It hardly seemed appropriate not to laugh. Then, he let slip with the remainder of the secret.

"Sue, know that part about kissing your sister being the same as a tie in a sports game.?"

"Um, yeah?"

"Well, it's not true."

Sue wasn't sure how to respond to this. Was Larry really telling her that he had kissed his sister? This was entirely too much information.

"Alright, Larry, I'll bite."

"Well, to be honest, my sister used to drink pretty heavily, and she was a really sauced at the prom. Fact is, she had a bit a thing for a friend of mine, Franklin, big black fella, football star. He had recently transferred in from some small farming town. He and I were friends on account of the fact that I tutored him in math, English, social studies, etc., etc., well, you get the picture. Anyhow, he needed me to help him maintain a proper grade point average so he could keep playing football, and I needed him to help me from getting my ass kicked every day walking to school."

He paused and seemed, to Sue, quite pensive and deliberate in his thought process.

"Larry, it's okay, no secrets between us, okay?"

He nodded, and then continued.

"Okay, well, my sister, who is a couple of years older than me, she had a real thing for Franklin. He's some sort of TV evangelist now, or something like that. Anyhow, I couldn't get a date for the junior prom and my sister said she would go with me. I didn't wanna go but somehow got talked into going and my sister I think figured it would be her turn to get a chance at Franklin. So, we get there, and by the time we get there my sister is half bombed. And by a few hours into the dance, she is fully well shit-faced. Then, right there in the midst of the event, she walks over to Franklin, picture this will you, I am sitting at my table in my finest powder blue tux, trying to look like I belong, but knowing I don't, when my sister walks over to the biggest, meanest looking football player in the school, who happens to be sitting with the homecoming queen, the prettiest girl in the school, Lena I think was her name, and my sister walks right up and says, 'Franklin, you can sit here all night with this high school skank, who ain't gonna let you anywhere near her pearly gates, or you can come get some of this', at which point she lifts her skirt and shows Franklin and the entire student body that she isn't wearing any underwear.'"

Sue was doubled over in laughter. Larry, for his part, was telling the story through a full-blown laugh himself and was having trouble holding the car straight on the roadway.

"So then Lena, who everyone thought was the most demure little blonde in school, well, it turns out she had a thing for very large men like Franklin and had apparently been giving him scenic tours of her pearly gates for sometime prior to the prom and was in the midst of telling him that one of his more recent tours of same had left her with child and she wanted to know what he intended to do about it."

Now, Sue stopped laughing, as she was sure that the story was taking a turn away from the bizarre.

"Well, Lena leapt out of her chair and slugged my 'sis hard across the jaw. My sister was a bit drunk and certainly tough enough and she took the punch and delivered two of her own in return. Franklin and I jumped in and separated them. Then, well, then, came the hard part."

Larry pulled over now. He put his arm up on the headrest and turned to face Sue. He removed his sunglasses.

"Franklin grabbed me and yelled in my face, 'Asshole, can't you control your stupid sister? Shit, man, bad enough I gotta put up with you for my tutoring, but then you embarrass all of us by bringing your sister to the prom'. Well, Sue, that hurt worse than anything anyone has ever done to me in my entire life. Worse than anything anyone had ever said. I snapped and said something I have regretted my whole life."

Sue sat patiently.

"I said something terrible. Everything slowed down. The music stopped. There I was, at the prom, the culmination of my entire terrible life in school, about to fight with my only 'friend' whom I

Standby

thought I embarrassed, and my sister was making a drunken spectacle of herself. I snapped. I said something terrible."

"Larry, tell me, let it go…"

"I pushed Franklin off of me and told him he was a 'stupid nigger who would've flunked out of school if he didn't have me to teach him basic arithmetic'."

Sue looked at Larry in silence.

"I've hated myself everyday ever since."

Sue stared at Larry and watched, unabashedly, as the tears rolled down his face.

"Everyone there thought he would beat the shit out of me. Everyone but me. I knew I had won the fight. I knew I had beaten him. I had called him out on the one thing he knew I was better than him on. His mind. No, he didn't kill me even though he could have done so. No, you know what he did?"

"No, I don't."

Larry paused.

"He hugged me. He whispered to me that he loved me and he was sorry about what he said. Then he looked at me and I saw tears rolling down his cheeks. Then he walked out of the room and I never saw him again. He got his diploma by mail. I was king of the prom for standing up to him. Later that night, my very drunk sister kissed me during the king and queen dance. It made me puke. All I could think of was the hateful thing I had said and the horrible thing I had done to that simple decent man."

"Larry, I'm so sorry."

"Sis' shipped out a couple weeks later. I saw her briefly at my brother's funeral. Then she went back to the 'Nam. She died in Vietnam. I've never seen Franklin again either, until two days ago in that hotel in Los Angeles."

"I'm sorry, baby, I don't follow."

Larry liked the way she had taken to using affectionate terms to talk to him. It made him feel as though he belonged. It made him feel welcome. He answered her.

"Franklin is now Reverend Thomas. Somehow he has managed to take on my case. Well, the case of whoever that is in the hospital. I can't fail him again. I cannot let my past mistakes destroy him. I think he believes it's me in that bed and he's trying to make things right, in the only way he can. And I have to do the same. I have to get to Miami, and soon."

Sue smiled and rested her head on Larry's shoulder. She knew that she was with a decent man. Larry pulled back onto the highway and continued his eastward route with the sun setting softly behind him.

Chapter 30

Their entire legal team had gathered in Sullivan's oversized office; an office in which almost half of the available office space was used for one office for an attorney who spent less than one third of the week actually in the office. It was an office designed to serve the truly massive ego of Clarence Darrow Sullivan. Overly ornate with massive floor to ceiling paintings of naked, barrel-chested men handling various "make work" projects made famous during FDR's new deal. Some in the office, in hushed voices, whispered about the real intent of the paintings in Sullivan's office.

Ronnie broke the silence.

"I have the CVR tapes."

Sullivan responded. "Excellent, what the hell is a 'CVR'?"

Franklin rolled his eyes at Ronnie and shrugged as if to tacitly acknowledge that they had tied their fortunes to a addle-brained moron.

"Cockpit Voice Recorder." Ronnie replied patiently.

"Oh, okay, well, let's have it."

"Well, first, I think you should know that its sort of garbled in places, and, well, as for whether or not it helps your case, well, I'm gonna kind of just leave that to you."

Sullivan had really had enough of this cloak and dagger. He was impatient, and, if he had ever allowed himself to spend time in a psychiatrist's chair, was the classic example of a narcissist personality disorder with obsessive-compulsive traits. Still, he knew enough and was still intelligent to know that he was getting in over his head. He needed to know what was on the tape. Then his speaker phone rang. The voice of his receptionist came over the intercom,

"Excuse me, Mr. Sullivan, it's Geoff, ah, excuse me, Mr. Padua calling on Line one for you."

"Tell him I will call him later," Sullivan replied impatiently and loudly enough so that everyone in his office could hear him even though he had turned his back to the room Sullivan's associate, Ramon, and Felicity, heard Sullivan anyhow, which was his intent.

"I sort of assumed you would say that, Mr. Sullivan, but he said he has an offer for you and I know you always take those sort of calls."

Sullivan paused. Again, he was smart enough to recognize that Padua could be laying a trap for him, but he also knew that he had an obligation to Felicity to hear what the man had to say.

"Put him through."

The line rang loudly in the now very silent office. Sullivan, practiced at the art of negotiation and always wanting the upper hand, let the phone ring exactly eight times, just enough to let Padua know he was busy, but not too many to be considered rude.

"Geoff, Clarence Darrow Sullivan here, what can I do for you?"

You could almost here the chuckle on the other end.

"Clarence, how are you?"

"Fine, Geoff, just fine."

"Clarence, pick up the phone, I don't like speaker, and I want to talk to you, lawyer to lawyer, man to man, without an audience."

Now Sullivan was in a pickle. Giving up the speakerphone meant giving up the control of the conversation. But he also knew he needed to get an offer out of Geoff and to do that would require following some instructions. He did as he was told.

"You're off speaker Geoff."

"Good, then let's make this quick and keep it strictly business." On the other side of the room Franklin went to pick up the muted extension. As he did, Geoff said, "If anyone picks up that muted extension of yours, I hang up." Sullivan shook his head violently at the preacher who put the phone down.

"Here's the deal. I've got you, Clarence, bent right over a barrel and nothing would make me happier than shoving it right up your ass. But, business is business. You never will get the same offer as the other families. Never. Your bullshit lawsuit and media theatrics

Standby

have seen to that. But, I can save your dignity. Imagine that, once again, Padua comes in and cleans up your messes."

"What is the offer Geoffrey?"

"One million dollars, paid by close of business today. Wired into your trust account. End. Done. Finished. Total Confidentiality. And before you protest, it's not negotiable and don't counter. If you counter, I lower it. I have an ace in the hole."

Sullivan thought to himself. He wondered how he could break this to his client. She had a chance, albeit a small one, at much more than what was being offered to her right now, even though she didn't know what was being offered, but his greed and rush to file a lawsuit weakened that chance. He was screwed, plainly and royally. He smiled at the assemblage in his office and shook his head slowly back and forth.

He acted immediately, impetuously and without the consent of his client.

"Geoffrey, your offer is rejected."

Padua didn't hesitate in his reply.

"I thought you might say that. See you in court. Enjoy the CVR tapes."

The phone went dead.

Sullivan spoke into the receiver.

"Stop whining Geoffrey, I taught you better than that." Then he slammed the phone down. Felicity brightened at the last remark.

Sullivan paused.

"They offered two hundred fifty thousand dollars. I rejected it. I'm sure more will be coming."

Franklin stared at Sullivan. Sullivan wouldn't make eye contact. Franklin knew he had lied. He imperceptibly shook his head at Sullivan

Sullivan was crestfallen.

Ronnie started the CVR tapes. "You guys will need to listen carefully to this, you
 know."

They all sat silently. All that was heard while the tape spun up was the sound of their collective breathing.

Voice of Captain:Roger Miami Central, DA 721 approach east at 15000. Maintain 500 knots and altitude

Center:Roger DA 721

Voice of Co-Captain: So what went on back there, anyhow?

Captain:(inaudible) guy gave me a lick. So I dropped him. Traffic on the right, low

Co-Captain:I got it. Tough guy?

Captain:Miami Control, requesting vector for approach, altitude and speed nominal.

Co-Captain:So?

Control:Deacon 721, continue approach, reduce altitude to 12000, speed to 480, be advised traffic on your right at 10000 and rising, passing at 2 miles to your right

Captain:Roger that Control. Reducing to 12000, speed 480. We have the traffic.

Co-Captain:So? Tough guy?

Captain:Focus please. Approaching 10000. Noise threshold. Not so tough. I've fought tougher. Strange fella though.

Co-Captain:How so?

Control:DA 721, please reduce altitude to 9000, speed to 400, approach vector 27 for landing runway 27A. Winds moderate from east at 8 knots.

Captain:Roger that Control. Reducing to 9000, speed to 400.

Co-Captain:Strange how?

Captain:Noise, please.

Co-Captain:(inaudible)

Captain:(inaudible) kept yelling at me about offering (inaudible), and he was important in the porn industry (inaudible)

Control:DA 721 you are clear to land, runway 27R. Welcome home.

Captain:Roger Control. Deacon Air 721, clear to land runway 27R, thank you and good night.

Co-Captain:Nice weather. Love the Miami approach. Wide open. Nice weather.

Captain:Noise please. Passing through 3000.

Co-Captain:Okay, I'll shut up. Passing 3000. Important in what industry?

Captain:Noise please. I don't know. Something strange. Passing 2500.

Co-Captain:Wow, look at that, looks like a whole flock of birds

Standby

taking off from that lake.
 Captain:(inaudible)
 Co-Captain:Something startled them. Must be hundreds.
 Captain:Adult (inaudible). Thousands more like it.
 Unknown speaker:Oh, shit, flying right towards us.
 Banging sounds followed by multiple warning alarms in cockpit.
 Captain:Miami control requesting emergency vectoring away from airport. Plane striking flock of birds, engine failure on number 2.
 Control:Are you declaring an emergency? Say which flight?
 Captain:Ah, ah, losing it. Help me, help me.
 Co-Captain:Shit. Shit. Shit. No, no, no.
 Control:Say flight please? Is this DA 721? Are you declaring emergency?
 Captain:Roger, 721, emergency, both engines dead, dead stick, say again, dead stick, ah….
 Co-Captain:Not now, please.
 Captain:Emergency. Brace. Brace. Brace.
 Unknown speaker:Help me hold it. Nose up.
 Co-Captain:Fucking birds. Aw, fuck, mother-fucking birds.
 Captain:Altitude 1000, dropping like a stone, help me lift the nose.
 Co-Captain:Shit. Here it comes.
 Tape ends.
 They sat in silence and looked at each other, each one more solemn than the next realizing that they had just heard the last sounds of a crew trying desperately to save the lives of hundreds of innocent people. They played the tape over and over again hoping to discern some clue to help them understand who the pilot was talking about. And every time they listened to it, they became more and more concerned that the pilot wasn't talking about Larry Jones.

The question was a strikingly obvious one. Even if you discounted Larry's penchant for non-violence, with the exception of the priest at his wedding, there was no way anyone would think the hangar industry was an important one.
 Franklin broke the silence.
 "Well, we certainly have a problem."
 Ronnie nodded his head. "Appears our boy ain't who he appears

to be, seems more like it, I think."

Franklin quietly chuckled at Ronnie's unique way with words.

For her part Felicity was stunned and silent. They all looked to her to see if she could offer them some information about Larry that they hadn't yet thought of, some way out of the mess that they now all found themselves in. Of course, she had nothing to offer. Still, it didn't keep her from trying to offer something.

"Larry's business was important, and, he could've punched the pilot, couldn't he?"

They all stared at her. Their collective thought was one of they would have all been better off if she had simply remained quiet.

Franklin stared at Sullivan. "Clarence, you're the trial lawyer. How are you gonna deal with this issue?"

Sullivan had less to offer than Felicity. But, like most egotists, he abhorred silence and felt the need to fill it with some comment, when the truly intelligent person would've kept their mouth shut. He hesitated for less than a second before jumping in with both feet.

"It's their burden. Here's what we know. One, Larry Jones boarded that plane. Two, Larry Jones is the husband of Felicity Jones. Three, according to the manifest, Larry Jones was in seat 1J, Four, the passenger who survived the accident was in 1J. QED, Larry Jones is the survivor from 1 J."

Sullivan felt rather full of himself; having made what he felt was a cogent, clear, concise, and compelling argument.

It took Franklin less than three seconds to respond.

"Mr. Sullivan, prudence would seem to dictate that you consider getting a real trial lawyer to argue in court, because if that is the argument you take in there, this judge is gonna eat your lunch, not to mention what Mr. Padua is going to do to you."

Sullivan reddened.

"Hey, I don't need to take that shit from you."

"Yes, you do!" roared Franklin, standing up to his full height and taking over the room and leaving no doubt who was now in charge of things. "You have made a mockery of this case and because of you the judge and especially Padua have turned you into a caricature of all that is wrong with personal injury lawyers. You have no control in the courtroom. That man in that hospital bed needs a trial lawyer, which you are not. Do you get it you insolent ass? Do you?"

Standby

Sullivan was also losing his temper. Quickly. He jumped out of his chair and walked right up to Franklin. "What the fuck is your problem? I'm the lawyer here. I run the show. Shit, you are just a mouthpiece!" What was worse than the words was the fact that Sullivan was emphasizing the words with repetitive pokes to Franklin's chest.

Ronnie knew what was about to happen. He could see the rage rising in his good friend's face. He also knew that he was the only one in the room who could put things to rest. He stepped between the two and pushed them apart. Sullivan continued to rage. Franklin calmed rapidly.

Franklin nodded to Ronnie and mouthed a "thank you" to him. Ronnie smiled.

Franklin turned his back to Sullivan, sat down, and spoke directly to Felicity.

"Felicity, we have a problem and this is what it is...

Sullivan interrupted, "Do not speak to my client."

Franklin spoke to Sullivan without turning his face to look at him. "Clarence, you made the mistake of annoying me once, you will not get a second chance to do that. From this moment forward, I am in charge. Let there be no doubt."

Sullivan began to speak and Franklin began to rise. Sullivan sat down and was quiet.

Franklin continued.

"Now then, we have a problem and I want you to listen very carefully because I think I know a way out but you are going to have to follow my directions explicitly."

Felicity nodded. She was prepared to accept the advice of whoever in the room took control.

"Alright then, first, we have to get out in front of this. That means a press conference. Now the judge has forbidden Clarence and I from speaking in public, but there is another way to get our message out. That is you, Felicity; you will have to speak for yourself. It will be a controlled press conference; we will only have reporters there friendly to our cause. Sullivan knows the local media so he can pick them. You will know the questions in advance, and you will know who to call on. I think three or four questions maximum after a two or three minute prepared statement. The court of public opinion is waiting to hear from Felicity. Of course, Clarence and I will have to distance ourselves from the press conference so that the judge cannot impose a sanction on us.

They were all listening.

"Here is the rest of my plan..."

Later that day, Felicity Jones stood before a bank of television cameras, in a new brown dress with modest makeup, all earth tones to better appear on camera.

"I have a brief statement to make. My name is Felicity Jones. My beloved husband is lying in a hospital bed fighting for his life. His name is Larry Jones. He is badly burned and has lost his hands. He cannot speak and every breath is a life and death struggle for him. I want you to know about him. He is my sweetheart. He works hard in an industry that he revitalized with his efforts. He is not a perfect man, but he is my man. I love him and wish that he could understand me now but he spends his days in a fog of drug delirium because otherwise the pain would be too overwhelming to handle. His name is Larry Jones, and I love him."

She paused for precisely eight seconds, just like the publicist had taught her when they practiced that "Impromptu" statement over and over again in his office.

"Now, I will answer a few questions."

Reporter 1:"Mrs. Jones, how are you managing?"

"I have surrounded myself with good people. My spiritual advisor, Reverend Thomas, is a remarkable help. I find strength in prayer and in the Lord. I know his plans are beyond my understanding, but I have not lost faith."

Reporter 2:"Mrs. Jones, what are your plans for the future?"

"I will stay with Larry. Forever."

Again she paused.

"I have time for only one more question." In Sullivan's office, Franklin smiled as he watched the television feed. This was going well, very well.

Reporter 3:Are you concerned he may die?

Felicity simply nodded her head. She did not give a reply.

Reporter 4:Have you ever cheated on your husband?

Franklin jumped out of his seat. Who the hell was asking that impertinent question? He immediately turned his glare towards

Standby

Clarence who seemed to be shrinking in his office chair as the seconds ticked past. It was Sullivan's responsibility to make sure only the handpicked reporters were at this "impromptu press conference". Clearly he had failed, because someone slipped through.

Felicity stared at the reporter open-mouthed.

"I, uh, am not sure what you are asking?"

Reporter 4:"Let me be clear then, ma'am. You are seeking a lot of money from an airline that is accepting responsibility for the crash and offering, by anyone's account, a very large amount of money to all of the victims. Yet, here you are, asking for more. So, after listening to you tell us about your wonderful relationship with your husband, I have a really very simple question. Have you ever cheated on your husband?

Franklin was about to explode. "Clarence, get her the hell out of there right now!!!"

"And how would you like me to do that? Judge has ordered that we can't go in front of the cameras!!"

"Shit, man, it's all collapsing. Ronnie!!"

"Yes, boss, right here."

"Get her out of there! Pronto!"

"I'm on it." Ronnie bolted from the room.

Franklin threw himself down in Sullivan's chair. Sullivan began to speak a protest but Franklin's glare made it clear that no such protest would be accepted.

Franklin stared at the TV and watched as Felicity tried to dance around the question. But the mystery reporter's tenacity would not be denied. Franklin looked at Sullivan. "How the hell did you ever get to be a lawyer?"

Felicity was in deep trouble. Even the friendly reporters sniffed blood in the water and were aiding the other reporter in moving in for the kill. This was too good of an opportunity to pass up.

"Did you cheat on your husband?"

"How many times?"

"Do you really love your husband?"

"How much money is enough for you?"

"Are you greedy?"

"Why did you hire a lawyer who has never tried a case?"

"Do you pick your doctors off the TV like you pick your lawyers?"

The questions were coming so fast now that Felicity's ability to respond was shutting down. She began to sob. Just then Ronnie stepped up on the dais and pulled her away announcing that the press conference was over.

"One last question ma'am, who is that? Another of your spiritual advisors?"

Franklin now knew that he would have to get Sullivan off this case. He was incompetent and every minute he remained involved in this matter, the value of the case decreased exponentially.

Across town, in another law office staffed by lawyers representing the airline, Geoff Padua smiled at the TV monitors. His planted reported had done a marvelous job. Now, to put the next step in his plan to work. He pressed a button on his desk phone.

"Marcia, get me Judge Berger's chambers, if you please."

Again, it was the Weasel who had to break the difficult news to Sullivan and Franklin.

"Excuse me, guys, Judge's assistant is on the phone."

Sullivan and Franklin were in the midst of trying to figure out a strategy to the latest bombshell, and now the judge was looking for them again.

"Yes Ma'am," Sullivan said after pushing the button on his speakerphone.

"It's Judge Berger, you nitwit, now pick up your damned phone, I speak to you, only you, and not your spiritual advisor. I want you in my chambers in fifteen minutes."

"But, your honor, I was in the middle of something."

"Ten minutes, you nitwit, ten minutes, my chambers, be there, bring the Reverend."

"Yes, Your honor."

"That's a good boy. Oh, and one more thing...."

"Yes, sir?"

"Bring your checkbook."

Chapter 31

Percy was still rolling around the trunk of the sedan. At the last rest stop he had convinced his handlers that he wouldn't scream for help. It took all of his strength not to scream in agony when Javis yanked the duct tape off of his mouth. Percy begged for something for the pain from having his nose shot off. In response, Javis nodded at his two goons, one of whom tossed a nickel bag of white powder to Percy, laughing all the while.

Percy didn't take kindly to the joke. "Cocaine? What the fuck am I supposed to do with cocaine? You shot my fucking nose off, remember?"

At that, Javis grabbed the stump of Percy's nose and gave it a squeeze. The pain was blinding for Percy. "I vould mind my tongue if I vere you." Javis grabbed the bag of powder, opened it and sprinkled some of the drug on Percy's wound. At first the pain was excruciating, then it went numb. Percy had to admit, at least to himself, that there was something to be said for this pain management technique.

He began to feel the more illicit effects of the drug and began to recall how he had gotten to this place.

He and Sue arrived in San Francisco, full of excitement at their respective futures. They found themselves a small apartment in Chinatown of all places. It turned out that Sue had a distant cousin who lived in that area and who was more than willing to give an extra bedroom to he and Sue once she learned that Percy's sexual proclivities did not include those of Sue's gender.

They were excited. The world was in front of them. Percy found fast employment in one of the bars in the Castro district. Sue enrolled at the University of California – Berkley. She shared an on campus room with a fellow student during the week and then shared the Chinatown apartment with Percy on the weekends. She came home on every weekend.

Percy enrolled in a local community college and was soon studying facilities management, hoping to get into the hotel business. His life was blossoming and his evenings were spent in an almost bacchanalian pursuit of pleasure. It displeased Sue tremendously and led to one of the first and only fights of their life.

"Percy, I need to speak to you, I'm worried about you."

"What?!"

"Don't be short with me, I care."

"Fine, I'm sorry, what?"

"Are you being careful? I mean I think its great that you are finding yourself here, and that the lifestyle is open for you, but, I mean, are you being careful?"

"What the hell, Sue, what do you mean? It's my life, stop being a nervous Nellie."

"I don't mean to pry Percy, but, you know, with AIDS and all, its dangerous.'

"I told you not to worry dammit, I know how to use a condom, unlike you I might add."

Sue slapped him. Hard, across the face. Percy reddened and spouted out, "Stupid bitch!" And walked out. They did not see or speak to each other for more than two weeks.

Each of them acted out in their own ways, all in some strange desire to hurt the other more, through acting out in some self-destructive way. Percy cut out the sex, and began snorting cocaine with a friend from the bar, while Sue stopped studying and began sleeping with her academic advisor, a man who was not only married, but was also twenty five years her senior.

It caused major strife in their friendship. Soon, before they knew it, they were seeing each other less and less. Then, when they were together they found their conversations to be very stilted, with each being antagonistic toward the other about the one thing they found most distasteful in the other, for him, it was her sex life, for her, it was his cocaine habit.

Standby

It was that cocaine habit which gave Percy his first introduction to Javis. One night, at the bar, as he and the owner, Francis, Percy's current love interest and supplier, broke the news to Percy.

"Percy, we gotta talk."

"What's wrong?"

"I'm sick."

"Huh?"

"I went to the clinic and got tested. It's not good."

"No, baby, are you sure?"

"Well, I got all the symptoms, I'm sick all the time, losing weight, these funny tumors you saw all over me, the fevers and sweats," he said through his tears.

Percy walked to him and put his arms around Francis. They sat there in quiet silence and didn't notice when the front door to the bar jingled its opening. They just sat and cried together.

"Aw, isn't this so goddammed sweet?"

They both started at the intrusion. Looking up, they saw the figure of a very blonde, very thin, man in a totally black suit with a very bleached and crisp white shirt.

"Javis, what the hell are you doing here now?" asked Francis.

"Francis, you know full well vy I am here."

"Who are you?" interrupted Percy.

"Francis, were I you, I would be telling my little love interest here to shut his mouth, and not to open it again until I leave and you and he are alone. I am here for my money."

"Javis, I'm sick, okay, and I haven't had a chance to get your money. Most of the product is behind the bar, okay, and I will go get it for you, okay?"

Javis stood quietly. Percy and Francis sat quietly at their table with Percy looking up and Francis sitting with his head down, still sobbing over his medical news from earlier that day. Suddenly, and with the quickness one would normally associate with a large cat, Javis shoved Percy off of his chair and, just as Francis looked up, he slapped Francis hard across the face. The blow was a stinging blow. The door jangled again.

Francis fell off of his chair and landed hard on his back. For Percy, this was too much to bear, and he leapt up off the floor and prepared to launch his fist at Javis' face. Even though he was gay, he still grew up with some tough Irish brothers who, although they accepted his lifestyle, made sure he could handle himself in a fight. Unfortunately, Percy must not have been paying attention when they were trying to teach him about the unseen assailant. He should given more attention to the jingling bells of the door.

As he moved on Javis, an enormous fist came out of nowhere and struck him in the temple, completely disorienting him. He dropped to his knees just in time to take another large fist in the mouth. Then, everything went dark and quiet.

When he awoke Percy had an enormous headache. While taking an assessment of his body parts, he realized that he was strapped to a chair and, for the first time in his life, had duct tape strapped across his mouth. He also noticed that Francis was in a chair much like his and was also strapped down in a similar fashion to himself. He guessed that Francis' appearance was much like how Percy felt.

"Now we are going to have a little chat, yes? Just the six of us."

Percy looked up. Six? The count was clearly wrong. He saw the two goons who had made short work of his face, there was Javis, and there was Francis. With him the count made five. Six? Who was six?

"What do you want, asshole?" Percy replied. His smugness caught Javis off guard. It also got him two short punches to the back of the head from goon number one.

Percy shut up.

"I vill make this simple for you. Francis was my dealer. I supplied him with product and he sold the product for me. Unfortunately, Francis became a bit too hooked on the product, dragged you into things and hasn't been making his quota every month. For this, Francis vill have to suffer. But now, Mr. tough guy, the problem is yours. You are now my dealer."

Percy was stunned. Not just at the news that his love was a drug dealer, I mean, he always knew that Francis had good product, but he didn't know what he was doing with that product, but Percy was also stunned that somehow he was being dragged into this.

"What the fuck are you talking about?"

"Simple, you are my connection."

"Your connection?"

"Yes, you sell the product I deliver to you. You keep the money I tell you that you can keep and you stand ready, all the time, to sell

Standby

my product. In fact, because I am a gracious man, I will give you Francis' bar, okay? Do we have, how you say, a deal?"

"I still don't understand what you are talking about? I am not a drug dealer, okay? Sure, I've used the stuff, but I'm not a dealer. I think this is all a huge misunderstanding, and I would really appreciate it if you would let us go."

Javis sat very quietly and stared at Percy. Then he laughed, a high piecing laugh that belied the severity of the moment. Then, with cat like motion, he reached into his belt, pulled out a very small gun and quickly put two bullets right into the center of Francis' forehead. Francis jerked back and then was still, forever.

Percy shouted "No!" and then strained with every fiber in his being to get out of his bindings.

Javis turned to him. "I suggest you stop fighting. You will not get free of the binds and you are beginning to irritate me, terribly. And, you still have not heard all of my proposal."

"Your proposal? You just killed my friend and I am supposed to worry about your proposal."

"Yes, you are very much supposed to worry about my proposal, unless you wish to very quickly join your dear departed friend."

Percy knew he was beaten. He knew that, for the moment, he would have to listen to what Javis had to say. He had no bargaining position. Then, his position went from bad to worse.

"Percy, I want you to look around you. Why did I say six, when all you could count was five, and now, just four with Francis' departure from our little group. I said six, who are you missing?"

Percy felt his heart begin to race. There was something ominous in Javis' tone. Percy frantically turned his head left and right trying to see who the other person was, with a deepening pit in his stomach over what he feared Javis was leading up to.

"Who is it? Dammit, just tell me, show me, something!"

"Misha, bring her out."

Just then, one of his two goons went into the kitchen and brought out what at first looked like a duffel bag, but which Percy quickly realized was a person, a woman. Sue. The goon dumped her unceremoniously at Percy's feet. She had her hands bound in front of her and had what appeared to be an old set of boxer shorts stuffed into her mouth as a makeshift gag, secured with the same duct tape across her face.

Percy tried to get to her but, of course, his binds wouldn't allow it. Instead, he whispered to her, "Sue, I'm so sorry, baby, are you ok?" he said through rapidly falling tears.

She looked at him with questioning eyes and her own tears.

Javis spoke.

"Sue, if you promise to be very quiet, I will remove your gag."

Sue looked to Percy, he nodded to her, and she then nodded at Javis, who quickly grabbed her hair, pulled it back while he yanked the tape off of her mouth with the other hand. She screamed for just a moment, which Javis responded to with a slap over her mouth. He told her again to be quiet, and, in response, received her rapidly nodding head.

Javis had them both quiet.

"Here is my proposal, Percy, you become my dealer, and Sue lives, fail me, she dies. In the meantime, she comes and lives with and works for me. At some time in the future, a time I will decide when she may leave me. She is, after all, such a beautiful flower, and I do love beautiful flowers."

Percy thought quickly. But he knew he was stuck. As much as he loved Sue, their relationship had become strained recently, he knew he couldn't fail her now. He was being dragged into a life of crime, but there was nothing he could do about it.

He nodded. Javis smiled. "Tell me your proposal."

Javis nodded to Misha, who took Sue outside to a waiting car. He then turned to Percy and told him the proposal. The deal was done.

Over the next several years Percy become quite efficient in moving the product through the bar. The lifestyle of many of the bar patrons allowed for greater risk and with that risk came greater profits. Percy often wondered what had become of Sue, but he certainly knew better than to ask either of Percy's goons who showed up every month to drop off product and collect the money. The counts were never inaccurate and, for his part, Percy had a nice supplement, albeit non-reportable, income.

After a time, Javis returned. It was late on a Saturday night, actually quite early on a Sunday morning, and Percy was finishing the cleanup. The door jingled. Percy yelled out "we're closed!"

The shrill voice replied, "Not for us, you aren't." Percy jumped at

Standby

the sound of that voice. Then he turned, and there, standing with his arm around Sue, was Javis. "Percy, my friend, I have come to return Sue to you. She's yours. However, in exchange, it is time for you to broaden the business."

Percy and Sue shared eye contact for the first time in years. She was older than he remembered, wizened in appearance, but more beautiful than ever. Still, she had a sadness in her expression that worried him. He answered immediately, "Anything you want just let her go please."

The next deal with the devil was sealed.

Chapter 32

Edsel continued to expand the business at a rapid rate, especially with the new capital that his deal with Javis had established. He was quickly moving westward and hiring employees to handle his east coast ventures.

Then, after around three years in the business, he got his first opportunity to open on the west coast. A small adult video store came up for sale through an estate sale. The property was part of a large family estate and was right near the Los Angeles Airport. An importing contact of Edsel, who supplied him with all the latest Asian pornography, called him to tell him that the owner of that small store had died suddenly in some strange circumstances involving some unique partnering, and his family, very wealthy, even by west coast standards, wanted to unload the establish the premises as quickly as possible. Furthermore, the family wanted someone from the outside, not local, to buy the premises, in order to try and silent the burgeoning scandal associated with his death.

Edsel was on the next plane to Los Angeles, his briefcase full of cash in the hopes of sealing the deal on one trip.

His friend picked him up at the airport in a very nice stretch limousine. On their way to the establishment, Edsel noticed two lovely young women in the car with them. "These are my new associates, Star and Galaxy. Ladies, please introduce yourselves to Mr. Dodger."

"Hello."

"Hi!"

Edsel turned and glared at his friend. Even though Edsel had no

Standby

qualms about the adult entertainment industry, he no longer made use of these services and his friend knew it.

"Edsel, relax, I know how you feel, but they aren't hookers, they're actresses and want to talk to you about producing a film they want to make. First option rights and all that crap."

Edsel nodded. "Okay, one thing at a time, let's go to the establishment first."

His friend pointed out the window. "We are already there." Edsel looked up. He hadn't been in the car for more than just a few moments and they were already in front of the store. He looked out the window at the establishment. It was small, to be sure, but it was fantastically situated right on a block of less expensive airport motels, and just a few blocks from the fancier airport hotels. Even more exciting was the massage parlor right next store to the store. He knew that he was looking at a gold mine. He smiled to his friend and exited the limo.

The jingling of the door chimes reminded his of his first meeting with Ronnie, all those years ago. Had Ronnie really found religion? He had heard that Ronnie was working with that big black Reverend, the Shadetree, or something like that. He smiled at the chimes.

Sitting behind the desk, looking over the books, was a squirrelly looking middle-aged man. He looked up, "What do you want?" Edsel smiled. He knew enough about negotiation now to be careful. "I'm here to talk to you about the establishment."

The man behind the corner smiled in clear relief. "Price is twenty thousand, including all of the inventory. Gives you full title, I can give you a discount if you're paying in cash. The estate lawyers wanted me to get a higher price, but quite frankly, I'm a bit sick of sitting around waiting for someone to buy this place. Not what I planned when I became an accountant, you know."

Edsel nodded, placed his briefcase on the counter and walked around surveying the inventory. It stunk. It was old and outdated. But that wasn't why he was here. It was location. Location and the large storage space in the back of the store. The place was perfect for his needs.

"Ten thousand."

"Excuse me?"

"You heard me, that's my offer, in cash. I want title transferred by close of business tomorrow, it's a final offer."

"Twenty was fair, but I can probably do fifteen if its cash."

"It's cash and you can do ten, because its all there in the briefcase, along with an extra thousand for you, and you only."

The accountant paused before responding. Who would know anything at all about an extra thousand dollars?

"Deal."

Edsel opened the case and handed the accountant the thousand dollars, which quickly disappeared into his pocket. "I will be here tomorrow at noon to close."

The accountant nodded. "See you then."

That was how Edsel entered the lucrative Los Angeles adult entertainment trade.

The deal closed the next day, on precisely the terms he had negotiated. Over the next several months, he bought up more and more locations, always on terms he negotiated, and always for cash, and always with the same accountant helping to finalize the transactions. To be fair, Edsel's war chest was significantly higher than any of his competition due to his other lucrative trade that he ran out of the back room.

It was during this time that Edsel truly began to understand the benefits of greasing the palms of government officials. Before long he found that he could provide all sorts of illicit entertainment to the local police and the local zoning commissioners. Through his dealings with the massage parlors he had a steady stream of young women who were more than willing to make some extra cash in other ways.

That was when he met Percy. Percy had moved down to Los Angeles from San Francisco after assigning his interest in the club to a new friend. Through their business dealings in Bolivian marching powder it was inevitable that their paths would cross. However, Javis, paranoid as always about some of his underlings moving in on his business, never wanted them to meet. Their business always took place through intermediaries. Percy secured the product through the ports from his growing list of various sailors and longshoremen, and he had it delivered to various dealers such as Edsel through a group of well-paid deliverymen.

They knew each other existed, were suspicious of the names on the powder train, but both were smart enough not to spend too much time trying to locate the other.

Before they both realized it, Edsel was the largest dealer of adult paraphernalia in Southern Florida and Southern California and was moving into the nation's heartland from both coasts. In addition, he was one of Southern California and Southern Florida's largest independent supplies of what he liked to refer to as "Booger Sugar". For his part, Percy was doing very well with the overland routes in cocaine supply and, after the airlines were deregulated, he got in on the ground floor of Deacon Air, a new start up airline from Southern Florida that was limiting itself to redeye service from Southern California and early morning routes from Florida back to California, having found through its marketing people that those were the routes that the business types and the celebrities wanted. In addition, Deacon Air created more first class seats and increased cargo space by limiting coach seats, thereby increasing their profit margin.

Percy started as a ticketing agent, and, with his personality and connections in the community, rapidly ascended to a supervising position. It was from this supervising position that he began to infiltrate the baggage handlers by first finding a sexually like-minded young man. With the promise of some additional cash, that young man began adding additional boxes to the cargo bins going on the plane, those bins then were picked up by a non-passenger in the baggage area at the Miami International Airport, after all, anyone who has ever flown through that airport knew what an unmitigated disaster the security was at that facility.

After that, the profits skyrocketed and with the increasing profits, so came the increasing demands from Javis. Javis found it easier to bring the bulk product in through the Pacific, with the Asian ports easier to grease than the European ports, what with Interpol all over those locations. So he continued to demand that Edsel store more and more product and that Percy find more and more ways to get the product to Southern Florida, with all of the demands of the starlets all over the South Beach hotels.

It was an arrangement that served their financial interests quite well.

Also during this time Javis forced Sue to work as a high priced escort for some of his better customers. Both Percy and Sue knew of the other's arrangements with Javis and both wished they could get the other out of their current situations. This, however, was not possible as Javis made it clear to both of them that if either of them tried to get out of their position, he would kill the other and then give them their freedom to live with their own guilt. They couldn't do this to each other and continued on in their current 'fields'.

Chapter 33

As they drove through the never-ending wasteland that was Texas and Louisiana, Larry and Sue said very little to each other. Several hours back she had shared her complete story with Larry, and he had done the same with her. At this point, all they knew is that they were both going to Florida. Sue in the hopes of saving her beloved Percy and Larry in the hopes of reaching some conclusion with his wife and trying to get his life back.

It was late, and they decided to stop for dinner. The restaurant was Cajun, the food was spicy and hot, and there was plenty of it, and the beer was ice cold and inexpensive.

They ate in silence, listening to the music coming from the two-man band playing on the stage. They drank their beers and each began to think about what to do about finding a place to stay for the night. Sue was tired and Larry looked sad.

"Larry?"

"Yup?" he replied with a mouth half full of crawfish and the best andouille he had ever tasted.

"You sure are hungry."

"Yup" and he belched.

They looked at each other and both laughed.

"I have another question."

Larry finished his beer, waved to the bartender for two more, looked at Sue and nodded his head.

"What?"

"What is it you want? Really want? To hurt her like she's hurt you? To embarrass her? Why not skip all that shit and just get away?

You and me, let's take what we've got and go somewhere, like a beach in Rio, or a cabin in Canada?"

Larry pondered the moment.

"Can't."

"Can't or won't? What gives Larry? I mean, hell, I owe my life in so many ways to Percy and it's all I can do to try and figure out ways to save him. See? That makes sense! I owe him, he is in trouble, and I have to go help him. We kept each other alive for all those years. Yes, we made sacrifices, yes, we gave into the worse demons in ourselves for far too long, but there was a bond there, there was always a bond." She was really sobbing now, the heavy throaty sob that actually quieted the other customers in the bar and caused one particularly drunk man to put down his beer and wander over.

"Hey, pal, why are you making the girl cry?"

Larry didn't lift his head.

"Why don't you just move along, asshole," Sue said to the man.

"Aren't you a spicy one missy? But if you don't mind, in these parts a woman shuts her hole and lets her man, if that's what this pansy ass is, do the talking for her." Then he turned his attention back to Larry.

"Asshole, I asked you a question. Why did you make the woman cry?" He hovered over Larry.

"Move away, please, sir." Larry replied, in a quiet voice that Sue had never heard before. It was like the low growl of a fierce dog that was being interrupted in the midst of a meal.

The man hesitated.

The bartender used the break to try and stop what was happening. "Hey, Shawn, back off, go outside and cool off before I toss you again."

"Shut the fuck up, Rudy!

The man flicked Larry in the ear. Larry snapped.

As the bartender again yelled at Shawn to back off, and as Shawn glanced away from Larry, Larry grabbed a nearly full beer bottle and swung it with all of the might, anger and frustration in his body, and cracked it right across Shawn's nose. Being fully intoxicated, Shawn had no fight left in him after he hit the floor, with his bloody face and his newly aligned nose.

Standby

Shawn's friend, the equally drunk Reggie, moved on Larry immediately. His error, of course, was in failing to consider Sue. Larry was entranced with looking down at the damage he had caused to Shawn and didn't see Reggie coming up from behind. Sue did, but a fraction of a second too late. Reggie's pool cue caught Larry just behind the ear, opening a neat gash and pitching him forward onto the table. Sue came around Larry suddenly and, using every technique in her repertoire, beat Reggie senseless, stopping only when the bartender fired a revolver in the air to get her attention.

"Miss, I suggest you and your friend leave immediately before I call what's left of the cops over here."

Sue looked at him curiously.

"That guy your buddy just smashed is the local sheriff and his buddy you just dropped is his deputy. One deputy left, he's at the station now, his night on duty I suppose. Were I you I'd be heading out of town in a hurry."

Sue and the bartender got Larry in the car. The bartender shoved an ice pack on the bloody side of Larry's head. He smiled at Sue and Sue smiled back and whispered a "thank you" as she jumped into the driver's seat. Larry fell quickly asleep.

Around an hour later, after they were safely outside of the parish where their scuffle had occurred, Larry finally awoke, moaning and nauseous. Sue wasn't sure that he didn't have a concussion so she made him stay awake for a while and asked him enough questions to be annoying but also sure that her new fighting buddy was with her in spirit.

"Larry, that was a very noble thing you did. Stupid, but noble. However, if you are gonna be a bar fighter, we need to work on the eyes in the back of your head. By the way, while you were out of it, the bartender told me the guy you cold-cocked is the local sheriff. Nice work cowboy."

Larry responded by begging her to pull over quickly so he could vomit. She did. He did. Then he turned to her and said, "Sue, I need to sleep, let's find a motel."

"You got it cowboy."

Another hour later they found the Honeymoon Motel on the side of the road. Larry went inside to check them in while Sue grabbed a couple of sodas from the machine. She hadn't seen glass bottles of pop since she was a kid, only plastic bottles trying to be passed off as glass.

"How can I help you, my friend?" asked a bespectacled old man in a dirty tank top t-shirt.

"Two rooms, please."

"Only got one."

Larry lifted his head. "Are you sure?"

"Shit, yeah, I'm sure, I'm the owner, proprietor, chef and chief window and bottle washer. Bought this place on my honeymoon with the missus, we stayed here you know, she's moved on now, you know, but I stayed."

"Sorry for your loss" Larry replied just as Sue was walking in the office.

"Oh, shit, she ain't dead, she just up and left one day, took the dog, and said she was going shopping. Ten years ago. I sure miss that dog." He laughed.

Larry laughed in reply. "Sue, man's only got one room."

Sue looked to the man. "Two beds?"

"One. Got a sofa though."

"Okay, we'll take it. Larry, you get the couch." She smiled.

Larry paid cash for the room. They were handed the key and a couple of towels.

Room 29 was pretty much what one would expect from a roadside motel. Threadbare sheets and pillowcases, very thin walls which enabled one to listen to all sorts of wonderful sounds from the other rooms, a television with the remote control bolted to the nightstand, like the clock, phone and lamp, and a sofa which had seen much better days.

Larry and Sue each showered and turned away while the other was changing, sort of silly since Sue had already seen Larry naked. By the time Larry was dressed for bed, Sue was sound asleep in the bed, her beautiful black hair curving around her chin and cheeks. Her face more peaceful now than Larry had seen it since meeting her.

Larry lay down on the sofa and contemplated everything that the day had brought him. He also contemplated everything that tomorrow would bring and where his life was taking him. He found that even though he was exhausted he couldn't sleep. He had too much pain in his head from the pool cue. His only hope was that the

Standby

asshole from the bar had more pain in his nose than Larry had in his head.

Since he couldn't sleep, he walked down to the office and went inside. The owner was still awake and watching TV. "Mind if I watch with you?"

"Sure, friend, don't get much company you know. Want some hair of the dog?" He replied as he waved a flask to Larry.

Larry shook his head. "Can I ask you something?"

The man turned the TV off and nodded his head. "How'd you manage it when your wife left?"

The man chuckled. "Now that my friend, is one story I've been waiting to tell for a very long time. How about I put some coffee on and we can talk a piece? I saw your wedding ring but didn't figure that beautiful young thing was your wife, of course, ain't my place to judge. Business is business.

Larry blushed.

"I will get to that coffee now and we can sit outside. Peaceful to listen to the owls I think."

Larry smiled and walked outside, sat in the rocker and waited for his new friend.

The owls were peaceful. Very peaceful. The night air was crisp and smelled like old, smoldering campfires. Larry enjoyed the quiet. He felt a nudging on his shoulder.

"Here's that coffee. Figured you might want a touch of something stronger in it, help with that mouse you got on the side of your head." The coffee was served to him in a mason jar, no handle. It smelled strong and tasted wonderful, and the added brandy was a welcome relief.

"Thanks, friend."

"My pleasure, like I said, I don't get too many visitors around here, least not the type I want to talk to much. You seem different though, like a good soul, someone who can understand what a man is talking about."

Larry sat quietly.

"Her name was Lucy. She was the local beauty queen. Short, thin, beautiful. Me? I was a grease monkey. Always was. Daddy owned the local gas station. That was back when a gas station was a service station. Pumped your gas. Checked your oil. Fixed your car.

Fixed your kid's bicycle tire. Simple and happy times.

"So my Lucy was the beauty queen. Now, you are wondering one of two things. One, I'm lying and giving her too much credit thereby giving myself too much credit or, two, how the hell do I end up with a beauty queen?" Larry smiled and nodded his head. "Well, I'm fixin' to tell you."

He continued.

"We went to the same school, small school, like a couple of hundred kids or something, and during our senior year we ended up sitting next to each other in home room. I didn't have any friends. She had nothing but friends. Everyone knew her. Everyone loved her or wanted to love her. Me? I just wanted to get a diploma and leave and join the army. Daddy told me I could join the army but only if'n I got me a diploma first.

"Lucy and Biff, yup, his name was Biff, all right, short for Biffington or something, family name I think, big oil and ranch family, well, she and Biff were a couple and had been for a couple of years. Everyone knew they would marry. He was a rock headed jock, you know the type, everything goes his way cause he's got money and status, plays great ball but lousy grades, but the beauty queen loves him cause that's how things happen in this here part of the south.

Larry found the story entrancing. He felt like he could listen to this man for hours.

"Well, believe it or not, in the last year of school, we had this progressive principal, Mr. Davies, well, he insisted the boys take one course that the girls usually always took and the girls take one course that the boys usually take. We were a small school, so me, like most of the boys, took a cooking class, while the girls took woodshop, autoshop, or something like that. Lucy took autoshop. I took cooking. I'm still a damned fine cook and make a good cup of coffee, I think."

"I agree. Best coffee I've had in sometime."

"True that, my friend. Well, anyhow Lucy takes autoshop. Don't know why. Could've taken woodshop like most of the other girls but Lucy liked a challenge. So she took autoshop. Well, it seemed like everyone was treating it like a big joke anyhow, laughing through the cooking classes and woodshop classes, me included I suppose. But

Standby

Lucy really wanted to learn. Anyhow, one day, in homeroom, she turns to me and says 'Leo', that's my name by the way, she says 'Leo, can you help me out on something for autoshop.' Hell, I didn't even know that she knew my name, but apparently she surely did. What could I say, I said 'Yes'. And there you are sir."

Larry looked up. "That's it? That's the story? No offense, Leo, but that can't be the whole story. Details, man, details."

Now it was Leo's turn to smile. "I knew I had your attention, just wanted to make sure.

Leo paused and took a deep drink of his brandy-laden coffee.

"Well, sir, I told her to come to the garage and I would help her out. Taught her how to change a tire, change oil, do a lube job. Well, hell, that woman took to it like nobody's business." He paused, a placid look coming over his face, as if fondly recalling a lost love. "We became friends too, if you believe it. I'm amazed myself, but over that semester she confided all sorts of things to me. I knew she hated her parents, and wanted to get away from this nowhere town like nobody's business. I knew she was tired of being the beauty queen and longed to be respected for her smarts, which weren't all that great but certainly more than most people gave her credit for."

"Sounds like quite a fine young lady."

"She was, Larry, truly she was." Larry looked up and saw tears welling in Leo's eyes. Leo continued, "anyhow, came graduation day and she comes over to me after we get our diplomas and she is crying and I ask her what's wrong and she says "Leo, I need help, please.' And I say 'sure, anything.' And she says ' I will meet you at the shop later.'

"And she does. Later that night, I don't even remember the time anymore although I'm not sure it matters, but she shows up, and its late, and she clearly been crying for a long time and I think she might'a been drinkin' too cause she seemed a little looped you know. And I ask her what's wrong and she looks at me, leans in and kisses my check and proceeds to tell me everything. She tells me how Biff talked her into having sex with him, and at first she didn't really like it but after some time she began to like it and they were doin' it quite regularly. She said they weren't using no protection and, sure enough, she found herself pregnant. She went to Biff and he called her a slut and told her that the baby weren't his. They fought, and then he hurt her. Asshole punched her right in the back, she showed me, he broke two of her ribs. She asked me for a place to stay, cause her parents weren't taking her in, I gave her my room and she stayed with me and my daddy."

Larry waited quietly. There was more to the story. Leo was looking to unburden and, for some reason he had picked Larry to do it with. Larry waited. Leo got up, went inside for a time, then returned to his rocker. He continued the story.

"After she had gone to sleep, I went lookin'. Lookin' for Biff. He and me had a score to settle. I found him at one of those ridiculous high school keg parties. Shit, he must've outweighed me by fifty pounds and was easily six inches taller than me, but I was pissed.

"I said to him 'Hey asshole!'."

Of course, he ignored me.

"'Asshole! I am talking to you. Why don't you tell us what you figure you get out of punching a woman?'"

Then the room went quiet. "I said, what the fuck you get out of punching a woman?"

Biff finally responded, "Piss off grease monkey."

"And I snapped. Just snapped. Jumped right on him. Imagine it, me half his size and I jumped on his chest like I was a long lost girlfriend, him holding me up with his arms yelling at me like a stuck pig, and me just hitting his face over and over again, and then I really snapped, bit his nose right off his face, can you imagine? And then he drops me and he's screaming 'gimme back my nose, gimme back my nose'."

Larry was rolling on the ground with laughter. So loud, in fact, that he woke Sue who came out to see what the commotion was, and saw Larry with tears rolling down his face. "So what did you do?" Larry stammered out.

"Well, I looked him right in the face, and I swallowed it."

"No! You swallowed his nose?"

Larry was dumbfounded. Leo was laughing hysterically.

"Yup, I sure as shit swallowed that nose."

"Well, what did he do? What did Biff do?"

"Do? Nothing. A man without a nose, tends to just run off. And he did. Last I heard he was tending bar in some other no name town in the panhandle. Family disowned him, running from a fight and all.

Standby

As for me, I was now most certainly the town crazy, swallowing the nose and all. Tried my hand at opening a restaurant, called it the 'Cannibal Grill' but no one wanted to eat there, tried turning it into a vegetarian place, thought that was a good joke, but a restaurant hereabouts that don't serve meat goes over like a fart in church.

Sue walked up, sat next to Larry and quietly laid her head on his shoulder. Leo continued on.

"I s'pose the good thing is that Lucy took to me after that. She never had a man stand up for her before. I knew about her problem and decided to marry her, right then and there, adopted that child, a little girl, just like she were my own. Lily, most beautiful girl you ever did see. Shortly after we had our own child, a boy, not much to look at, called him Ronald, Ronnie. He was sort of squirrelly as a child and never amounted to much, folks around here called him "Weasel" cause he liked to catch snakes and eat 'em. Strange boy. Loved 'em both anyhow.

"Eventually I sold the garage and bought this motel. Thought the kids would take it over, they didn't, they moved off once they finished high school, and once Ronnie graduated, Lucy left. The day after he left. I came home from the store, found a note on the desk in her hand, it said 'Thanks', that's it, nothing more, and she was gone, never saw her again."

They all wept.

"Truth is, I don't think she left because of someone else, I figure she just felt like she and I were now square, and it was time for her to try and find a life elsewhere."

Sue turned to Leo, "She was a lucky woman to have you."

Leo nodded. A tear fell from his face.

"Good night Leo."

"Night Larry, night pretty lady, we don't get many around here as beautiful as you, Larry is a lucky man, even if he don't realize it yet."

Sue bent over and kissed Leo gently on the cheek. Then she took Larry's hand and they walked back to the room together. They laid on the bed and then, after looking at each other, quietly made love with their eyes open.

Chapter 34

Edsel was still in that haze between asleep and awake. When awake he prayed for sleep because of the terrible pain he was in. When asleep, he was bothered by the strangest dreams.

Airplanes.
Falling Chairs.
Boxing rings.
Punches.
Floating teeth.

All had a loaded message. But all the messages were on the periphery of his consciousness. He couldn't grasp them. All that he knew for sure was that he was in pain. Terrible pain. Teeth chattering pain, except he had no teeth.

The other thing he knew for sure was that some strange, plump woman kept coming to his bed and calling him "sweetheart", and "my love" and, even more strangely, "Larry."

"Who the hell was Larry?" he thought. "And who the hell was this strange woman?" Well, he was too well doped on whatever was pumping through that tube in his arm to much worry about it. The only time he wasn't well enough doped was when they stuck him in that damned whirlpool. That was pure hell. And this strange lady certainly wasn't around when he was going through that.

"Was he married?" Edsel thought not but the events of the last couple of days were so surreal that almost anything made sense. Was this all really just a dream? A nightmare?

It had to be a nightmare. He remembered a plane ride.
A plane ride.

Standby

There it was. The medication was wearing off just enough to allow him to remember the plane ride. He made it to the plane at the last minute and convinced that little gay guy to bump that useless standby passenger off the plane. Who was that guy? What was his name? In the back of Edsel's mind was a thought. Somehow he believed, truly felt and believed that that guy from the plane in LA had something to do with why he was here, in unimaginable pain, repeatedly visited by some woman who kept showing him affection.

Dear God, could he possibly know that woman? No, it wasn't possible.

And then he slept again.

Chapter 35

Sullivan, the Reverend Thomas, and Padua were all in the courtroom well before the scheduled hearing, Sullivan having learned that he better not be late. Ronnie sat in the back of the courtroom, behind the glare of the television lights that were shining all over the courtroom. He was inconspicuous. No one noticed him, which was how he liked it. Lily was even in court for this hearing. She had a horrible sense of foreboding about this hearing and wanted to be there to support her husband. She knew, in her heart, that she had to get him back on the straight and narrow. She also knew that there was more to this case than simply his greed. It was too personal. She needed to know, felt entitled to know. And so she was here.

Padua walked over to the plaintiff's table.

"Clarence, the hearing starts in around eight minutes, and you know the judge is always on time. I want to talk straight to you for a minute, okay?"

"Geoffrey, go away, I'm getting ready, alright? And I don't appreciate it when you try and distract me. Stop playing for the cameras!" This last part said just loudly enough to get the attention of the reporters who directed their cameras right at Sullivan, just where he wanted them.

"Clarence, you don't get it, do you? For a while, I will admit, this was fun for me. Taking you down a peg or two. But this, what happens here, in these courtrooms, this is real life, serious business, done by serious lawyers who know what they are doing. You have skills. You have a TV face and a great voice and you are a hell of a

Standby

businessman, but you know less about what to do in a courtroom than my dog. And it is about to destroy you. Six minutes now..."

Sullivan lost his cool.

"You arrogant little shit! Everything you have you have because of me. I made you and I am about to break you!"

Geoff paused, collected himself and replied.

"Clarence, I appreciate the opportunities you gave me, but I have a client to represent. You have five minutes now to accept the offer I made you on the phone."

At this Franklin stepped up.

"Offer? You call $250,000.00 an offer? That's bunk and you know it Geoffrey." He boomed. The reporters were taking everything down.

No one had called him "Geoffrey" in years and something about the way this man said it was soothing in a way that discomfited Padua.

"Two fifty? That wasn't the offer."

Sullivan blushed. Then, instantly, Geoff knew. "You never told your client what I offered you?"

Franklin turned to look at Sullivan, his mouth open in question. A question that was never asked.

The bailiff boomed.

"All Rise!" For the first time in his career, the judge was early.

Judge Berger glared at Sullivan, who had difficulty raising his gaze to meet that of the judge. He was still stunned by what had taken place just before the hearing began. He was in a rapidly descending spiral now and he knew it.

"Mr. Sullivan, you are in contempt. That little stunt you played with using your client when I forbade you and the good Reverend from speaking to the press. So, you tried to play cutesy with me. Well, let me explain something to you, sir, I am the Judge, you are the lawyer, in only the most base of terms, you are a lawyer, and you have over-stepped your bounds. You are in contempt."

Lily was in agony over what would happen next, just as the judge turned his attention to her husband.

"Reverend, I will not hold you in contempt because even I do not need the bad karma of putting a man of the cloth in contempt. Of course, to call you a man of the cloth is about as much a joke as calling that jackass a lawyer. Get me?"

Franklin had faced physically tougher men on many football fields and locker rooms, but never had he been so intimidated. However, unlike Sullivan, he found his voice.

"Yes, your honor, and I am sorry. I am guilty as charged, and I am sorry."

The courtroom was silent. Lily had never been more proud of her husband. That was the man she married. A humble man forced to act to make a life for himself after he was abandoned by those who used him but who he could no longer serve.

The judge was disarmed. He stared at Franklin, who held his gaze. Man to man they stared. Then, surprisingly, the judge blinked. "Well, Reverend, I thank you for that. I trust this will be our last conversation on this matter. You may continue to serve as Mrs. Jones' spiritual advisor, if you wish, but I assume that I will not hear press conferences from you."

Franklin smiled. "You have my word, your honor."

"Very well, then."

The judge turned to Geoff.

"Mr. Padua, I am curious if there is any chance of settlement of this matter?"

Geoff rose to respond. He thought for a moment. He knew that his prior employer had failed to tell his client about the real offer. He just was lost about what to do. The only thing he could do was tell the truth. His client had instructed him that the offer was gone once the hearing began. The hearing had started. His instructions were clear. Sullivan's failures were his problems.

"Your honor, no, there is no chance of settlement of this matter. My client has withdrawn their offer and wishes to proceed with the hearing. We believe that the person in the hospital is not Larry Jones and ask that the court order Mr. Sullivan to prove the identity of his client. If he is right, we will offer what was publicly offered to all the other families. If he is wrong, and it is not Mr. Jones there in the hospital, then the case must be dismissed, with prejudice, and we can all move on."

The judge nodded.

"Okay, then, Mr. Sullivan?"

Sullivan finally found his voice.

Standby

"Judge, Mr. Padua's position is outrageous. I have, quite simply, never heard of having to prove identity of my client in a courtroom."

"Mr. Sullivan, I'm not sure you have ever heard of anything in a courtroom, seeing as how you've never been in one before this case."

The entire gallery broke into laughter, especially the reporters.

Sullivan blushed noticeably.

"That being said…"

"Mr. Sullivan, enough. It is Friday. On Tuesday, we hold the hearing. You must prove the identity of the man in the hospital or show me good cause why you cannot yet do so."

Sullivan nodded. "Yes, sir."

"Very well, ten am, here, Tuesday. Is there anything else?"

Geoff rose again. "Your honor, I wanted to advise the plaintiff's that we also are now filing our motion to dismiss this matter. In the interests of fairness."

"Very well."

Sullivan spoke again. "Judge, its Friday, how am I to address this motion?"

"Don't like working weekends?"

Again, laughter from the gallery.

"I'm afraid I have one more piece of bad news for you, Mr. Sullivan, you are in contempt of my court. You will be a guest of the county for one night, tonight. It will give you plenty of time to plan your arguments."

"Guest of the county?"

"Yes, sir, you are going to jail. One night. Bailiff, secure Mr. Sullivan." The bailiff grabbed Sullivan by the arms and began walking him out of the courtroom.

"See you Tuesday."

"All rise."

Chapter 36

*L*arry and Sue were having another silent drive. Each in their own thoughts. Interestingly, if they had shared their thoughts, they would have realized that they were very much the same. Both had enjoyed the night before much more than they thought.

Sue broke the silence.

"Larry, do you want to talk about it?"

Larry drove in silence for a bit.

"Talk about what?"

"Why, last night of course."

"Hmmm. I suppose we could if you feel like we should."

"I'm not sure why it happened. I mean, I like you. I liked you when I first met you, but that felt like it was about more than just sex, didn't it? I know what sex feels like, that was different."

"I don't know Sue. Been so long for me, I can't answer the question you are trying to ask. Only thing I know is that it sure was different than anything I've ever experienced before."

"So that's a good thing then I guess."

"Yes. I think it's a very good thing."

They were crossing Alabama now, just a short stretch from cutting into Florida around the Pensacola area. It was the part of the drive on Interstate 10 that always amazed people driving into Florida. That they could drive for days to cross an entire country and then get to the Florida border and feel that they should be just a few short minutes from Miami, only to learn that they were still a hard day to day and a half of driving away from Miami, since Florida was such a large and long state. To Larry, he likened this to his favorite

Standby

piece of trivia, that being that Florida had the second longest coastline in the United States, the longest being Alaska. Most people didn't know that and assumed that Florida must be first. Trivia always intrigued Larry.

"Wow, the Florida border. Where do you think Percy is now?"

"No idea. But I'm guessing he is heading in the same direction we are. Seems to me all roads lead to Miami."

"Larry, do you think he is okay? Percy, I mean?"

"Sue, to be honest, I don't know. However, it strikes me that Javis wants him alive. I am guessing that if Javis had no need for him, he would've killed him back there instead of shooting him in the nose, only. After all, anyone who could do what he did to Percy could certainly kill a man if he needed to. So, I think Percy is alive, and I think he is going to Miami."

"Thanks Larry."

"Let's go find your friend. You owe him that much."

Chapter 37

Percy was still in the trunk. It was stifling hot and he was dehydrating rapidly. His nose hurt miserably and he was suffering from a desperate need for more cocaine. It was this last pain that troubled him the most. After a five-year cocaine habit he had spent a small fortune and went to the best detoxification clinics in the country and rehabilitated himself from cocaine use. Now, Javis throws the cocaine on his facial wound to numb the pain, which it did with the terrible side effect of triggering a response in Percy's brain causing an ache for more powder.

He shivered miserably in the trunk. It was stifling hot, yet he was shivering. He knew he had been here for at least two, and maybe three days. He knew this because during the day there was some ambient light in the trunk and during the night it was pitch black. He knew when they stopped because he could hear them talking outside of the car and could smell the fumes when gasoline was added to the car.

For sometime now they had stopped letting him out of the trunk for bathroom breaks. He knew that he had soiled himself several times and, for this fact alone, he was thankful that his nose had been shot off because he stopped being able to smell himself.

He prayed they were getting close to their destination, wherever that may be. He drifted to sleep and began to dream.

Javis came to him with the demand that he, in order to save Sue, begin to ship bags of cocaine to the east coast. It was simple, almost too simple.

Then, one Sunday, which was a very busy travel day and to

Standby

Percy, one of the easiest days to place a few extra bags on the redeye flight, a man approached Percy and said, "Percy, we need to talk."

Percy turned to the voice. There, in the fading sunlight of the west coast, stood a man in a brown suit, with mirrored sunglasses. It wasn't his appearance or the menace in his voice that rattled Percy. Rather, it was the very large badge and ID card that he held up for Percy to see.

"Someplace quiet we can talk, Percy, or would you prefer to head downtown?"

Percy nodded. He was stuck and he knew he was stuck. The man was a federal agent, that much Percy quickly gathered from the badge and identification that had quickly been put away.

"Percy, here is the deal, ship those three bags, we are gonna let 'em go through with a tracking device inside, of course, but you and I are gonna talk. Here is my card, the address where we are gonna meet along with the time and place is on the back. Be there."

Again, Percy nodded. He was caught. There was no alternative.

Three days later, Percy sat with DEA Agent Simpson to discuss his future. They met at a coffee shop right across the street from Edsel Dodger's first Los Angeles adult emporium. Percy enjoyed the irony.

"By our calculations, which I am sure are very conservative, you have shipped over thirty million dollars or so of cocaine to Miami via baggage that you and your boyfriend slipped on to Deacon Air flights. If I arrest you, you are going to jail forever, young man. And I am about this far away from arresting you." At this he snapped his fingers.

Percy stared at his rapidly cooling bowl of oatmeal. He was not hungry but knew he had to eat.

"Eat your oatmeal." Damn, it was like this guy could read minds.

Agent Simpson continued.

"See, Percy, but here is the thing. I don't want you. I want that asshole Croatian, Javis."

Percy looked up in shock that the DEA knew about Javis, that they knew his name.

"Yeah, you scumsucker, I know all about Javis. I know all about his Miami lawyers and his island money launderers. Been watching him for years, but can't get close enough to nail him. I need someone inside. Then, strange thing happens, he goes into this gay bar in San Francisco, owned by a guy who was alive and well before Javis goes in, and then is never heard from again. It was sort of lucky, see we were all set to bust the bar, then Javis shows up out of the blue and we change our plans. Quite flexible on our part I might add."

Percy found some courage.

"Agent Simpson, I appreciate the stroll down your memory lane, but what does all of this have to do with me?"

Simpson practically leaped across the table. He grabbed Percy by the nose and slammed his face into his oatmeal, then pushed his back into his faux leather chair.

"Percy, I could've busted you five years ago, but I've been watching you ever since. Do you understand? I have enough information to send you to Leavenworth forever. That's not a country club, that's hard core, baby, and they would just love you there, get it?"

Percy wiped his face and stared back down into what was left of his oatmeal.

"So, here is the deal, we want Javis, and those two goons of his. We are nailing him on drug, racketeering, and murder charges. You help us get him, and get him convicted, you get immunity. Fail us, we charge you and send you away. See, we don't need any witnesses to nail you. But we need you to nail him. Get it?

Percy slowly nodded his head.

"Oh, Percy, one more thing, refuse us and we nail that girlfriend of yours, Sue, is it? Well, refuse us and we nail her for prostitution and conspiracy. Get it?"

Percy stared off outside the window. "I understand."

"Good, then let's talk about your wire."

"Wire?"

"Shit, yes, from today on, you wear a wire, twenty-four seven, you are wired. You take a dump, we know about it. You shower, we know. You get laid, we know. Get the picture? This way everything Javis says is recorded. We want you to get close to him, real close. Remember, we hear what you are saying. So don't try and fuck us, get it?"

"Sure, I get it. But I got a question."

"I'm sure you've got plenty."

Standby

"What happens if Javis or one of his goons gets wind of what I'm doing? Who's gonna save my ass and how?"

"Don't worry, we give you an emergency signal button. Hit it and we come swooping in.

Percy nodded in thanks.

"Provided, of course, we are close enough to save you."

At this, Agent Simpson laughed heartily.

"Now, Percy, let's get to work."

The DEA made Percy their ace insider in the developing case against Javis. Percy played his role and played it well. He wore the wire as instructed and, for his own amusement, made as much noise in the bathroom as possible to try and cause discomfort for those listening in during those inopportune moments. He was successful.

The information came rolling in. Percy was a fountain of information for this DEA investigation. Javis, normally exceptionally careful with his information, spilled his guts to Percy. It was assumed that he did this out of a mistaken belief that that Percy would be totally loyal to him because of Javis' threats regarding Sue. DEA Agent Simpson had struck right to the heart of this threat by promising safe passage for Sue if Percy cooperated. For Percy, the threat of death for not complying with Javis was outweighed by the promise of freedom if he cooperated. He only hoped that the DEA lived up to their end of the bargain.

Hundreds of hours of taped conversations were put together from Percy's contact with Javis and his two goons. The DEA was ready to move in and make their arrests when the crash of Deacon Air 721 took place. Then suddenly Percy disappeared and Javis disappeared. The DEA was playing catch-up. Percy still wore the wire in the belief that the DEA was still following.

Simpson heard the entire interchange between Percy and Javis right up to the point where Javis shot Percy's nose off. Then, in being taped and manhandled, his wire had broken and now Percy was truly alone.

When he awoke in the trunk of the car, the two goons lifted him out while holding their noses at the stench of him. He hadn't eaten anything in three days and he was hungry, dehydrated, feverish and in agony. Misha complained to Javis about the smell. Javis told him to take Percy into the hotel room and strip him and throw him into the shower. Javis told Misha's brother to go to the store and get him some clothes. Misha threw the much smaller Percy over his shoulder and took him into the room to clean him up.

Percy passed out from the pain.

He awoke several hours later, quite disoriented and extremely uncomfortable. It took him a moment to gather his bearings. He was in a dark hotel room. He was clean, that much he could tell. He was also seated in a chair and couldn't move. He also realized that he was gagged and when he looked down and saw that the clothes he was wearing weren't his he knew with absolute certainty that Javis had found out about the wire. He was in trouble, very big trouble.

Javis pulled up a chair right in front of Percy. "Something you vish to tell me my old friend?"

Percy just stared back at him. Where was that damned button Simpson had given him? He had pushed it over and over again in the trunk, with no help coming. Now, here he was, duct-taped to a chair in a hotel room and his worst nightmare coming true. Javis knew. He was dead, he was sure of it.

"Percy, Percy, Percy, I trusted you, you sunofabitch!" And with that, Javis slapped him hard across the face, back and forth.

Javis then shoved the wire in front of Percy. "Why? Who? Give me information now! Right now or I will find Sue and destroy her! So help me God!"

Then, for the first time since he had met him, Percy saw fear in Javis' eyes. It was unmistakable. It was fear. Javis had lost control of a situation. He didn't know where Sue was. He also knew that without Percy's assistance, the cocaine shipments had to stop, his cash flow would disintegrate, and whoever he had to answer to back in whatever country he was from would not be pleased with Javis, to put it mildly. Javis was in a world of danger right now. The wire had seen to that. Now, if Percy could just figure out a way to stay alive. He mumbled, as forcibly as possible, to Javis to remove the tape from his mouth.

"If I remove, and you scream, I vill shoot you in the balls."

Percy nodded.

The tape was removed. Percy held back the scream with every fiber of his being.

Percy lifted his head, mustered his courage, and spoke.

Standby

"You still need me, and you know it. Kill me and you are toast. I can figure something with the DEA, get it? They need me to testify. Kill me and the only hope you have in court dies with me. Get it?"

Percy had overplayed his hand and he knew it instantly. Javis had no intention of sticking around the country. He probably wouldn't even go back to where he was from, content instead to head off to some island with no extradition and a private bank.

Javis sneered at Percy. "Kill him slowly," he said to his goons. "I am leaving and vill call later."

He turned and walked out without looking back at Percy. The punches from the two goons began raining down from all directions. Percy tried lifting his head to show some pride, but after a time drifted to that state between conscious and unconscious thought.

Javis sat in a restaurant across from the hotel. Two things caught his attention. The first was several clearly government issue cars pulling into the parking lot with agents spilling out and heading to the room where his goons were hopefully finishing off Percy. The second was a small sports convertible stopped for gas down the street. A man and a Chinese woman chatting quietly. Could it be? Was that Sue? The karma of the moment was breathtaking for him.

He dropped five dollars on the counter and walked to his sedan and drove off.

In the fracas between the police and his assistants that followed, Misha's brother was killed, Misha was captured, and Percy was saved, badly hurt, but still alive. Simpson had his star witness. Now he had to capture his crook.

Chapter 38

Larry was pumping gasoline while Sue went into the store to get them each a snack. Larry found that he didn't have much of an appetite lately, and he noticed, with some degree of pleasure, that his clothing was getting looser. He had a lot on his mind.

Where was this all going to end?

What did it all mean?

He was heading for Miami, to confront his wife and handle that issue, and still he had to help Sue with the Percy issue, after all, Percy had saved their lives. What did it mean?

Was Percy even still alive?

"Larry, cookies or chips? All they had."

"Neither, Sue, not really hungry."

Sue smiled at him. He was no longer the man she had met that first night in Los Angeles. There was a quiet confidence in him that was growing each day. She was attracted to him. Even though he was unlike any man she had ever met or been with, he was gentle, chivalrous, and intelligent. She liked him, and that was all there was to it.

"So, Larry, what's next."

"Well, we're in Tampa, I figure another five hours to Miami. But I'm tired, and that last stretch into Miami is a rough one, straight across the Everglades, nothing to look at, easy to fall asleep, dangerous road. I say we get a hotel, get some rest and get up early and hit it. Sound good?"

"Sure. Give us more time to figure out what we are gonna do."

That night Larry and Sue ate dinner at one of most exotic

Standby

steakhouses in North America, the sort of place that was clearly designed for an all-male clientele but had modernized with the times. The meal was fantastic, and they both ate ravenously. Then, they were escorted upstairs to the dessert room. The after dinner wine list was amazing and given their current cash situation, they decided to splurge on a bottle of Civil War era wine. It cost almost ten thousand dollars for the bottle and the owner of the restaurant himself came out to be sure that they wanted it, as once it was uncorked, they purchased it regardless of the taste.

Larry paid in cash. The wine and dessert came.

The wine, of course, had turned a bit. It was a Union bottle. Larry told Sue the Story of Felicity's family lineage to the Civil War and the story of her ancetor's "wound." Sue laughed hysterically and, even thought the taste was a bit off, they finished every drop.

They left, checked into a hotel, and rather than sleep, Larry was treated to a night of lovemaking he had never imagined.

Neither of them noticed the black sedan parked just across the parking lot from their car. It was there all night and followed them when they left the hotel in the morning.

Chapter 39

Sullivan had never seen the inside of a jail before. Not as a lawyer, and certainly not as a client.

He was tired, he was grumpy, and a bit hungry. The food the guards served him wasn't really edible, not that he had much of an appetite when the "meal" had been brought in by a giggling guard who said "Hey, I know you, you're that TV lawyer, ain't you?" and dropped a tray of some sort of creamed something or other. Of course, that was several hours before, and time doing what time tends to do, it passed, and with nothing else to do his mind began to turn to food.

He lay down on the concrete slab which served as a bench and bed in this holding cell in the bottom of the jail and began to dream of food. His appetite was very well known; he liked the finer things and almost always enjoyed a shrimp cocktail with his meals. That was what he was thinking about when his cell door opened and his associate, Ramon, came in nervously.

"Ramon, thanks for coming man, I'm really hungry, got anything?"

"Sorry, bossman, I didn't bring any food. I will see what I can do for you, ok?

"Okay, sure, but get me something please. The food here ain't worth shit."

"Ok, will do, boss, gotta talk to you. Things are getting real bad out there."

"Why? What's going on?"

"Well, Mrs. Jones, Felicity, she and the Reverend want to come

Standby

to the office, asap, to collect her file. She says she's lost confidence in you and is gonna hire another lawyer. I don't know what to do."

"What are you? Fucking stupid? You stop them. You don't give them their file. That's the biggest damn file in the office and you can't let it leave. Dammit, I'm stuck here until tomorrow and there ain't anything I can do. Stop them. Get out of here. Stop them or don't come to work on Monday!"

Ramon was out the door in an instant.

All thoughts of his grumbling stomach left Sullivan, for the moment.

Reverend Thomas and Felicity were, in fact, at Sullivan's office, and they were, in fact there to get Felicity's file. The decision had been made at a semi-private meeting at Thomas' office, attended by Felicity, Lily, Ronnie and the Reverend.

"Felicity, I have to discuss something delicate with you."

"Yes, well, I thought you might after that hearing and all."

Franklin was surprised. Felicity was apparently capable of more insight than he had at first thought possible. So, what was on her mind?

"Franklin, I think the judge doesn't like you guys very much. Like he favors the other lawyer."

Franklin sat quietly. She was, of course, quite right. The judge disliked him very much. That was not really too much of an issue since he would not be making any arguments in court. Those were the domain of Sullivan. The larger concern was that, at every turn, Sullivan had alienated the judge. That, alone, was not too much of concern. Of larger concern was his seeming lack of legal ability.

She continued.

"I watch Mr. Sullivan, and he just doesn't seem like the guy I see on television every day. He seems to be getting pushed around, and, well, um, I don't know how to say this…"

"You can say anything here, darling, no one is going to tell him what you said." It was Lily speaking. Franklin smiled at her. She always had a way of relating to people who even Franklin, with his considerable people skills, could not manage.

"Yes, well," Felicity continued, "it just looks like Mr. Sullivan doesn't know what he is doing in that courtroom and that other lawyer, Mr. Padua, seems to know just what to say and when to say it, and, well, I'm just wondering if maybe we shouldn't have tried to settle the case for that offer they made to all the other families.

Franklin, and now Lily, in whom he confided everything, knew they were all treading on thin ice. They had gone along with Sullivan's plan, some might say they actually triggered the plan, to file suit in a hurry, to be the first one to the courthouse. That took them out of contention for the 2.5 million dollar offer all of the other families were receiving. Now, they knew, although Felicity didn't, that the airline had offered her one million dollars. Sullivan had lied. Plain and simple. He lied. Told them all that the offer was only a quarter of that. He had violated who knows how many ethical rules in failing to disclose the real offer to Felicity. Of course, that really was Sullivan's problem, not Franklin's. Franklin's problem was that the deal he had made with Sullivan for a portion of the fee was not enforceable under the law, and both of them knew it.

Franklin was at a crossroads. He knew that he had already taken a step towards the crossroads when he distanced himself from Sullivan in the courtroom by apologizing to the Judge. Now, he needed to take the final step. He owed it to Felicity, it couldn't be about money anymore. It was time for the truth.

"Felicity, you need to sit down, I have to tell you the truth. The whole truth."

Felicity did as he asked. For the next hour, Franklin told her everything. He told her about Sullivan's plans, about the offer that he rejected without first having a discussion with her. And then, in the end, he told her all about his relationship with Larry. All the way back to high school.

He told her how he knew that he owed it to Larry to come forward and help him. He had to make right what had gone so wrong all those years before.

Then he stopped talking. He sat down heavily in his large chair. He wept. Lily came and sat in his lap and held his head and whispered quietly in his ear.

Felicity spoke.

"Reverend. I appreciate everything you have told me. Truly, I do. But, quite frankly, I don't give a shit about your conscience." Her voice was getting louder and more shrill by the moment. "You will help me get this matter settled, you will help me get the money I am

Standby

entitled to, or, so help me God, I will see you and Mr. Sullivan in jail for a helluva lot more time than one night on a weekend. Now, you have more invested in this than you thought. That useless excuse of a husband of mine wasn't worth shit. Now he's worth at least a million dollars and I expect you to help me get it.

She paused and stared at Franklin, who, for the first time in his life, found it difficult to make eye contact.

"I expect you to help me get it," she repeated slowly and deliberately, "and I expect you to charge me nothing for it. Are we clear?"

Franklin sat quietly, content to lay his head on his wife's shoulder.

It was Ronnie who found his voice first.

"Mrs. Jones, there is something I think you may be forgetting."

"What? What the hell do you wanna tell me now, you little weasel?" Felicity's shouts shattered the silence of the room.

Ronnie hesitated. But he was tired of being the standby in the room. "What if Mr. Padua is right?"

"Right about what?"

"About whether that is really your husband in that hospital bed?"

"Of course it is, that's the most ridiculous thing I have ever heard. Why, its really just the airline trying to avoid paying what's fair."

"Fair? Hell, they offered several million dollars to every family, and then after you sued, they still offered you a million dollars."

"Yes, but I didn't know about that did I? You all saw to that, didn't you? And now, if I don't win at least that much, you all are going to make that right, aren't you? If I lose, you all owe me a million dollars."

Franklin had had quite enough.

He stood and his sheer size silenced the room. "Felicity, the offer was made to Larry, not to you. If that is, in fact, Larry in that hospital bed, the offer is to him, not you. The offer is not made to you, its made to him, and there won't be an offer, to you, unless he dies and only if you can prove that is your husband in the bed. So, I would genuinely appreciate it if you would just shut the hell up and sit down so that I can think. Got it?"

"Why, I never…"

"Not according to what I have learned. Shut up woman!!!"

Felicity did as Franklin said.

He sat quietly for a time and then picked up the phone and dialed.

Geoff was sitting in his office, discussing testimony with a pathologist who he might call to testify at the hearing regarding the techniques for identifying the man who was in the hospital, the man who was the center of the current firestorm. His phone buzzed. He had instructed his assistant not to disturb him unless it was an emergency. Geoff had had all sorts of legal assistants in his career. This one was special. He knew what constituted a real emergency.

"Yeah."

"Sorry to bug you Geoff, but I think this one is important."

"I'm busy, who is it?"

"Reverend Thomas."

Geoff paused. "Okay, put him through."

Geoff immediately picked up the phone. Rather than say anything, he waited to hear the Reverend speak. It was a little ploy he had learned over the years. If the caller was really under pressure, he would try to fill the dead air after the phone connection had been made.

The silence was audible. Their breathing began to synch with the clock ticking on the wall.

"Uh, Geoffrey, uh, Mr. Padua, are you there sir?" You could still hear the power in the man's booming voice, even over the telephone.

"I'm here Reverend Thomas, Geoff is just fine, sir. What can I do for you?"

"Well, I'm calling on behalf of Mrs. Jones, you know."

"Franklin, I sort of assumed that as you and I don't have any other business together and I'm certainly not one of your parishioners."

Franklin bristled at the insolence of that lawyer calling him by his first name, especially without first asking permission. Of course, he realized he was no where in a position of negotiating from a position of strength. What was worse is that Geoff knew it as well.

"No, sir, you are not."

"Well, Reverend, the question still stands. What can I do for you?"

"Mrs. Jones would like to settle this case. There it is, sir, as

Standby

directly as I can put it. Now, I am not her lawyer, just her advisor, and I do not speak for her lawyer, but I do speak for her. Her demand is two point five million."

Geoff sat quietly for a moment. "Reverend, this is a damned impertinent call and you know it. Mrs. Jones has a lawyer, and whether he is competent or not is not the issue, he is her lawyer. I speak with him, and only with him, until such time as I receive notice that he is not her lawyer. That is it. It's that simple. I do not negotiate with you sir."

"Sullivan isn't gonna be her lawyer much longer, I think we both know that."

Geoff thought quietly for a moment. This was a moment with grave consequences, that he knew. Ethically he knew he could not negotiate with this man.

He responded after another moment.

"Well, that is not my concern. This call, Reverend Thomas, is over."

"Wait, put the million back on the table."

Now Geoff hesitated. Just as his finger was about to hit the disconnect button. This was a dilemma. The plaintiff in a potentially explosive case was vacillating. There was weakness.

"That offer is gone. The best I could do is maybe half that. Of course, you understand I am not negotiating with you. You want to put a number in writing, do it, from Sullivan, or his client."

"Alright"

"And Franklin."

"Yes, Geoff."

"This conversation never happened." The line went dead. Franklin looked over at Ronnie who was quietly hanging up the extension and turning the tape recorder off.

Geoff called the CEO of Deacon Airlines and asked for an emergency board meeting. The CEO, with the mounting evidence of how successful Padua's plan had been so far, went along and called the directors in. Those who couldn't make it were hooked up via a videoconference. Not one director missed the meeting. Each was becoming more and more intrigued by how successfully the lawyer's plan had come together at every stage.

The CEO called the meeting to order. As usual, he got right to the point. "Geoff, what's on your mind?"

"Well, as you know, the plan to settle the cases quickly is going very well. Something like sixty percent of the victims have already settled and around half of those didn't even hire lawyers. The remaining families are mostly in negotiation with us and again, about half of those haven't hired lawyers. Publicly, the stock of Deacon Air is holding somewhat steady. There was some drop after the crash, but the stock price has held and will likely rise again. The FAA and NTSB are probably going to clear the airline of any wrongdoing. Complete fluke, flock of birds. Just pilot error. Too busy talking below the noise threshold. The union will hem and haw like they usually do, but they will back off because they know the airline, and therefore the jobs of their members, will be saved."

At that, each of the directors nodded their heads. The plan, to date had worked brilliantly. Most start-up airlines would have collapsed from a crash like this one. By all accounts, Deacon Air was going to survive this terrible event. As for Padua, he already knew that his stock with the company was soaring and he, therefore, needed to choose his next words very, very carefully.

Numerous heads around the table were still nodding in assent at the news about the stock price. They all just wanted to hear about the stock price, anyhow, since that is where they each saw the bulk of their income.

After taking a very deep breath, Padua continued.

"Really only one matter remains open. The case involving Larry Jones, the fella who may or may not be in the hospital."

The loudmouthed Texan jumped in.

"What do you mean 'may or may not be in the hospital'?"

"Well, we just don't know. He was assigned seat 1J. His name is on the manifest for that seat and that is the seat he was found in, still handcuffed. Now, I've bought us some time on this issue by convincing Judge Berger that Sullivan has to prove his client's identity in court. That's really just a procedural issue, isn't it, after all. So, let's assume he does prove it, let's assume Sullivan suddenly figures out a way to prove that that man is really Larry Jones laying there in that bed, with the burned face, and the missing hands, etc., then there is the problem. The case is huge. Its worth millions."

Again the Texan.

Standby

"Wait a sec, there, counselor, you told us you could whip that Sullivan's ass in court, that his case was full of holes, etcetera etcetera etcetera, and we bought into your plan and gave you a helluva lot leeway in how you handled this case. Your first case, I might add, for this airline. We've paid a lot of money and now I am starting to smell fear in you. Is that right, you afraid to get your hands dirty?"

All sorts of murmurs of assent and dissent went around the boardroom.

Geoff swallowed his growing rage before continuing.

"I am not afraid of the courtroom. Unlike Sullivan, I've lived in the damned courtroom. So, Henry," he said right to the Texan, "I would appreciate it if you would shut the hell up. I am your company's lawyer and I am trying to give you some damned advice."

Henry was quiet.

"So, here is what I want you all to know. There is dissention in the ranks over on Mrs. Jones side. Her lawyer is in jail, and she has her spiritual advisor caving in to the judge in open court. There is no strength on that side anymore. This case can be settled, and settled cheap. If that is what you choose to do."

He paused, deliberately, to allow the moment to settle it.

"And that, ladies and gentlemen, is precisely what you should be doing."

He knew this would bring a chorus of questions, questions that he was prepared to answer.

"Folks, if you would all just settle down. Please be quiet and I will explain. As you lawyer I am obligated to give you sound economic and legal advise. And that is precisely what I am doing by telling you that you can and should settle this case quietly and cheaply, as quickly as you can.

"Here is what I recommend. Offer her a quarter of a million dollars. I know it sounds like a lot of money but it's a tenth of what we are paying on the death cases. And it sure as well will help us with the insurance carriers who are paying big money right now. Might even help us re-up with some of those carriers when the policies expire. We pay the money out of airline funds, hell, pay them in airline stock for all I care, whatever.

"Anyhow, that's my proposal, and I welcome your questions."

For a moment, the room was eerily quiet. The CEO spoke first.

"Geoff, seems to me that there is one question on all of our minds. And I think you know what it is. Why the change of heart? You went from wanting this trial to now recommending settlement. What gives, young man?"

"Well, sir, it's like this. She hired a shitty lawyer, I think we all know that. But the fact remains there is a very badly hurt man in that hospital bed and if this case gets to a jury, that man will get a ton, and I mean a ton of money. Remember, we have no defense."

"Hey, asshole," the Texan shouted, "we have no defense because you waived it."

"No, asshole," Geoff roared right back, "you have no defense because you have no defense. The pilot error is still Deacon's responsibility. So, do me a favor, hell, do us all a favor, and shut the fuck up please and let me work here!"

The entire room went silent, not so much at Padua's upbraiding of the Texan, but at the drama of the moment.

Geoff regained his control.

"Settle this case. Settle it now and settle it quietly. I can make a call right now and get this thing done for a quarter million. Eventually Sullivan is going to get his act together and realize that he is in over his head, he will get a real lawyer to represent this woman and that lawyer will get an accommodation from the judge and get more time and then the sky's the limit."

"Gentlemen, that is my advice."

The CEO spoke first, "Geoff, we need to vote as a board, can you excuse us for a moment?"

"No."

"Excuse me?"

"No, I am the company's attorney and I will remain for the vote."

"Let him stay." This time it was the Texan. "the boy has balls, bull sized balls, and I admire that. He can stay."

Geoff nodded his thanks.

"Well, I suppose we need to vote on the plan proposed by Mr. Padua?"

Geoff's cell phone rang, disrupting the moment. "Excuse me, I should have turned this off, but I will take it real quick."

The directors all murmured to each other while Geoff took his

Standby

call. His expression changed dramatically while he listened to the call. He thanked the caller, whoever it was, and closed his phone. He paused for a moment.

"Forget everything I just said. Pull the offer. Pull it right now and offer nothing."

Now the CEO lost it. "Geoffrey, I can't seem to understand you. You change your mind more often than any woman I've ever been married to, and there have been a few."

Geoff nodded. "You're just gonna have to trust me. Pull the offer, offer nothing. Trust me."

And with that he bolted out the door leaving a rather confused Board of Directors behind him. Only the Texan spoke,

"Well, fellas, that sure is one strange lawyer we got ourselves there. Strange. But dammit I sure as hell like the kid."

Chapter 40

Sullivan was bailed out of jail at five the next morning. He had not even spent a full night in jail, but the time he had spent was the worst dozen or so hours of his life. Meeting him outside of the jail building was his associate, along with a surprise visitor. There, in direct contrast to Sullivan's disheveled appearance stood Geoff Padua, in a freshly pressed suit and clean white shirt, no tie. He walked over to Sullivan.

"Clarence, I took the liberty of bringing you some fresh clothes and an electric razor. You can change in my car. We are due in Judge Berger's chambers at seven am. Emergency hearing."

Sullivan's heart began to race. He knew very little about the machinations of the courthouse, but he did know that any hearing set for seven o'clock in the morning, on a weekend, had to be serious. "What do you mean seven in the morning? I just got out of jail after all. I need a shower, a meal, some decent sleep…"

"Clarence, what you need is to be in chambers at seven o'clock, on the dot, freshly shaved and dressed and with your most apologetic look on your face. I will swing you by your house so you can get cleaned up, quickly, and then I will take you to the courthouse. This way you won't be late."

"Geoffrey, I don't know what to say, I thought you had gone off the Sullivan reservation and that we were no longer on speaking terms…"

Geoff let out a long breath.

"Clarence, let me be perfectly blunt. I don't like you, never have. You are the example of everything that has gone wrong in the legal

Standby

field. You are an ambulance chaser. You hold yourself out as the lawyer who handles the case, which we know is completely untrue. I mean, if your clients do nothing more that watch this trial on television they will know what an incompetent ninny you are. And then they will run from you like roaches scattering when the lights come on."

"Geez, Geoff, that was a little rough don't you think"

"Clarence, I'm just getting started."

"Screw this, pull over, I'm leaving" and with that Sullivan tried to open the door.

Geoff felt his hackles going up.

"No, Clarence. You can't leave because I promised the judge you would be at that hearing. Then I was persuaded to post your bail, which I did. Of course, anyone would think I am a complete jackass for helping you out like this."

Sullivan paused for a moment to reign in his anger and collect his thoughts.

"Okay Geoff, I have many faults but ingratitude is not one of them. I'm sorry."

Geoff paused for a moment, torn temporarily between hubris and sympathy for what Sullivan's life was becoming. At this early hour of the morning, sympathy won the battle over gloating.

"Apology accepted."

Now it was Sullivan's turn to sit quietly and think. After a few moments he spoke.

"Why?"

"Why what?"

"Why did you pick me up? I mean I could've taken a taxi, called a car service, gotten someone from the office to get me. Why did you come out and get me and, more importantly, why did you bail me out? Why? If you hate me so much, why?"

Geoff nodded quietly in the car before responding. "A fair question. Truth is, while I detest you and everything that you stand for, knowing that you would sooner sue your own mother if she caused an accident than actually get your hands dirty in a courtroom, that in spite of that you did give me some of my first opportunities. Now, the fact remains that I helped make you hugely successful and gave you legitimacy, and you repaid that with contempt. But, at a minimum, I feel like I owe you something so I decided to bail you out. Now I think we are even."

"Geoff, that was the strangest explanation I have ever heard. But I accept the sentiment, even though it really doesn't suit you."

"Fuck you, Clarence."

"Better."

After that they drove in silence to Sullivan's house. Geoff waited in the car listening to the early morning news shows to hear if there was any news on his case. There wasn't. That was good, very good. It meant that his company was winning the public relations war. Geoff intended to keep it that way. He smiled when he thought about how he might be able to parlay his success with this disaster into a lucrative board position with one of the big commercial airlines. Around fifteen minutes later, Sullivan got back into his car.

"Hey, Geoff, why can't I just drive my own car?"

"Not a chance in hell. I promised the judge I would bring you there and I intend to abide his instructions. Buckle up."

Again they drove in silence for a time.

"So, the suspense is killing me, what's really on your mind, Geoff?"

"Clarence, let me be blunt.

"Oh, but of course, Geoffrey, be blunt…."

"Clarence, shut up and listen for once in your life. Ramon called me a little while ago and asked me to help get you out of jail. He asked me to talk some sense into you. You are going to lose this case. You are going to lose and lose huge, and I think you know that already. You're arrogant, and pompous and full of yourself, but you aren't dumb. So, I won't belabor that obvious point. The reason I'm here is to help you save your dignity. Take our offer and get this thing settled."

"The offer? I thought it was off the table."

"The last offer was off the table and the one I am about to make you is one that I will go back to the board with as having come as a final demand from you. See, I have recommended they offer you nothing. Not one dime."

"Okay, let me get this straight. You want to tell me a number, have me take it, and then you go to the board that it was my demand and you are recommending it?"

Standby

"Yup, that's about the size of it."

Sullivan stared out of the window for a few moments. He could see the courthouse coming up.

"What is the number?

"Fifty."

"Fifty thousand?"

"Yes, and fully confidential on both sides. No press. The parties quietly settled. Oh, it will get around the airline industry what happened, but that shouldn't affect you since I doubt you will ever see another mass tort case again. You are too smart to take them anymore, forgetting for a moment that no client worth his or her salt is going to come to you with a mass tort again, face it, you've burned that bridge with your frank incompetence. I will protect you in the local legal community. 'He did right by his client, that sort of BS', Stick to bullshit whiplash cases. Make your million a year. Just get out of this."

Sullivan bristled.

"Geoff, what you are suggesting is blatant malpractice. Shit, I might as well just tell my own malpractice carrier that it is time to pony up if I go through with your bullshit plan."

"Your plan, not mine. Remember, I am authorized to offer you nothing. The only reason we are together is because, out of the goodness of my heart, I decided to do something kind for my old boss and bail him out of jail on my recognizance."

Sullivan laughed. His laugh became louder and louder until Geoff thought he would double over. Geoff pulled into a parking place, turned off the car and looked at Sullivan.

"The offer, if that is what we are calling it, expires as soon as I get out of this car. You have an ethical obligation to that whore you call a client. You are going to lose. Lose the case, fine, there will be others. Don't bet everything on this horse, you can't win. Take the money."

"Take the money so I get my pride? You get the glory? Fuck you. As for your deadline, let me give you my answer right now." And with that, he opened the car door, slammed it shut and began walking to the courthouse.

Geoff nodded grimly. "I was hoping you would do that, you stupid fuck. Now we end this. Checkmate."

Chapter 41

Felicity was in the hospital at her lawyer's suggestion. Dressed in her Sunday finest and doing her best to look the part of a grieving and worried wife. A face torn with angst as she held the hand of the man she "loved" as he lay in agony. All the while Edsel went in and out of his morphine induced haze and wondered who this woman, this horrible woman, was who kept a vigil next to his bed.

The press sneaked into the room.

Cameras and flashbulbs popped. This happened every day or so, to Edsel's calculations, and after a few minutes a nurse would come and shoo everyone off. However, Edsel was still alert enough to spot when either that horrendous woman, or that scummy lawyer of hers, slipped the nurse (always the same nurse) an envelope. An envelope that seemed to be getting thicker every day. The wages of sin grow with each passing hour, Edsel mused to himself, causing himself to chuckle inwardly.

Or so he thought.

Felicity's head popped up. "Larry, did you say something?"

Who was Larry? why did people keep calling him Larry?

"Aagh." Edsel felt himself choking on something. Something hard was in his throat, interfering with ability to swallow. He began to panic and thrash about the bed. However, the more he thrashed the more severe his pains from the burns became and the more he gurgled in pain.

Felicity was, of course, completely at a loss for what to do. She stepped back and stared in horror at the man she believed to be her husband struggled in agony in the bed. The equipment alarms were

Standby

going off at frantic levels and Felicity just stood and stared. All the while, a local news cameraman shot the scene from just behind the curtain of the bed adjacent to Edsel's.

The medical team rushed in and first gave Edsel a rather large dose of morphine and valium. He quickly settled down and fell back asleep. The doctor turned to Felicity.

"He seems to be waking up. This is exciting. Don't be concerned, they all fight against the breathing tube when they start to wake up. We will remove that once he is better sedated. So, just so you are aware, this is wonderful news. He is really making progress. His situation is critical and he is far from out of the woods, and he could still expire at any moment due to the severity of his injuries, but this is progress."

After hearing this, Edsel drifted into the deepest drug induced sleep he had ever experienced.

Felicity nodded.

The cameraman raced out into the hallway and yanked out his cell phone. "Tommy, it's Mack, get the boss on the horn. Hey, boss, that crash survivor is starting to wake up and I've got footage. Alright, I'm on my way back to the studio right now."

Chapter 42

Judge Berger walked in to his courtroom at precisely 7 AM. Geoff was seated at defense table. With him this early morning was the Texan from the Board, sent by the Chairman, much to Geoff's chagrin, as the representative of the company. Sullivan was on time and waiting for the judge.

Reverend Thomas was nowhere to be seen.

"Gentlemen, good morning."

Geoff rose. "Good morning, your Honor."

Sullivan spoke from his seat. The judge glared at his over the frames of his glasses. Sullivan rose, "I'm sorry your honor, good morning."

"Okay, gentlemen, where are we on maybe getting this thing resolved."

Just as Geoff was about to speak, Sullivan jumped in. "Judge, just this morning, the plaintiff rejected the Defendant's ridiculous offer of $50,000.00 to settle this. We look forward to airing our issues in court." All the while, the cameras whirred behind them.

"Mr. Padua, is this true?"

Geoff rose and glanced at the Texan, who stared at him through dead eyes that seemed to be asking him for information about this mystery offer. "Your honor, I'm afraid I don't quite understand where Clarence, excuse me, Mr. Sullivan, is coming from. I have no settlement authority from my client nor can I, in good conscience, recommend that it offer any money to Mrs. Jones or her husband, assuming that is, in fact, him in that hospital, a fact which we still dispute."

Standby

"Judge, he is lying."

At this, the judge banged his gavel down. "Mr. Sullivan, unless you wish to spend another night as a guest of the county, I strongly suggest that you watch your mouth and refrain from improper accusations against your opposition. An attorney, I may remind you, who served your clients quite well for many years."

Sullivan was stumped. He had no response to this, so he sat down.

Geoff sensed the weakening and knew he had to take another shot at Sullivan. "Your honor, I am very concerned about Mr. Sullivan's airing of our private conversations in open court. I will acknowledge that he and I had settlement discussions, and have had many over the last few days, as most companies will do to hold down litigation costs, but we just cannot, in good faith, offer him anything. Indeed, since he has opened the door about what we discussed, it is my recollection that we talked about what sort of 'nuisance value' this case could be settled for."

The judge stared at Sullivan for quite a while this time.

"Mr. Sullivan, why are you disclosing offers and demands in my courtroom?"

Sullivan was at a loss of words. He simply stood and shook his head.

"Mr. Sullivan, in my courtroom I expect that opposing lawyers will have the opportunity to speak to each other candidly, without fear that their words will come back to haunt them in here. Am I clear?"

Sullivan nodded.

"Am I clear?!?" thundered the judge.

"Yes, your honor."

"Alright then, what is before me now?"

Geoff stood again. Sullivan looked to his right and saw Geoff pulling out a large set of documents from his briefcase. The other shoe was about to fall.

"Your honor, at this time, the defense files its Motion to Dismiss and for Sanctions for Fraud Upon the Court. I have copies for the plaintiff's attorney and for the court. The original has been filed."

"Mr. Padua, this is a serious motion and I assume that you are not expecting an immediate ruling."

"No sir, please take whatever time you feel is appropriate."

Now it was Sullivan's turn. "Judge, this is, quite frankly, an outrage. I mean, I come here after a night in jail, get rushed to a seven am hearing, and now this gets thrown at me."

Geoff responded. "May I remind counsel for the plaintiff that it was his decision to file this lawsuit? My client has the absolute right to defend itself. Perhaps if had done the appropriate investigation into this case, all of this misery could have been avoided."

Judge Berger nodded.

"He's right, counselor. You picked the fight. So, how much time do you need to respond to this motion?"

"I don't know your honor, because I am not even sure of what is the gist of his motion."

"Oh, well, Mr. Sullivan, that seems simple enough. Padua here is telling me that the man in the hospital is not Larry Jones, your client's husband, but rather some unfortunate fellow named "Edsel Dodger'…. Did I get that right Mr. Padua?"

"Yes, your honor, you sure did."

Sullivan felt the world spinning around him. If the man in the bed wasn't Larry Jones, then he had no case, the lawsuit would be dismissed, and he would be the laughing stock of the legal community.

"So, Mr. Sullivan, the question stands, how much time do you need?"

"I just don't know your honor. This is all so sudden. I mean, this changes many things, you know."

The judge tightened the noose.

"I know, like foremost whether you even have a case or not. Like whether you should have done some research into your case before you rushed to file it and secure more publicity for yourself, among other things which I am sure will come to light."

Sullivan squared his shoulders and looked at the judge. "Two weeks your honor."

"Two weeks?", responded the judge incredulously.

"Yes, sir."

The judge shook his head. "No way, you have forty eight hours. Back here in two days. I will let Mr. Sullivan sleep a little later. How is 830 AM?"

Standby

"That's fine, your honor", responded Padua.

"Fine, judge," responded Sullivan while trying to ignore the snickering from the press pool. Sullivan again found his voice. "Your honor, one more thing, would it be possible to remove the cameras from the courtroom?"

"Denied."

"But judge, I, uh....."

"Mr. Sullivan, you asked for the cameras when you thought you had a case, now that it is spinning away from you, you want to slink away in private? Denied."

"Judge....."

"Dismissed."

At this the Judge rose form the bench and began to walk to his chambers. Just before entering his office, the door opened and his clerk, a beautiful young woman who was studying at the local university, was there to whisper something to him and hand him a piece of paper.

Judge Berger opened the note, not knowing what to expect. He turned back to the courtroom.

"Gentlemen, a moment, please."

Both Geoff and Sullivan turned, unsure of what to expect next.

"Yes, your honor."

"Seems we have a strange turn of events here. Seems that Mr. Jones, or Mr. Dodger, whoever that gentleman in the hospital is, has died."

Chapter 43

Franklin was at his desk trembling in quiet rage. Even the strong work of his wife's hands on his neck weren't enough to ease the tension. He had tied himself well and good to a falling star. He knew that now as clear as day. His association with this case was getting out of hand and there was no clear way out of this mess.

Now, to top things off, that man in the hospital was dead and Franklin had no idea who it was, or what it would all mean.

"Baby."

"Yes,"

"Where is Ronnie?"

"I think he is tracking a few things down for you. Said he should be here in about ten more minutes or so."

"Alright."

Then the phone rang.

Franklin hit the speakerphone button.

"Yes."

"Franklin, its me Ronnie, I am out here chasing down a few things but I just heard that the patient died. Is it true?"

"Yes, it is."

"Wow, that sure is some strange timing, I betcha. Anyhow, I was wondering if Mrs. Jones was there with you?"

"No, she isn't, why do you ask?"

"Well, she left the hospital with a couple of reporters and no one has seen her and no one knows if she knows that her husband is dead. And everyone here at the hospital is trying to track her down to let her know and there are some rumblings that it is awful strange

Standby

that she isn't at the hospital now, you know what I mean?"

"Ronnie, slow down. Let's take this one step at a time. That man is dead."

"Yup."

"Felicity is nowhere to be found?"

"Yup."

Franklin thought for a moment before responding.

"Well, Ronnie, I suppose that is all we need to know for now. Let's just wait a piece and see what else transpires, okay?"

"Sure, boss."

"By the way, Ronnie, what are you out there running down?"

"Oh, just a couple of odds and ends, checking on some things, I will be in touch, don't you worry."

"Okay, Ronnie, be careful, my friend."

"Sure thing, boss." And the line went dead.

Franklin continued to sit in his large leather chair, with his eyes closed, trying to relax but also trying to figure out who would make the next play and what it would be. He knew there would be no settlement and he knew that he was going to take a hit on this but he also believed that he would walk away relatively unscathed. First, however, he needed to distance himself from Clarence Darrow Sullivan and the case. Then the phone rang again.

Franklin hit the speakerphone again.

"Yes, Ronnie, what did you forget..."

"Franklin, is that you?"

Franklin almost fell out of his chair. He knew the voice as intimately as he knew his own.

"Larry?"

"Yes, Franklin, its me, and I need your help."

Chapter 44

Larry Jones stood at a pay phone with Sue by his side, frantically pumping quarters into the machine so the connection wouldn't be lost.

"Franklin, there are some very bad people chasing me and I don't know where else to go."

"Larry, after all these years, why are you calling me?"

"Because I don't know where else to go. I can't call Felicity and drag her into this. Besides, she is frankly so stupid that she would end up getting me caught, and if I get caught, I am dead."

"Dead? What the hell are you talking about Larry?"

"Franklin, listen, I don't have a lot of time, but I am begging you for your help, okay? Somehow, I have managed to get myself into a very strange situation. There are some real bad people after me and I don't know what to do anymore. I don't know where they are now and I don't know when they are going to find me. But I saw on the news that you were involved and I thought there was no one else to call. Please, help me."

"What, I mean how? How am I supposed to help you Larry? Where are you? What sort of trouble are you in? And, hell, for that matter, who the hell is it that just died in that hospital bed?"

The line went silent.

"Died? He died?" Larry's voice was barely audible.

"Yes, he died, Larry. Now, who the hell is he?"

"Franklin, all I know is that his name is, or was, Edsel Dodger. He was into some bad shit, some seriously bad shit, and now whoever it was that he was into that shit with is chasing me, thinking

Standby

I am him, and, oh hell, do you have a television on?"

Franklin grabbed the remote control and turned to one of the all news channels. There was Larry's face, with the years of his life underneath and the words "Dead?" posted next to his name.

"Oh, Jesus, Larry, they think you are dead now."

Larry was too dumbfounded to respond.

"Larry, wait a second, we need to think this through. Give me the number where you are and I will call you in five minutes."

Larry obliged him and the line clicked dead.

Franklin turned up the volume on the television.

"... recent developments in the Deacon Air crash. That poor victim, Larry Jones, who had been comatose at a local hospital since the accident has succumbed to his injuries and died this morning. Neither his wife, Felicity, nor his attorney, an advertising lawyer named Clarence Sarrow Sullivan, could be reached for comment. This last fact, of course, quite strange as neither of them has shied away from the spotlight since the accident.

The TV reporter paused, evidently quite pleased at her turn of the phrase.

"However, in what is an even stranger twist on this already strange set of circumstances, the attorney for Deacon Air filed a Motion to Dismiss Attorney Clarence Darrow Sullivan's case and has alleged that the gentleman who just died is not actually Larry Jones but is actually a man by the name of Edsel Dodger. Little is currently known of this Mr. Dodger other than that he apparently was, or is, very successful in the adult bookstore industry, has his own line of adult toys, and that there are rumors that he has been linked to the Croatian drug trade.

"A curious story, with a tragic end, or perhaps a tragic beginning, continues. Back to you George."

Franklin flicked the channels around and found more and more of the same on all of the news channels.

The lights on his phone were ringing frantically and he watched as his wife ably fielded the calls and deflected the questions. She sent him a person-to-person message on his computer. "Press conference? ASAP?"

Again his private phone line rang.

"Larry?"

241

"Larry? Boss, you lost your mind? It's me, Ronnie…"

"Yes, Ronnie, I, uh, I'm sorry. Things are getting a bit hectic here and I am trying to deal with that poor man's death, you know."

"Yeah, boss, I know, but hey, you need to get your mind around something new. We are in serious, no bullshit, stuff here."

"What is it?"

"Well, I called some people I know who knew this Dodger character. In fact, I actually knew him, long time ago. Seems as though he was into some pretty shady crap. Not just the porno stuff, but also the importing of illegal drugs. He is tied into some really bad characters."

"Okay, and how exactly does that affect us?"

"Well, seems as though these Croatian fellas, most particularly this Javis fella, think that Dodger had some sort of deal with our Larry, some back handed deal to screw them out of some money. So, they seem to think that Larry, and here is where it gets hairy, anyone affiliated with Larry, have either their, um, product or their money, either one of which, or both, preferably both, they want back. And soon. Franklin, this is no bullshit. I know these guys, especially Javis, and this is hardcore bad!"

"Ronnie, Hang on, I think I know where you are going with this. Hold the line I have to make a call."

Franklin frantically dialed the other line.

"Franklin?"

"Yes, Larry."

"Shit, man, you said five minutes. It's real bad out here."

"Larry, I am not going to sugarcoat this. You need to run. Now. You need to call me as often as you can, I will give you my personal cell phone number, it will be on for you all the time, twenty four hours a day. But run, right now. Those people after you are for real. They are not bullshit. They are real bad guys. Run. Call me in a couple of hours and I will have a plan worked out. Larry, do you understand?"

There was no answer. The line had already gone dead.

Franklin paused to collect himself. He pushed the other line.

"Ronnie, come to the office right now. We have to get started on a plan."

"On my way, bossman."

Chapter 45

Larry and Sue were about to jump back in the Corvette that was currently parked behind a rather seedy strip club near the Tampa Bay Buccaneers football stadium. That was when Sue saw him.

"Larry, oh my God, look, carefully, across the street."

"What?"

"Just look…"

And there he was. Javis. The man who had been chasing them ever since Los Angeles. He had somehow tracked them here and was starting to come across the road. He was accompanied by two new thugs. The ones they had seen before were gone.

"Sue, we need to ditch the Corvette."

"I know."

"We need something less conspicuous, less obvious."

"I know, but how the hell are we gonna get any wheels. We still don't have any identification, and no credit cards that we can use."

"Hang on, Sue, I have an idea. Oh, and by the way, you still have that bathing suit in your bag?"

"Yes, but…."

But Larry was already headed through the back door of the strip club carrying Sue's bag on his shoulder. "Larry, what's on your mind???"

As they passed through the door, a very large man, probably a bouncer, grabbed Larry by the shoulders and said, "Just where in the hell do you think you are going?"

Larry smacked the man's hand aside and responded, "Hey

asshole, this here is your feature performer and get your goddamned hands off me."

The bouncer stepped back to collect himself. "What the fuck man? She ain't the feature act at all. The feature act is Holly Swallow. Who the fuck is this?"

Larry didn't miss a beat.

"Hey, asshole, have you ever met Holly Swallow?"

The bouncer shook his head in response.

"Then who the fuck are you to tell me that this gorgeous creature isn't Holly Swallow?"

"Well, I've seen her in the films and she ain't no Asian chick."

Again, Larry didn't miss a beat.

"You are a seriously dumb fuck. You know that? You are telling me you can identify an actress by what she looks like on TV? Fuck, that's all airbrushing and lighting. This is Holly Swallow, and all she needs is a dressing room to get ready."

Just at this time the supervisor of the club wandered over.

"What seems to be the problem gentlemen?"

The bouncer responded. "No problem, boss, its just that this guy here says that this chink there is Holly Swallow, and I don't think its her and I am not about to let her into the club until I know who she is…"

The supervisor stared at all of them for a moment. "Fuckhead, I don't pay you to think. That is Holly Swallow and she needs to be onstage in about eight minutes or I am firing your ass."

The bouncer stared at the floor as Larry and Sue walked past. As Sue went off toward the dressing room the supervisor grabbed Larry by the arm and pulled him into a side office.

"Okay, pal, I know that isn't Holly Swallow, so let's just cut the bullshit, alright? Holly called here around an hour ago that her car was broken down on the expressway and she wouldn't make it until later. So the way I see it, that gook in the changing room ain't Holly and you sure as shit are a lousy bullshitter. Tell me where I am wrong."

"Uh, just one thing….."

"And what is that?"

"I'm actually an excellent bullshitter."

The supervisor looked Larry up and down and then smiled at

Standby

him. "Fair enough, Mr. Bullshitter. Name is Beaver. Don't ask why."

"Nice to meet you Beaver"

"You too, pal. So, anyhow, here is the deal. That chink of yours either gets on my stage and blows it away or I kick your ass. Understood?"

Larry realized he was out of options.

"Deal."

"I know you two are running from something. Don't ask me how I know, I just do, alright. Now, your girl does a good job and me and a few of the fellas will help you out, She fucks up, I toss your ass to those funny lookin' dudes just came into my club," and with that Beaver pointed at the two men who Larry and Sue had just spotted outside. They were now inside looking for Larry.

"Again, Beaver, deal."

"Stick with me, pal. You stick right by my side."

Larry followed the larger man as he darted across the club to the DJ booth. He couldn't overhear what was being said to the DJ but Larry imagined it had something to due with Sue and her impending appearance on the stage. He was right. The music quieted, temporarily.

The DJ spoke.

"Alright, fellas, give it up for Mary Jane in her Mary Janes! Remember she is a working girl. Tip her right and she will treat you right! Next up, our feature act. All the way from LA! Last year's winner of breakout performer at the porn star awards. Stand up and make some noise for Holly Swallow!!!!"

The crowd literally went wild. The lousy strip club music started and Larry watched the curtain draw back.

Sue came out in the typical stripper attire of g-string, bikini top, feather boa, and ridiculously high Lucite heels. But, the piece de resistance, the one part of the costume that saved the day for them was the feather mask expertly applied over her eyes. Larry knew it was Sue as he was now intimately familiar with her body. But, unless you had that familiarity, you wouldn't know her from any of the other women in the club because you couldn't see her eyes.

The goons were staring at her and pointing, but it was clear to Larry that they weren't yet sure whether it was in fact Sue on stage.

Sue seemed a natural on stage. She spun on the pole, accepted the appropriate gratuities, flirted (much to Larry's unsettling dismay) with the patrons, and danced like a woman who had been on the stage before. Then, for just a moment, she and Larry caught each other's eyes and Larry saw, for the first time, something that looked like contempt staring back at him.

The crowd was going crazy. Catcalls and hoots were shouted from every corner of the room. Larry turned to Beaver and caught the first sign of a genuine smile on his face. The DJ was cranking the music louder and louder and Sue twisted and turned with the music as she disrobed and the crowd loved it. Even the goons were so distracted by the moment that they had given up their search for Larry and Sue and were watching, quite intently, the show.

The DJ then announced that Holly Swallow would be taking a short break for a costume change and that the club had decided to extend the two for one drinking hour for another hour. The patrons also answered this with a great deal of applause.

"Looks your gal pumped up my club just fine. Who is she?"

"Just a friend."

"Friend my ass. Two things I know about women pal. Only two things, that is, and I think that knowing those two things puts me ahead of most other guys."

"Yeah, what's that?"

"One, that woman knows her way around a dance stage. She's done some hard work in her life."

"Maybe."

"And two, I think she loves you and believes you let her down."

"How's that?" Larry responded with a degree of surprise.

"I saw it in her eyes. Sure, it was a strong bit of contempt. But mostly she was hurt cause she feels like you let her down and she had no choice but to do what she was doing for both of you. Anyhow, deal is a deal. You lived up to your end of the bargain. I have to as well. Here are my keys. It ain't much, but it will get you wherever it is you have to go. Don't worry, you'll have a good head start from those yahoos.

"How did you know I needed a car?"

"I can tell someone on the run, been there a few times myself."

"Beaver, I can't pay you."

"Just let me know where the truck is and I will have it picked up.

Standby

I got friends all over. Truck is out back. It's the black one. Just go out the back door. One of my boys is out there to take care of you. See that you get off safe."

"What about my friend?"

"She's already in the truck."

"Thanks"

"No problem."

With that, Larry shook his hand and began walking for the back door.

"Hey Larry!"

Larry turned.

"Yeah, I thought it was you."

It was then that Larry realized he had never told this man his name.

"Um, how did you know?"

"So you are Larry Jones? That guy from TV?"

Larry nodded.

"Shit man, you are a lucky son of a bitch. Someday you are gonna have to tell me how you got off that plane."

Larry smiled.

"It's a deal."

Larry jogged out the back of the club and jumped into the driver's seat of a simple, but nice, pickup truck. Sue was sitting next to him, clearly angry, but busy trying to remove the layers of stripper make-up from her face.

"Fuck you Larry!"

"Sue, I know, I'm sorry, but let me get us on the highway first."

Larry pulled onto the street and soon had them on the highway, headed south, for Miami. For home. For some undetermined ending to his saga.

Larry turned to Sue.

"Sue, I'm really sorry for putting your up to that. There just wasn't any choice."

Sue was very quiet and Larry turned to see her face. Her eyes were puffy and red and she had evidently been crying very hard.

"Larry, just drive the car please."

Larry nodded and pulled the truck onto the expressway.

Chapter 46

Sullivan called an emergency meeting of all of his associates and law clerks as soon as he returned to his law office.

"Folks, we have a real problem here. Judge Berger is gonna dismiss this case, and, what's worse is he wants to do it publicly. So, I need your help. I hired you for your brains and now you are gonna have to prove it."

Ramon spoke up first.

"What do you want from us boss?"

"What do I want? Well, shit, isn't it obvious? Find me a way out of this mess!"

"So you want us to find a way to beat Padua's motion?"

"Beat the motion? Shit, you are too fucking stupid to be a lawyer. Beat the motion? We can't beat the motion and do you know why?"

Ramon was flummoxed. He had never seen his boss so upset. Sure, there had been times when he was upset before but those were typically when cash flow was down and he actually had to come in and work for a couple of hours a week. Of course, those times usually led to Sullivan starting his "Dialing for Dollars" program where every case in the office that could be settled was settled, often times for less than the case was worth. Of course, if the clients ever found out what Sullivan was doing, he could be in a world of hurt, but hell, he never really cared as most of them didn't speak English and he was content to keep taking a third of their money for as little work as possible.

"Ramon, are you there?"

"Uh, huh, yeah boss, I'm here. Sorry, I was thinking."

Standby

"Well forget thinking, it was thinking that got us in this problem here. Now it is time to act."

"Well, actually boss, if you remember, you were in a hurry to file that lawsuit and Geoff always warned you about being impetuous."

"What are you? My mother? Shit, you are about as useless as tits on a bull. Fuck it. Get out. I will handle this myself,"

"Get out?"

Now Sullivan was furious. He jumped out of his chair, leapt across the table and grabbed Ramon by his lapels. "Yes, out, you are fired!!! I knew your loyalties were always to Geoff. They were always with him and not me. Shit, I am just the guy who signs your paycheck. Fuck you! Get out!!"

For the first time in his life, Ramon found his own courage. "Fuck me? Fuck me?!? No, fuck you! I quit. You can't fire me. I quit. You are a scumbag and I wish to God I had never spent any of my career with you. Career? Ha! That's a good one! All I have ever done as a lawyer was settle bullshit whiplash cases for whatever I could get. Shit, do you even realize that half of your clients are here on their second, third, or even fourth car accident? What are the odds on that one, asshole? You're a joke! Only you aren't capable of getting the punch line. Well, here it is in plain words that even a hack like you can understand. I haven't learned shit from you other than how to milk the system for thousand dollar settlements. My god man, have you no shame?"

Sullivan snapped. He punched Ramon right in the nose, breaking it and sending blood everywhere. Ramon fell to the floor.

Ramon quickly got off of the floor and brushed himself off. Then he simply turned and began walking out of the conference room. He called back to Sullivan over his shoulder, "By the way Clarence, two things I want you to know."

"I told you to get out!!!"

"Fine, one thing. You know how you can tell the ship is sinking?"

Sullivan's curiosity was piqued.

"How, asshole?"

"The rats are all jumping overboard."

"What the fuck is that supposed to mean?"

With that, Ramon tossed a computer printout on Sullivan's table and walked out. Right behind him went Sullivan's other two associates leaving only Sullivan and his secretary at the table.

"Well, I guess our rats have left. But this ship ain't sinking."

His secretary spoke up. "Uh, Sully, I don't think Ramon meant he and the other two."

Sullivan was now definitely confused.

"Well, then what? Who are the fucking rats?"

"Maybe you should look at those notes."

Sullivan did.

"Yeah, so, it's a list of about forty of my clients. So what."

"Ex clients."

"What?"

"Those forty clients have all fired you as of this morning. The reason they are getting out is that they don't want to be represented by a lawyer who ends up in jail instead of court. Fact is, Sully, the phones are still ringing but it's always clients calling to fire you."

Sullivan's head dropped to the table. "Oh, Jesus."

"And boss...uh, one more thing."

"What."

"The bank called this morning."

"Why? There is nothing wrong with my accounts," Sullivan said, still oblivious to the collapse around him.

"Not that." Now she was crying. "It's not that. The Bar froze your trust accounts."

"Fuck."

Sullivan was left alone by his secretary. He poured himself a large glass of very expensive vodka and swirled the clear liquid in his Waterford crystal glad. Then, after swallowing the vodka in one gulp, he poured himself another and began staring at the computer printout for almost an hour, shaking his head in disbelief. A sudden knock on the conference room door broke him out of his stupor. Sullivan looked up to see his secretary standing there weeping with two police officers behind her.

"What's this all about?"

"Mr. Sullivan, Ramon Scola, your associate, called in a complaint of assault and battery against you. We are here to arrest you."

Sullivan simply nodded his head in meek acceptance.

Standby

"Now, sir, do you, as an attorney, know and waive your rights, or do you want them read to you?"

Sullivan stood and headed for the door, "That won't be necessary." His head was hanging towards the floor as his secretary came in.

"Boss…"

Sullivan didn't respond.

"Boss, please don't think of me as a rat."

Sullivan looked over at her, trying to ascertain what she was referring to, then he saw the box in her hands, full with her personal effects. Again, he simply nodded. As he walked out of the office, hands cuffed behind his back, he looked around his office and noticed that most of the desks were empty and had been cleaned off. His empire was rapidly crumbling.

Chapter 47

Franklin was seated behind his desk with Ronnie nervously pacing the room.

"Holy shit, Shadetree, this is fucking A unbelievable."

Franklin was beyond getting annoyed with Ronnie over the "Shadetree" reference. He knew it only came out of Ronnie at moments when Ronnie was particularly flustered. It was involuntarily, made Ronnie comfortable, and came without malice.

"Yes, Weasel, we sure are running down the rabbit hole."

Ronnie snapped his head up looking upset at being referred to as "Weasel." Then he saw the smile on his friend's broad face and relaxed. "Uh, sorry about that Franklin. Old habits and all."

"So, Ronnie, what do you think? Larry is an old, old friend and he is in trouble, not of his own making. What do we do?"

"Well, I suppose we can all assume there is no money coming from the airline, so that part of all of this is behind us. But there is your ministry to think of, isn't there?"

"Yes, there is. But, more importantly there is my friend to think of. Please don't forget that."

"I won't boss, I promise. If he is your friend, he is my friend as well. Simple as that. That means he gets all my best efforts."

Franklin stared at this strangest of his friends. He knew Ronnie would now walk through fire for Larry, and he hadn't even met him. "So, Ronnie, any ideas on strategy?"

"Boss, I am gonna be totally honest. I got nothing. Been rackin' this pin brain of mine and I just can't figure anything out. You?"

Standby

"Yes, my friend. I have a few ideas. First a press conference, hear me out."

For the next hour Franklin relayed to Ronnie his plans for the mess they found themselves in. Ronnie nodded feverishly and told Franklin he loved the plan and would back it all the way.

Then the phone rang.

Franklin answered.

"Yes?"

"Franklin?"

"Larry, thank God. Where are you?"

"Let's leave where I am alone for right now, lets just say I'm closer to you that I was a few hours ago. But until I feel safe I am telling no one where I am."

"Sounds reasonable. Do you need anything? Money? I could wire you money if you need."

"Thanks, no, I'm all set in that department."

"So, what can I do?"

"Franklin, I'm only saying this one time, because if you ask me any questions I am gone."

"Got it."

"Remember that place where we last saw each other."

"Yes."

"Midnight, tonight, in the back. You come alone."

"Done."

The line was quiet.

"Larry, anything else?"

The line was dead.

Sue stared across the car at Larry. "Larry, do you know what you are doing?"

"Nope. Sue, honestly, I haven't known what I've been doing for a while now. And, strange as it may seem, I feel more confident now than I ever have."

She nodded at Larry. He smiled back at her. They held hands as the car drove closer and closer to Miami. Closer and closer to whatever ending lay in store for them.

Chapter 48

Franklin stared into the black night. There was no moon and it was cloudy so there were no stars. He could hear the whispering of the ocean breaking in the distance and could smell the salt air. He had no idea where all of this was going, and no idea of how it would get there, but he know it would get there tonight. He continued to stare into the distance as he struck a match to his cigar.

"Those things will kill you, you know."

Franklin started to turn around.

"Don't turn around Franklin. It's me, but don't turn around. Please."

"Okay, Larry, I won't turn around, but I have to ask you. What do you have in mind? I'm not real particular about standing in a dark alley with a man I haven't seen in years standing behind me telling me not to turn around."

"Wait two minutes, count it in your head, then open what I left for you. I'm trusting you Franklin, because you came alone. Please. I need your help."

"Larry, wait, what do you want from me???" But Franklin could hear the footsteps running away from him. He counted the two minutes in his head then turned around. The alley was still dark, but there was a rather petite Asian woman standing in front of him holding an envelope.

"This is for you. It's from Larry." She handed him the envelope. Franklin took it and slid it into his jacket.

"Who are you?"

"Who I am doesn't matter. That I am here does matter. That

Standby

Larry needs you help does matter. And that he turned to you, for whatever reason, really seems to matter. Can you help him?"

Franklin didn't hesitate. "Yes, I will help him, and you. Whatever I can do."

"Thanks."

She turned and walked away.

Franklin watched her walk away and then waited a moment before heading for his car. When he reached the street he opened the envelope.

Dear Franklin

My friend, it's been years since we've spoken. I realize that this is a very strange way for us to communicate but I am in trouble, big trouble and I don't know where else to go. As you probably know by now, I wasn't on that plane that crashed. Some guy named Edsel Dodger was on the plane and somehow our boarding passes got switched.

Long story short, I was in such a bad marriage that I thought I would use this as a way to get out. Hell, she seemed to be in a good place with you on her side.

Then, I started getting chased by some very bad people who seem to think that I have something to do with this Dodger character. It's been really rough. This guy was apparently into some very bad stuff.

Anyhow, the woman I am traveling with, who she is isn't important, her best friend is mixed up in this somehow, and he saved our lives. Another long story. I think the only way she and I get out of this is to find out what these people are after and get it first. Here is what I know.

His name is Javis. He is Croatian. Very tall and thin, wears black all the time. And he is into drugs, cocaine I think.

That's it.

Cryptic enough?

Call me at the number writted at the bottom of this letter. Memorize it, right now and then burn this letter. These are bad people, Franklin, very bad people. Only you have the number. If you don't call I understand. Only get involved if you want to. Please find out what this is about.

Long strange trip, eh, my friend???

Larry

Franklin took a long drag on the cigar and used the embers on the end to light the letter on fire. When it was all consumed he dropped the last remnants to the street and used his shoe to crush the burning ashes. He took his keys of his pocket and walked to his car.

For the first time in his life, Franklin didn't see the hit coming.

He was unconscious before he hit the ground.

Larry and Sue shared take out Chinese food on the bed of a cheap motel on Miami Beach. She had mentioned that she wanted to go to South Beach, but Larry convinced her that the hotels were way too expensive, even the cheap ones. Instead, they sat in a room in the motel where Versace's assassin had stayed so many years before.

Larry kept that part of the tour to himself.

They sat and ate in silence, waiting for the cell phone to ring.

Chapter 49

Padua worked late that night, finalizing his arguments for the hearing scheduled the next morning in front of Judge Berger. He knew it was a fait accompli. He knew he had won the case. Now it was simply a matter of getting the order signed. He also knew that he had succeeded on another level, a much more important level to him, personally.

Sullivan was finished. From what Geoff had learned, he was in jail again for assaulting his associate and this time there was no one to bail him out. The rumor was that the bar was already planning a raid on his office to seize all of his files as someone had tipped them off that for many years he had been paying kickbacks to doctors for cases. There was even a new rumor circulating that he had been setting up some shady offshore bank accounts. Yes, Sullivan was finished. He wouldn't even be in court tomorrow unless Judge Berger worked some magic and had him brought in.

In the back of his mind, Geoff hoped that his ex-boss would have an epiphany and would come to court, dismiss the case and throw himself upon his sword. Of course, he knew better. Men like that simply weren't capable of self-awareness.

His phone rang.

Geoff looked at the phone. It was late, very late. Who could be calling him at this hour?

"Geoff Padua here."

A nasally whiny voice responded.

"Mr. Padua?"

"Yes."

"Sir, my name is, uh, Ronnie James, you may not know me…"
"I know you, you work with Franklin Thomas."
"Right, sir, so I am sorry to disturb you."
Geoff was confused.
"What can I do for you Mr. James?"
"Well, I think we need your help."
"We?"
"Yes, me and, uh, Franklin's wife."
"What's going on?"
"Well, sir, Franklin has gone missing and I think it's cause of this case."
Geoff felt the cold sweat on his back.
"What do you need me for?"

Chapter 50

Larry stared at Sue sleeping on the bed. He thought her the loveliest woman he had ever laid eyes upon. Here, in the midst of all of this chaos, she laid peacefully sleeping.

The phone rang, startling him out of his reverie.

Larry flipped open the receiver. "Franklin?"

"Mr. Jones, I think ve need to meet," answered a strange voice with an even stranger accent that Larry could not immediately place.

"Who is this?"

Sue awakened and stared at Larry.

"I said, who is this?"

"You have something of mine. Something I vish to receive back and when you deliver it, I vill deliver your friend, all in one piece."

"What are you talking about?"

The voice on the other end of the line grew more angry. "Do not play coy with me, Mr. Jones. I know who you are, I know who your girlfriend is. I have your friend Franklin, and I know where your wife is, or shall I say, where she will be tomorrow."

Larry knew he was stuck, but he also knew that he had to buy some time here.

"Listen, I, uh, want to help you, really I do, but I'm confused here. What do you think I have of yours?"

This was answered with a scream. Someone on the other end of the line, Larry didn't know who, was screaming. The voice came back on the phone.

"Your resistance to following my directions just cost your friend one of his fingers. Should we make it two??"

"What friend? What are you talking about?" Larry was becoming progressively more frantic.

"This friend." Larry could hear the phone being passed.

"Larry, its me, Franklin."

The phone went dead.

"Hello, hello? Are you there? What do you want from me?"

Sue interrupted Larry.

"Larry, who was it?"

"That guy with strange accent, the one who shot your friend. But Sue he has Franklin and I think he is hurting him, and, oh shit, he says he knows about you and about Felicity, and, oh shit, what do I do?"

"Larry, calm down, please…"

Larry sat on the bed and put his head in his hands.

The phone rang again. Sue reached for it but Larry had it before she could get it.

"What?"

"What? Mr. Jones, be polite please or your friend gets hurt again. You will meet me at the freight docking station, pier 12K, by bin 16-2882, at noon tomorrow. Bring with you Dodger's bag. You come vith the girl. You bring me vat I asked for or your friend dies, and then your wife dies."

"Okay, I will be there?"

Again, the line was dead.

Larry again stared at Sue. "We have to call someone. We need help on this."

"Okay, I agree, but what do you have in mind?"

"Lets talk in the car."

They walked out of the hotel room, got in the car and drove.

Ronnie James walked into Padua's office late in the evening, accompanied by his sister. Geoff ushered them into a back office and sat down. "What's up?

Ronnie sneered.

"What, no coffee? Where's your manners?"

"Hush, Ronnie…."

Geoff stood. "Mr. James, unless you have something particularly relevant to me or something I need to somehow get involved with, I suggest we just dispense with the formalities and get on with it."

Standby

"Fair enough. Franklin Thomas has been kidnapped. I don't know by who but I know that it has something to do with this damned plane crash. And, quite frankly, we just don't know where else to turn." His nose whined.

"Have you tried the police?"

"The police? Ha! Then we get into a whole discussion of why Larry didn't come forward sooner, etcetera etcetera and I think we would all rather avoid that."

"We?"

"Sure, you are in this mess as well. I know you listened to Franklin negotiate with you when you should have ended the conversation immediately. From where I am sitting that sure sounds like it might be an ethical violation. Sullivan is already going down, no doubt, in large part because of you. I know you always hated the guy, but Jesus, you really set his ass up. Shit, you are definitely not a guy to piss off."

Geoff began pacing the room.

"Your point, Mr. James?"

Ronnie stood his entire small frame right up Geoff, "My point, exactly, is that we need your help to find Franklin. You help us, we don't go to the judge with what we know, you don't help us, then this disaster of a case will see the destruction of two lawyers. Personally, I almost hope you go that route, the world will be better off without two more lawyers."

Padua stared at Ronnie, attempting to gauge the sincerity of the man. The path was chosen.

"What do you need?"

Ronnie nodded his head.

"We need your help. Franklin went to you in confidence. That means he must've trusted you. So now we need to trust you. We need you to help us find him, and help us get him back."

"And how exactly am I supposed to do that?"

"Well, here is my idea."

Geoff listened to the plan from this odd little man. It was simple, direct, and with enough luck, it might just work.

He sat and thought for a moment and then grabbed the telephone and began making arrangements. A lot of people were going to have to wake up to make this one happen.

Chapter 51

Geoff stood before a bank of press lights which all seemed to blink on at the same time. Behind him stood the CEO of the airline along with the big Texan, who rushed in for this press conference. He was definitely the man out in front now and he was not altogether sure that he enjoyed the experience.

The time had come to start the press conference. There was no turning back.

"Ladies and gentlemen. If I may have your attention?! I have a few prepared comments to read and then I will be happy to take your questions.

The men behind Geoff, the CEO and the Texan looked exhausted and confused. Both were roused from the beds late the night before and flown here for this press conference. Both had been briefed on the plane about what was about to happen. Neither was thrilled about it but both understood that there were no other realistic options.

Geoff paused, breathed deep and stared into the cameras in front of him.

"For some time now Deacon Airlines has been quietly assisting federal drug enforcement agents in a sting operation designed to stop the use of the airlines for the shipment of drugs and drug funds across the country. Recently, Deacon airlines learned that one of our regular passengers, Edsel Dodger, a man with a somewhat unique employment history, was using our airline to move large quantities of drugs and drug money back and forth across the country. Upon learning of this, the DEA was notified and, with the cooperation of Deacon Air, Mr. Dodger was put under surveillance.

Standby

"Unfortunately, as you all know, just a few days ago, a Deacon Air flight tragically crashed on its way to Miami. What I am about to tell you was only known to the few people who now stand on this podium with me. Due to some confusion in the boarding process, Larry Jones – the gentleman reported to you as having been the sole survivor of the crash – was not actually on the plane. Instead, his seat was taken by Mr. Dodger."

At her home, Felicity Jones was watching the press conference. When this information was disclosed, she dropped her rather large plate of food and collapsed on the floor in a faint.

There were growing murmurs in the crowd. Questions were already being yelled out.

Geoff continued.

"Folks, if I can ask you to hold your questions for a just a few moments."

The crown quieted.

"This is a complex story and I ask you all to bear with me while I give you the rest of the details.

Again he paused.

"Mr. Dodger was the sole survivor of this regrettable crash, a crash for which Deacon accepts responsibility and for which Deacon has now settled with nearly all of the victim's families.

"However, again at the request of the DEA, even though Deacon knew that it was Mr. Dodger and not Mr. Jones in the hospital, we had to play out the charade a while longer to get the remainder of the players in this drug trade. For that information, I turn this press conference over to Dale Sampson, the President of the airline. Mr. Sampson flew in here from Pennsylvania last night to be here for this conference. If you could please give him your attention."

Sampson stepped up to the microphone. Truthfully, with a voice as booming as his, a microphone seemed a bit redundant, but he enjoyed playing to the crowd.

"Thank you Geoffrey. And who would've thought that a lawyer could actually be helpful to society?" he said to the laughs of the gathered crowd.

"I want to thank Geoff and the board of directors of the airline for having me here today. This is an important day for Deacon Air and, more importantly, for the country as a whole. With our cooperation, a major drug ring is being put out of business." He continued to drone on while Geoff sneaked off the backside of the dais, walked down the stairs and slid into the back of the waiting car.

"Thanks for coming Mr. Padua."

"You must be Agent Simpson."

"I am, now let's go finish this thing."

The car sped off toward the port.

Chapter 52

Larry and Sue stood at the end of the pier, holding hands, each consumed in their own nervous thoughts.

"Mr. Jones, do you have the package?"

Larry startled at the voice. The speaker was nowhere to be seen and in the middle of all of these freight boxes, the voice seemed to be coming from a dozen different directions.

"Come out where I can see you!" Larry shouted with a bit more courage than he thought he could muster.

"I ask you again, and for the last time, do you have the package?"

"And I ask you again, come out here where I can see you! You have us here at the end of the pier, there is nowhere for us to run, come out here!"

Larry heard a groan and glanced to his left, just in time to see Franklin pushed out from inside a freight box. A freight box whose number matched the number inside Dodger's bag. He was bloodied and had clearly been beaten rather severely but it was definitely Franklin.

"Sue."

"I'm on it Larry." Sue went to Franklin's side and held him in her arms.

"Mr. Jones, you are running out of time."

With that Javis walked out of the freight box holding a rather nasty looking machine gun. To his left, two of his henchmen spread out so that Larry was now covered from three different angles.

"Mr. Jones, where is the fucking package??"

"Javis? Yes, you must be Javis. Well, I'm afraid I don't have it."

"Don't have it? Don't have it!" Now Javis laughed. It was an eerie and decidedly evil laugh. "Well, why is that? Why don't you have it?" Javis nodded at his men, both of whom began walking to Larry, who began imperceptibly to move towards the dock. The guns were cocked.

Sue was whispering to Franklin, who looked at her and nodded his head slowly.

"Javis, I don't have the package. I never had the package." This, Larry knew, was a lie, he knew what the package was but the way he figured it, he was keeping the money.

Javis walked quickly up to Larry and smacked him, hard, on the right side of the face. Larry dropped to the ground, lifted his head and quickly nodded to Sue.

Franklin stood up quietly behind Javis and his two goons. He knew that there were only three of them, having spent the last dozen or so hours in their company. He also now realized why Larry kept moving back toward the dock, as he had managed to position Javis and his two men so that their backs were to Franklin. Javis had unwittingly created a poor position for himself by having had Franklin's shoes removed earlier. Franklin could now move silently.

And he did.

Franklin took a deep breath, said a quiet prayer, and stood up. He began to run towards Javis.

Demonstrating the quickness he had, for so many years, demonstrated on the football field, Franklin covered the fifteen yards between himself and Javis in seconds, quiet seconds filled with anger and frustration and a brief sense of exhilaration just before the impact with Javis' back that sent him flying.

Franklin was smart enough to hit Javis first, sensing that the goons would be too confused to act and that, hopefully, before they figured out what to do, Larry and Sue would have escaped from the area.

That is exactly what happened.

Javis was down, something was definitely broken in his back and his gun had clattered away. Franklin was moving for the gun.

Larry yelled to Sue, "Now!" The goons were confused and looking in all different directions. They turned to Sue just in time to

Standby

see her jump off the pier. They fired at empty air and then turned back to Larry just in time to see him to do the same from his side of the pier. Again they fired at empty air. Javis muttered breathlessly, "Kill them all!" They turned toward Franklin.

A gunshot sounded and one the goons dropped to the ground. The other turned to the sound and saw a small, weasely looking man come out from behind one of the freight boxes, along with a rather small woman coming out from behind one of the other boxes. Both of them were armed and he knew he was covered. He dropped his gun.

Franklin stared at them in disbelief. "Ronnie, Lily? How?"

"Oh Franklin..." Lily yelled as she ran toward Franklin. In the distance the sound of sirens grew louder and overhead a helicopter now hovered. A loudspeaker growled

"Javis Kaneps. Drop your weapons. This is Agent Simpson of the DEA and you are under arrest. Our snipers cover you and if you move even an inch, you will be shot. Tell you assistants to also put down their weapons."

Javis couldn't respond. He was now unconscious from the vicious hit that Franklin had delivered to his back.

Franklin looked at him and knew he had delivered the hardest hit of his life.

"Oh Franklin, are you okay?" It was Lily. "Franklin, I am so happy you are okay."

"I'm alright Lily. Been through worse. I guess I should thank you and Ronnie, you saved my life, again...."

"Aw shit, Shadetree, what are friends for?"

This time Franklin didn't care about the nickname. He laid his head on his wife's shoulder and wept.

Agent Simpson came running up. "Where is Jones? Sue? Where are they?"

Franklin just shook his head.

He was picked up and put into the ambulance. Lily climbed in right behind him. The ambulance drove off.

Padua stood at the end of the dock watching a small boat speed away. He smiled.

He turned back to the resolving chaos behind him. "Agent Simpson, if it's okay with you, I could use a lift back downtown, I'm due in court in thirty minutes and Judge Berger doesn't take kindly to anyone being late. Just another loose end to tie up."

Simpson nodded to one of his agents who took Padua back to Court.

Chapter 53

The court marshal bellowed.

"All Rise. The Honorable M. Ira Berger presiding. Draw near and be heard. God save this Court, the Great State of Florida and the United States of America!"

Judge Berger sat down heavily in his chair. He was clearly weary from a night without sleep, having been awoken rather early with several strange requests, among them an emergency request for a wiretap warrant, which he granted after rather brief consideration.

Geoff was surprised to see Sullivan in court, and dressed in a suit, neatly pressed, showered and shaved. Geoff said hello, Sullivan ignored him.

Felicity was present with a young man who must have been her new attorney. He looked familiar but Geoff wasn't sure if he knew him which really didn't amount to much since there were so many lawyers in Florida.

There were dozens of reporters in the court room along with numerous police officers, probably court officers from around the courthouse, coming to the courtroom like vultures to see how this most odd story would play itself out.

"Well, Mr. Padua, I can see by the news that it has been a most interesting morning."

"Yes, sir."

Sullivan jumped up. "Your honor I demand to know what is going on! Right now!"

Padua shook his head. Sullivan clearly wasn't here to fall upon his sword. The man's ego knew no end.

"Sit down right now Mr. Sullivan! I will get to you soon enough."

Sullivan sat.

"Mr. Padua, before we begin with your motion, I believe Mrs. Jones wishes to be heard. Any objection?"

"No, judge, no objection."

"Alright then, Mrs. Jones."

The young man with Mrs. Jones stood up.

"Uh, actually, your Honor, if I may be heard? My name is Ramon Scola, I'm new counsel for Mrs. Jones."

At this, Geoff started. He, of course, knew Ramon, but the bandages all over his face had hidden his appearance. Ramon glanced at Geoff and smiled. Geoff nodded and smiled back.

"Any objection Mr. Padua?"

"None, your honor."

"Well, I object, I am her attorney dammit!" Sullivan yelled at the court.

"Not anymore you aren't" Ramon responded quietly as he passed some paperwork to Sullivan and to Padua. "Your honor, here are the papers necessary to have Mr. Sullivan replaced as counsel by myself."

"Again, any objection, Mr. Padua?"

"None, Judge."

"Mr. Sullivan I assume you object and you can assume I have overruled your objection. You are no longer Ms. Jones' attorney, but you are not relieved. Remain in your chair! Court officers, secure Mr. Sullivan!"

At this all of the officers in the court stood behind Sullivan. Padua now understood why so many officers were in the courtroom.

"Mr. Scola, you may proceed."

"Thank you judge. Your honor, as you know, before you today is the defendant's Motion to Dismiss. At this time, Ms. Jones has no objection to the motion."

Geoff looked up.

"She has no objection to the motion provided that the defendant is willing to release her of any responsibility for fees and or costs from this matter. This is her personal request and has no bearing on any sanction which the court might have against Mr. Sullivan."

Standby

Judge Berger tapped his fingers against his nose. "Any objection to this Mr. Padua?"

"Judge, may I be heard?" It was Sullivan, rising to speak.

"Mr. Sullivan, were I you, which I sure as hell am glad that I am not, I would be quiet right now."

"I wish to be heard. If I had known, I wouldn't have ….."

"Sullivan, shut up!" The judge bellowed.

"Mr. Padua, do you have any objection?"

Geoff knew he should get his client's permission for this agreement, but he was feeling confident this morning.

"None, your honor."

"Fair enough, the deal is accepted by the court. Case dismissed!"

All Rise!!!

Chapter 54

Geoff walked into the sunlight bearing down on the courthouse. He felt a tap on his shoulder. It was Ramon.

"Geoff, gotta second?"

"Sure, Ramon, sure."

"You know she was sort of duped into all of this. I mean, she did think it was her husband on the plane, but Sullivan, well, he, well, you know."

"I know."

"Anyhow, I just wanted to thank you for agreeing in there. Its good to see you, I've missed you."

Padua nodded.

"Me too, but I guess we will be seeing more of each other now."

"How's that?"

Padua reached into his briefcase and pulled out a file. "I have a new client."

"Great. Hey, on another issue, I was wondering if you might be interested in partnering up?"

Padua shook his head. "Not possible, mi amigo. Conflict of interest and all. We represent clients with competing interests."

Ramon was confused.

"What are you talking about, Geoff?"

Geoff handed him the folder. "It's a fair offer, consider it. Lets get this over with."

"Offer? What are you talking about?"

"The divorce of Larry and Felicity Jones. I represent Larry. Just filed the paperwork with the clerk."

Standby

Geoff walked off.

Ramon chuckled and opened the file. He turned to his client, "Felicity, let's go back to my office, we need to talk."

Chapter 55

Sullivan was taken down to a holding cell. As the time went on, he was becoming more and more familiar with holding cells.

In walked a man he had never seen before.

"Mr. Sullivan, my name is Roger Simpson, I am an agent with the DEA. You can assume that you have been read your rights."

Sullivan felt the sweat begin to trickle down his back. He now knew for sure that he was well and truly finished.

He looked down at the table.

"Mr. Sullivan, you and I need to talk about something. Actually, someone. One of your investors in your side businesses. Someone you opened an offshore account for? A man by the name of Javis Kaneps. Know him?"

Sullivan was in a full sweat now. Then, finally, he said the first intelligent thing he had said in years.

"I think I need to speak with an attorney…"

It was Simpson's turn to speak.

"I thought you might say that" he said as he walked out of the room. As the door began to close, he was pretty sure that he heard Sullivan begin to sob.

Chapter 56

It was a typically rainy afternoon in Louisiana when the rented sedan pulled up in front of the Honeymoon Motel. The car parked and out stepped the oddest grouping of people that the old owner had ever seen. Two of them looked very familiar, but the third man, while he also looked familiar, was confusing to the proprietor.

The old man walked out to the parking lot.

"How can I help you folks?"

"We need two rooms, sir, if you please," replied the lovely woman.

"Of course, no problem. You folks aren't from around here are you?"

Now it was the man's turn to speak.

"Not in some time now," he paused, "dad."

A sob caught in the old man's throat. "Ronnie, after all these years, you've come home."

"Yes, dad, I'm here."

The old man and Ronnie shared an embrace while Lily wept in Franklin's arms.

Lily spoke first, "Daddy, I want you to introduce you to my husband, the Reverend Franklin Thomas."

The old man took out his handkerchief and blew his nose loudly. Another sob caught in his throat. It rapidly evolved into a laugh.

"Well, I'll be, my new son-in-law, the 'Shadetree', as I live and breathe."

Franklin joined in the laughter.

Chapter 57

Larry and Sue sat on a private balcony of a luxury cruise ship as it sailed. They stared at the sunset, holding hands while sharing a bottle of champagne. A very expensive bottle of champagne.

"What now Larry?"

"Fred."

"What?"

"Get used to calling me Fred. Agent Simpson said it would be my new name; they are still working on one for you. Fred Smith. My new identity. Pretty neutral name don't you think?"

"I don't get it"

"Witness protection program. Federal. Good thing is we get to keep the money."

"Money?"

"Yeah, money. The money in the boat we took off in. Something like three million dollars. It was Javis' money, but Simpson said he'd work it so we could keep it."

Sue sat quietly. She thought about the witness protection program and whether she wanted it. She realized it was her best option. Everyone she loved in life was gone now. She intuitively knew that she would never see Percy again; he was gone to the Witness Protection system himself. She knew her life was with Larry now.

"Larry?"

No response.

"Larry?"

Again, no response.

Standby

Sue smiled.

"Fred?"

"Yes, ma'am" he replied with a faux Southern accent that made them both laugh.

"Fred, I think I would like to be called 'Ginger'."

"Ginger, huh? I like it."

"Fred and Ginger."

Now they both laughed.

"Fred?"

"Yes, my love…."

At this, she smiled. She knew it was true.

"Fred, let's go inside and start our dancing lessons. I have a few things I want to teach you."

"Just a second, hon, be there in a second. Don't start without me."

She threw a laugh over her shoulder as the cabin door closed behind her.

Larry stood at the balcony and looked out at the expansive sea.

He smiled, closed his eyes and breathed the salty air deep into his lungs. He chuckled as he realized that this was just the second time he had drunk champagne.

He tossed the glass overboard, turned, and opened the door to his cabin.

THE END